To Kerry,
All

One accident and five lives changed forever

[signature]
2024.

Other Books by Jim Ody

Lost Connections
The Place That Never Existed
A Cold Retreat
Beneath The Whispers
…Just South of Heaven
Noah's Lament
Mr Watcher
The Revenge of Lisa Lipstick
Mystery Island

<u>Hudson Bell Series:</u>
A Lifetime Ago
Come Back Home

<u>Tall Trees Series:</u>
Little Miss Evil

<u>Joel Baxter Series:</u>
The Crazy season

A Lifetime Ago

(Hudson Bell book 1)

?

Question Mark Press

All rights reserved. No part of this publication may be reproduced, distributed or transmitted in any form or by any means, without prior written permission.

This Second edition published in 2021 by Question Mark Press
First published in 2020 by Question Mark Press

Copyright © 2020 by Jim Ody

?
Question Mark Press

This is a work of fiction. Names, characters, places, and incidents are a product of the author's imagination. Locales and public names are sometimes used for atmospheric purposes. Any resemblance to actual people, living or dead, or to businesses, companies, events, institutions, or locales is completely coincidental.

A Lifetime Ago/ Jim Ody. – 1st edition
ISBN: 9798622663826
Cover design by: Emmy Ellis @ Studioenp
Promo by: Donna's Interviews, Reviews and Giveaways
Blog Tours by: Zooloo's Book Tours

If only I could see that smile one more time

Chapter 1 - Hudson

He didn't want to be here. It was a Tuesday evening. A dark winter's veil wrestled any light away on his long walk, wind battering his face with sharp-cold air, and him quick to find solace in the most unlikely of places. A generic eyesore of an underfunded building that was no more welcoming than the weather outside.

The apologetic reception area silently blamed everything that kept people away. A Netflix television binge won out to socialising at the various clubs that used to be on offer at this community centre.

The paint on the walls had grown tired, peeling away like a tactical retreat; or left for dead in forgotten piles of small chips on the floor.

Abandoned staples were the aftermath of some staple gun killing spree. The act of a self-medicated volunteer with too much enthusiasm for the mundane. One who couldn't care less whether or not the small bits of metal would ever be removed. In years to come they might be the only thing that kept the walls together. That and melancholy-induced nostalgia, and dirty regrets. Ghostly apparitions of kids smoking spliffs, drinking sweet cider and snogging would be all that was left from over a decade of youth clubs that no longer existed.

Inconsequential paperwork adorned a noticeboard. Dog-eared, and aged, a lot of it now out of date. Jumble-sales, charity events, weight-loss meetings and other historical groups nobody gave a shit about anymore.

Then through the swinging doors, that the police had battered their way through on more than one occasion, sat a soulless group in a frigid atmosphere. The sprinkling of people had been forced together through bad luck, and tragedy. A random cut of society, who with the best will in the world would never choose to be in a social environment with each other. Ever.

Uncomfortable plastic chairs were haphazardly dropped around on the wooden floor. Neither in a sloppy semi-circle, nor in rows. It had been years since the floor had been varnished. Memories scratched into it and trampled down for evermore. The meagre budget carefully spent elsewhere.

Hudson Bell sat quietly at the back of the room waiting for this shit to be over. He'd only been there five minutes, and was already bothering his watch by counting down the time left. He was desperate for a cigarette. He'd not smoked in five years, but these idiots were driving him with the desire to fill up his lungs with something toxic. It wasn't their fault. They were, by circumstance, extremely self-centred. But this support group was not doing it for him. Each one of them had a sorry story to tell. He didn't want to hear it. He was still too raw to care about them, or what they had to say. He wished them well, and a speedy recovery, but honestly, he couldn't give a shit about them past that.

His name was scribbled in marker pen on a lopsided label he'd slapped onto his chest. Not because he wanted people to know his name, but because it was part of the rules. *Nobody is anonymous*, they were fond of saying. Ironically, that was all he wanted to be nowadays.

This was his third meeting. The regulars told him it would get easier. He found that hard to believe. Not unless they started to introduce alcohol, drugs and loose women. Now that would be a meeting worth attending. Even on a fucking Tuesday night. However, looking around the room at the slapped-arsed faces, it was easy to see they'd freak out if fun and excitement made an entrance.

He hated the way everyone looked at him. It was like he had victim printed on his T-shirt. The forlorn looks of sadness and pity. They willed him to speak. To stand and nervously relive each grim detail, maybe shed an emotional tear for effect, but he refused to accept their regular invitation.

He remained silent. Tight-lipped and frustrated as they all uttered their tales of woe. Most spluttering through tears, or at least a wobble of lips or voice. That would be humiliating for him. He didn't need his masculinity questioned. He felt bad enough as it was, so how could telling a bunch of judging strangers make him feel any better?

Jim Ody

He looked up to the ceiling. Some part of him willing a release of happiness like rain, and have it wash down upon them all. He sighed, and noticed a woman catching his eye. He stared for what might seem too long normally, but his feelings were mixed. Part of him well past caring. Was she disappointed in him? Intrigued, perhaps? Did she feel sorry for him? Maybe she just thought him to be an unsociable dickhead. She'd not be wrong if she did.

She smiled, but again this meant nothing so he turned away, focusing on the skinny guy with a makeshift beard who was currently depressing everyone with tales of how his wife had died from cancer. Great, this was going to be a crowd warmer.

The guy gulped, and tried hard to compose himself. Then, struggling to talk continued as best he could. "It consumed her… she lost so much weight, and… I saw the life disappear from her eyes… the flames no longer flickered." Depression had a way of turning you into a poet.

Hudson looked around at everyone nodding like some religious group, soaking up the words from a sermon. Gulping it like air. He just didn't get it. He struggled with the pity. He really thought a free bar would be a lot better. People would probably talk more, and if not, then he'd just get blind drunk.

A middle-aged woman hadn't stopped crying since the meeting began. Perhaps she was going for some Guinness Book of Records accolade. Though more than likely dehydration and a migraine. She was certainly dedicated to the constant shed of tears.

A tough-guy with a goatee had shuffled uncomfortably throughout. He dabbed his eyes when he thought no one was looking. His hair was wild and stuck out in tufts. He clearly had no one to help him use a brush properly. Or a mirror that didn't lie.

A teen, who seemed too young to be there was beside herself. Her face ruddy with tears. It almost seemed against her human rights to make her stay.

A man with glasses nodded to every word, and wrote in a notebook. Silent, and stern faced, he was either a serial killer, or about to go home and top himself.

What a way to spend a Tuesday night.

Hudson found himself huffing. He hadn't meant to, and it was subtle enough that no one heard. He glanced over to the woman who'd caught his eye earlier. She grinned, and then supressed her smile. She was more than a breath of fresh air. Her smile contraband and likely to cause her trouble. He loved a rebel. Especially in this sea of sour-pusses.

He grinned back. Maybe he'd found a similar soul. Maybe she'd been made to be here too.

Twenty more long minutes and he was stood pouring the free coffee into a paper cup, if for no other reason than to stop himself from running headfirst into one of the walls.

"You wanna pour some misery for me too?" the voice said from behind. It was high-pitched, and he expected to see the teen, but instead it was the grinning woman.

"You keep smiling and we'll both get kicked out of here," he said deadpan. "Comedy night is Thursdays."

She made an over-exaggerated attempt at keeping a straight face. "I'll try. But I might then cut my wrists."

It was his turn to grin. Until he saw her wrists. She'd pulled up her sleeves to shock him. The white zig-zagged scars tattooed both. She was masterful with a blade.

"I'm sorry," he said before stopping himself.

She frowned. "What for? Me not succeeding, or me in general?"

He quickly poured her a coffee. "For my insensitivity."

She rolled her eyes. "Christ, you're not going to give me your story now, are you? Do I need a tissue? Shall I brace myself?"

He shook his head. "If you don't tell me yours, then I won't tell you mine, deal? I've heard enough sad stories for a lifetime."

She liked that. He could see her warm to him. She took his outstretched hand and shook it. It was neither limp, nor firm. Normal, he guessed. And he'd shaken hands with a lot of people.

"I'm Laura," she said.

"Hi Laura. I'm Hudson."

"Like the river?"

He shrugged. "If you like."

A Lifetime Ago

And for the first time since the horrible incident, Hudson felt something he'd not felt in a long time.

A glimmer of hope.

She nodded and walked away.

Just then his phone buzzed. He glanced down and saw it was from his friend Jez. A video message.

Hudson was a former policeman. He'd loved his job, right up until the morning of the incident. The one that would lead him right here.

He now consulted for the police. He had a pile of cold cases that couldn't wait. They were hardly going to get any colder, but that wasn't the point. His old department was stretched as it was. A high-profile murder investigation had sucked the life out of the team, not to mention the overtime budget. His ex-colleagues were running on empty, a couple in dire need of a holiday. Who was going to pick up these cases?

No one, that's who. So Hudson, with a fragile mind, and a tired body stepped in.

Jez was already an IT consultant for the police. With his skills in computers, CCTV and digital footprints, not too many people could remain invisible for long with him on the case.

Hudson pressed the video, and waited for the incriminating evidence to come through.

However, what he got was a video of Jez's wife, sat naked on a yoga ball and singing Miley Cyrus's 'Wrecking Ball' song. The normal angry woman was certainly to be seen in a different light from this day forth.

Jim Ody

Then suddenly he received another text from Jez.

Whoops! Wrong video. Lol! Sending the right one now!

Jesus, Hudson thought. The guy was nuts. At some point, he'd bagged up his social skills and put them out with rubbish.

The next video was of more interest. He felt relieved. Another paedophile would now be off the streets.

Hudson had had a gut feeling about the guy. That was how it started. From there, he'd done the background checks, and then watched him.

He'd learnt over the years, these evil people had habits, and that meant they had daily routines and patterns that were easy to track. They rarely deviated, especially if they found things worked, and they felt they were in the clear.

It had been a set-up. Hudson himself had struck up the friendship with fifty-three-year-old Wesley Loughlin. It had been awful, and Jez had offered support when Hudson was all for going over and beating the sick bastard up.

The things that Wesley wanted to do should never be spoken out loud.

The team were deliberate in setting up the sting operation when Hudson was at the group therapy. They all knew he couldn't be anywhere near the guy when he was caught.

Relieved, Hudson replied back to Jez with:
Good work, mate. Send it to the boss. But make sure it's the right video!

A Lifetime Ago

    Almost straightaway Jez sent a winky-smile emoji. At least he had a few things in his mind to occupy his thoughts whilst he sat through this suicidal bunch. So there was that.

Chapter 2 - Hudson

The night swallowed him up as he left. With hands deep inside his pockets, and the collar tight against his cheeks, he walked at pace to get away from the group. No offence to them, but he was now in dire need of getting some distance between himself and them before he added to a list of possible suicide solutions. He had well over three hundred. He wondered if there was a world record for such a list.

He lost himself in a Tesco Metro before noting he'd not made an effort to speak to Laura again. He felt slightly guilty, but satisfied himself with the knowledge they'd see each other again next week. His mind had been on the video from Jez. The one that didn't feature his friend's wife.

His mind was deep in the details of his current case, the cogs all turning inside his brain, and he was second guessing himself. He was sure the evidence was enough. The van slowing down outside of the suburban house a number of times. The clear view of the number plate. The suspect seen walking past the house on several occasions in one evening, even though he had no reason to be near the property. The van was owned by the suspect. And having been caught a year earlier for exposing himself to a minor, and bothering children, he'd been registered on the sex offenders list.

Hudson knew they needed more. A good QC could argue that it was all coincidental and circumstantial. He wondered how QCs and solicitors were able to go home to their families at the end of the day, when they'd spent their efforts and energy on keeping a guilty man out of prison. There was a moral obligation that Hudson just couldn't get past. Was it really the money? Or the challenge of winning the unwinnable? Either way, they fell upon the darker side of the law, a complete contrast to where he kept himself.

Hudson wasn't sure what had drawn him in to the shop. An unconscious desire for something of comfort, he suspected. A quick easy shot of calories he knew he didn't need. Chocolate, or alcohol. It didn't matter which.

A young couple were hovering around the condoms, pretending it was the deodorant that held their interest. Hudson smiled at them. He'd been young once. A nervous trip that promised such a reward. Give him a few years, he thought.

A guy shuffled around suspiciously. He was dishevelled and looked like he might grab and run at any time. He was probably just a hard luck story waiting to be told. In the grand scheme of good versus evil, this guy was of no concern to him.

Hudson squeezed past a woman dressed in a onesie. She seemed perfectly at ease with this dress code as she grabbed a bottle of cheap vodka.

Her lipstick smeared around her face, and more than likely be around the neck of the bottle opening soon. Her hair though, was strangely perfect. What a strange order of priorities.

Hudson's eyes were drawn to the bottle of rum on the shelf. Dark and inviting it called out to him. He didn't have a problem with alcohol, but then that's what people with a problem often said. This particular brand held bad memories for him. Ones that made him feel like a cliché. You could dress it up however you wanted to, but that was just what it was. Before he was made to go on leave, he worked on cases that messed you up inside. He didn't clock off at five, go home and wind down like his friends did. He was left staring at crime scene pictures, debriefs with colleagues over the next course of action, or just sat under poor lighting in an empty office with his own thoughts. So many cases of violence and neglect. Then eventually, with eyes that were dry with tiredness, and a body ready to drop, he'd drag himself home. But when he closed his eyes his mind was still actively working the case.

His girlfriend at the time was understanding. She knew the hardship of the job. But sometimes she wanted more. And who could blame her? And then sometimes turned into most times, until she felt neglected and by then it was too late. Soon, the good times lost themselves to the past, and the future no longer held a couple bonded by love. The rum took the edge off everything. It gave him the sharp tongue to respond to her frustrations. It fuelled the verbal fighting between lovers that just wanted to be loved, but for separate reasons were unable to do so. Circumstance sent her into the arms of another man. The incident saw him put on leave pending further investigation, and eventually voluntarily leaving the force. And whilst later on he'd join again as a consultant, his troubles tugged at him as he tried to move forward. Eventually, he conceded and began therapy, which later led to the support group.

Fuck it. He grabbed the rum for one more last one. He'd sleep it off in the morning before looking at another case. One he shouldn't be looking into, but he'd not turn his back on those children.

He was in his own little world. He glanced up just in time to see a skinny white lad in an oversized grey T-shirt, and wearing a black baseball cap hovering around an old woman. She was squinting, and doing her best to extend herself to a higher shelf in the pharmaceutical section. It was obvious that the very act was an effort for her. Age and health were no longer on her side.

Without worry, the lad swooped in like a predator and grabbed her bag. He pushed her and made a run for it.

Hudson kicked into action. He didn't need to think about it. He didn't shout *stop!* or any other warning, instead, with the bottle of rum sat like an abandoned date on the well-worn floor, Hudson pumped his legs and ran in hot pursuit.

Out of the shop, Hudson saw the lad heading left down an alleyway that was sandwiched between the shop and a bookie. He desperately ran with everything he had. The lad had slowed assuming he'd got away, but his eyes grew wide when he turned and saw Hudson bearing down on him. The lad was everything to Hudson now. He was the target and Hudson was gaining fast.

At the end of the alleyway, the lad hesitated and then turned right. Hudson was on him in a flash, seven feet; six feet; five feet…and then he launched himself with a tackle straight out of Twickenham. Hudson's weight knocked the lad over like a skittle onto the hard tarmac below.

"I didn't do nuffin'," the lad said, trying to wriggle undeath Hudson. His face was all too familiar. He had more mugshots on the system, than a mother had of her firstborn.

Both of them were out of breath. "Well, well, well, if it isn't Craig Trowbridge," Hudson said slightly out of breath.

"You can't do this. You ain't even a copper anymore!"

"It's a citizen's arrest," Hudson said with one knee in the lad's back. He pulled out the plastic wrist-ties from his pocket. *Never leave home without them*, he often grinned to people.

"Hands behind your back!"

"Nah, mate. Ya got it all wrong. It's my nan, innit?"

"Yeah, and I'm the Duke of York!" Hudson got him to his feet, and called it in. Then, even without ten-thousand men, he marched him back to the shop, but this time via the road and not the alleyway. Too many bad things happened in alleyways.

A Lifetime Ago

The old lady was grateful with her returned bag, but was clearly shaken up. That was what really saddened Hudson. A senseless act that would rattle her nerves every time she left her house.

"Let me get what you were looking for," Hudson said, reaching for the medicine.

"Thank you so much," she said gratefully, after Hudson paid the shopkeeper.

Hudson turned to Craig and gave him the change. "Don't thank me, Craig here paid for your medicine, and to say sorry, he paid for these groceries too."

"Really?" she said and flashed a forgiving smile at him.

Craig nodded and looked guilty. It would do for now. Craig would be taken to the station and continue to repeat 'No comment' for as long as both parties could stand. But that wasn't Hudson's pain anymore.

Craig was well on his way to being a career criminal. His childhood was but an apprenticeship for what he'd eventually evolve into, having been born into a family tree whose branches reached most of the prisons in Britain. Unfortunately, even at his young age, being locked up held no fear to Craig. Criminals were all he knew, and made up his complete social circle. They were his peers and heroes alike.

A few minutes later and a couple of officers arrived at the scene, rolling their eyes at the young offender. Hudson nodded a salutation to them, as they greeted Craig like a long-lost son.

Rehabilitation was futile, so instead they'd continue to just go through the motions.

Hudson looked back at the bottle of rum sat lonely and discarded and then walked out empty handed into the night. He'd make do with a cup of tea instead.

Hudson had a pile of case files that were growing colder by the day. He was their last hope at being solved. He dragged the heavy pressure of that all the way back to his flat. Weight seemed to increase by the day.

But it was the news of the missing boy that dominated his mind. It had been two months and nothing.

Officially, it was not his case, but the media had now grown bored, having squeezed as much as they could from the story. The shock value had diluted, and the sensational headlines were replaced by Z-listers sexual exploits. With nothing new, and all the leads having dried up, the papers had moved on. All that was left was old footage, and the look of complete and utter devastation on the tear-soaked face of his mother.

Tomorrow was another day. But maybe tomorrow would be too late.

Chapter 3

Two months earlier

The morning had been dark. Black thunderclouds had marched overhead and bullied away the sun. The skies had opened like only Britain skies could. Eventually the wall of water had stopped, and the sky conceded with apologetic fluffy whisps of cloud. Relieved, the sun was then smiling high over everyone again, and doing its best to coax people out of hiding, whilst diligently drying up the ground.

Sophie Hughes had one love in her life and that was her four-year-old son Darren. Her relationship with the boy's father had been brief, and not that memorable. A drunken night out had ended with an unprotected liaison in the back of his work van. She blamed the vodka, not to mention her friends, for allowing her to leave the pub with him. Her memory was hazy, but she did remember the uncomfortable feeling of work tools pressing underneath her. It was a pity that more than a hammer poked her body that night.

Casanova had made himself scarce from that point on, and she'd done her best to erase him from her life. Darren was the only thing left of that night.

Sophie and Darren lived in a new area of Swindon, a stone's throw from her parents and a handful of her friends.

That morning, she had an interview in the town centre. The job wasn't much, but it would give her some money, and more still, a purpose in her life. Not that her son wasn't enough, but she wanted to work. In fact, she needed to work, even if it was a part-time administrative role. Her parents had money, and even as a one-parent family, she was determined to provide as best she could.

Her brother Simon agreed to look after Darren.

Simon was a lot younger than his sister — still just a teen himself - but time with his nephew was important to him.

On the afternoon in question, Simon took Darren to the park. He knew how much the lively little lad enjoyed it. And who wouldn't want to see that smile light up his face?

The park was busy with desperate parents happy to be able to unleash their children into the outside world. Many had a trail of destruction left behind in their houses or flats, and this was also the perfect opportunity for the parents to meet up for a gossip, and to complain about their incompetent other-halves. Part of Simon's reasoning for going to the park was because of meeting young mothers. He was a young male after all.

Darren was already pulling on Simon's arm as they got nearer. He was so excited to be there. For twenty minutes, Simon pushed the boy on the swing, and watched him go up and along the climbing frame. Then Darren went to sit in the play house, his arms outstretched pretended to steer the make-believe car.

Simon glanced over at his large bag sat on its own. He didn't want to lug it around the play area, but now, he noticed two ladies were looking to sit down.

He trotted over to remove the bag.

"I'm sorry," he said apologetically. "Let me move that."

They smiled and nodded thanks, both taking in the helpful young guy that he was. He liked that they assumed him to be the father. He couldn't see him officially playing that role for many years, but it was nice to pretend.

Then his mobile buzzed.

"Hey Si! Everything okay?" Sophie said in her excited voice. He could tell by her tone that the interview had gone well.

"Yes, we're fine. We're just down the park. Darren's pretending to drive the car."

He could see her smile and picture the grin, the one almost identical to her son's. "I got it!" she burst out, and then went on to tell him about the interview, and the answers she proudly gave.

Simon glanced over to Darren. Whilst he couldn't see him, he could see the arm of his blue jacket moving. Satisfied, he glanced away.

He was so pleased for his sister. The park was heaving by the time he'd finished the call. He picked up the bag, and began to walk towards the little house under the climbing frame.

"Darren! Time to go now buddy!" he saw the arm still moving, and as he got closer the outline of the boy came into view. The little boy's head turned and his stomach dropped.

The boy was not his nephew.

"Darren!" he shouted dropping the bag where he was. He turned on the spot, his head twisting and turning as his eyes scanned every child.

"Darren!" he shouted louder, and parents and children all stopped and stared at this sudden spectacle.

"Have you lost your son?" A hipster mother asked, her dreadlocked hair pulled back with a huge hairband.

"My nephew. Yes," he corrected, her now suddenly irritated with everyone. He began to move around but without purpose or direction. He looked at all of the children again, but it was no use. They weren't him.

Darren had disappeared.

Phone calls were made, and soon everyone knew about the missing boy called Darren Hughes.

Despite searches, televised pleas by Sophie and Simon, interviews with parents at the playground, none of the leads went anywhere but a bulging folder grasped by a number of head-scratching detectives.

One day turned into a week, then two weeks and then a month. With each passing day, the statistics of finding Darren alive reduced.

A Lifetime Ago

By the second month, there had been a murder, and an arson attack, and suddenly little Darren Hughes was no longer the highest priority, and his case folder became nothing but a hot potato.

Chapter 4 - Hudson

Sleep wasn't something Hudson found easy to come by. His mind was permanently switched on. That was part of the problem with cold cases. A small detail or even a hunch could start up the fire again. It was all about getting that break.

He lay there gazing into the darkness, but to turn on the lamp was to give up on sleep. And that was one of things he really needed in order to break the cases.

Night time was a lonely time, and if he wasn't frustrated trying to piece together puzzles, then he was thinking about a woman who should've been laid there next to him. The clichéd one that got away.

It wasn't even the incident that drove her out the door. She'd already wandered into his neighbour's bed weeks beforehand, not that he was aware of it at the time. Hudson was always quick to take the blame; to say it was his work that made him neglect her, rather than admit she'd cheated on him through her own free will.

He was a haunted soul, forever full of regrets. Wishing he'd not been so distracted that morning.

A Lifetime Ago

At some point in the night, exhaustion smothered him into a comatose state. He fell deeply asleep. However, not long after the witching hour, he was tossing and turning.

He was re-living it over and over again. When he woke up, he was close to tears. Despite the therapy, and even the grief counselling group sessions he didn't feel like he was getting better. Talking about his feelings and breaking it all down did nothing but upset him further. What he needed to do now was give back to the community. To go that extra mile to help those children that appeared to be beyond help. Only then could he even consider the possibility of redemption, and maybe he could finally forgive himself.

No sooner had the sun appeared in the sky than his mind kicked back into action. A flick of a switch bringing him to life like Frankenstein's monster.

It was early when Hudson got out of bed. That wasn't unusual. His mind refused to relax even in the morning.

He put the kettle on, and made himself a strong coffee that would clear any remaining cobwebs from his mind.

For the most part he was a tea drinker, but in the morning, he enjoyed the jolt of strong caffeine. It was his current drug of choice.

His flat had two bedrooms, and the second one he dedicated to his work. It was his life. The only way he felt he could truly mend inside.

Jim Ody

As soon as he opened the door he was met by the face of little Darren Hughes. His picture was blown up and on the wall as a reminder. Darren wasn't alone. The whole of two walls was a sad gallery of missing or vulnerable children. Each had a backstory, and whether or not they'd had a happy upbringing, the fact of the matter was everything about their current situation was bleak.

Hudson sipped his coffee and slowly scanned each picture. Each day he looked into the two-dimensional eyes of each child. He knew they were only pictures, but they deserved to know that someone was trying to help them.

Hudson's mobile rang, and it frustrated him that he hadn't got to the end of the pictures.

"Hi Pete," he said, the real feeling was evident.

His friend, and former police colleague was his direct contact with the police. He would go back into police headquarters for meetings, but despite the past, he'd now be considered just a civilian. Everything he was told had to be authorised first, that was just the way it worked.

"We found the body of Tristan Burns, Huds."

"Are you sure?" Hudson said as he walked up to the picture of a toddler with baked bean juice smudged around his face. Tristan was three. He was smiling in the picture. A mischievous grin. Hudson wondered whether that made things better or worse.

Apparently, he'd been taken from his front garden. And as often was the case, that was a lie.

"We have no doubt, mate," Pete said slowly, and careful with his words.

Pete called Hudson a couple of days a week to update him on any case developments. Hudson was under no illusion that Pete was also tasked with keeping an eye on Hudson, ready to raise the alarm if his mental state began to deteriorate. As a police contracting consultant, it was the only major clause he had written into his employment contract.

Tristan's case was a classic. No witnesses and no idea how or why it had happened. The case had been cold. Very cold. And now it was no longer a missing person case, but a murder case. The body of the little boy had been found buried in a garden. The back garden had been owned by one of the grieving parents. It had been that simple. The crocodile tears had rolled for the cameras, but dried quickly when the lights were turned off.

"Send me the details." Hudson ended the call just like that. Pete fully understood, they'd worked together for many years.

Hudson walked up to the picture. He bent down to the level of the small boy, and whispered, "I'm sorry." Each case was personal.

He wouldn't remove the picture until after the court case. And even then, it was with reluctance that he took it down. The minute he removed the Blu Tak from the back, and placed the picture into its folder then it felt like he'd officially given up and lost.

He completed the ritual of looking at each of the pictures, and then stood back, as if addressing them all at once.

"I'm sorry I don't have more time. I promise I will do my best."

He wanted to save every one of these children, even though it would never bring back the one child he wanted more than any.

Four-year-old Luke Southall.

The boy he knocked down and killed.

Chapter 5 - May

Over the past four years, May Southall felt like she'd aged considerably. In the mirror, she looked at the sad bedraggled woman staring back at her and wondered whether it was a manufacturing defect with the glass. Surely the reflection was utter lies.

She used to be pretty. Her long red hair had a natural wave to it. Her eyes were grey and she'd been told they were hypnotising. Her ex-husband Robert had told her as much on many an occasion. Strangers had too. She was still athletic even if her body had suddenly attracted a few pouches. Clothes hid a multitude of sins.

Each day was now spent covering her woes with products claiming to reverse the signs of aging, or cover enough skin to make herself look acceptable.

At some point the sides of her eyes had begun to droop, and lines had formed at the side of her mouth. She'd stayed inside more and more, and the once healthy glow in her cheeks was nothing but a memory. The only glow she got now was anger through frustration or from wiping away the sadness that spilled from her eyes.

Each step outside of her door was another bombardment of emotions. Everybody could tell she was no longer a happy woman. She didn't always want to pretend anything else.

She was fed up of the sympathy that people felt the need to give her. Their sad resigned faces as she moped by. The poor woman who lost her son and her husband on the same day. One went to heaven, and the other she cast to hell. Both were dead to her.

People only wanted quick small talk. They swooped in and then were gone just as quickly. Nobody wanted to be burdened with her sorrow. She sucked the life out of wherever she went.

After that awful day, she'd moved away from her house. At first, she moved in with her parents, she needed to be looked after, but after a few months they assumed she'd be cured. They assumed their stacks of cash would somehow heal her shattered heart, reboot her mental state back to the factory settings and she would suddenly be normal again. It didn't work like that. Days and months rolled into one. Until she had to get away.

They'd gone from years of saying how wonderful their son-in-law was, to telling her now how they knew her husband would eventually stray. And now, her mother had the audacity to hint that perhaps May wasn't pleasing her man. That was the last straw.

She fell out with her parents, and eventually bought a house on the other side of Swindon.

She was truly alone. Well, sort of. Her husband had left her with a departing gift. For many nights she had laid crying herself to sleep, shaking hands on her stomach as the fatherless-child grew inside.

Now she sat at her laptop staring at faces of men she may never meet. It felt so desperate to look for a man this way. Not to mention judgemental. In an instant she would look at them and decide whether or not the two of them had a future together.

She was picky. She couldn't help it. Each smiling face only hid the deception behind it, and their profiles were more than likely littered with lies and fabrication. She knew that each man had some emotional baggage kicked just out of shot of their profile picture. The ugly ones were desperate. The handsome ones too good. The middle-of-the-road wanted something better. It was a whole minefield. And that was even before she'd made connection.

Every night when she sat down to look at the hopeful faces, all she saw was one. Her ex-husband Robert. He wasn't that handsome, and he wore a few extra pounds but when he pulled her close, she felt safe. He was dependable and perfect. Right up until the point he wasn't.

Before she knew it, she was scrolling his profile and keeping up to date with his life. She hated it. She hated him. Everything was so sickeningly perfect. The death of their son should've brought him back to her. It should've been the emotional tie that kept them forever bound. Although, the legality of their marriage didn't seem to hold much water, so why should loss?

Robert just ran further into the arms of his lover and that was what really stung.

In the pictures, Nadia, of course, looked great. Her dark Indian skin was blemish free, and her long black hair straight and silky. May hated that Nadia's body still looked like a teenager's. The way she always accentuated her breasts, only taunted May who always felt short-changed in that department.

May heard the beep and saw the smiling icon appear as she received an instant message from a guy called Greg. She'd recently been speaking to him having seen his profile online. He was handsome, and as far as she could tell had minimum baggage. He was divorced with a child.

Hey Gorgeous! The message began. She didn't know whether to feel complimented, or guarded to such lies.

Hey Handsome! She responded, and so it went on. He was up there with what she wanted. He wasn't Robert, but that was only because Robert was still alive.

Greg lived on the Devon and Cornwall border. He'd given her the town he lived in, and from there it had been simple. The internet can get you any information you want. It was that simple.

She felt giddy when she talked to Greg. He was smart, kind and funny. He was the leading man in her movie, and she, the awkward woman who wanted to experience romance again.

She couldn't help it. Her thoughts were mixed up; her emotions were all over the place. She wasn't bipolar, but since that day, she'd wondered how differently that disorder would make her feel. She took another swig of gin. Not a sip, a swig. It was dangerous. She knew that. She'd stopped seeing the mental doctor when he demanded she pull back on the emotional substitutes she was indulging in. Alcohol and prescription drugs. Now speaking to Greg, it was another euphoric shot around her body, and with every high, she'd experience the deep lows too.

When Greg was gone, she'd fall hard. Her thoughts became dark. Very dark.

By the light of her monitor screen, she turned and glanced at the bedroom door of her son, now four-years-old. The name on his birth certificate was Sonny, but she couldn't help it, she didn't want to call him that.

So she always called him Luke.

Her boy was here again and this time he wasn't going anywhere.

She screwed her face up at the profile of her ex-husband, closed down the lid on him for the night, and wished to God she could remove him off the face of the earth too.

Chapter 6 – Robert

18 months after the incident

The house was lovely. No, that wasn't right. The house was perfect. Small and quirky, it sat back into the hillside, almost invisible from the surrounding area. It was the perfect getaway. A place to forget your past and build memories for the future. And more importantly, far away from people they knew.

His job was stressful. He no longer had the daily commute into London, but he was still up early every day. After a quick jog, he showered and had breakfast before the day ahead where he was usually making calls and living online. That was the world of investigative journalism. And for a large national magazine to boot. But even back before the incident, he'd taken advantage of the shift to no longer sit in an office to write, read and research. There were too many distractions, and now he could do it from home. The world had changed and evolved.

Then, with some money saved up, he began to

A Lifetime Ago

do freelance work. It meant he got to write about stories and issues that he believed in, and not what had been decided by a monotonous Monday morning meeting with out-of-touch old-school editors, and managers.

His life had changed suddenly the previous year. Everything he'd known had been blown apart. He'd got up that day in exactly the same way he always had, not knowing that life would never be the same again.

He now looked out over the flat sea. Yesterday, the waves had been huge. The silent roar of water violently crashing upon itself. Almost exciting. A force of nature untamed. Man could do nothing against it.

He couldn't help thinking back. This was the perfect place for contemplation, and invariably that meant thinking about the past. Whatever his feelings, Robert knew it shaped him and to a point outlined the future. In the city, he'd locked that day away, never facing it head on. His life was too busy. He never relaxed. That was what he wanted to do now. But with that slow pace came the worry that he would spiral out of control.

"Are you okay?" she said peering over the top of a paperback.

He glanced over with a small smile at his partner Nadia. "Of course," he lied. He was never alright when he thought back to then.

She knew. "You don't have to forget your past, Robert. As long as you're happy now?"

"I know," he said probably with too little conviction. He was happy, that was the truth. Very happy in fact. But there was always the part of him that would never get over what had happened.

"How's your book?" he asked, not only to change the subject but to include her in his thoughts. She was his future now. His co-conspirator in life.

She reached over the sofa bed and stroked his leg. "You don't really want to know, do you?"

He laughed. "Of course, I do!"

She raised an eyebrow then said sarcastically. "Really?"

He nodded. "I'm sure it's not clichéd at all."

He knew he was flying close to the wind. She loved his sense of humour, but reading was incredibly important to her, and she hated him being so trivial about it. He needed movie pictures, whereas words were enough to spring visions alive.

"Go on, then. Tell me what you think it's about oh wise one!"

He turned to her, and in a dramatic Morgan Freeman voice began, "It was a grisly murder. None like anything that had ever been seen before. A serial killer on the loose leaving a telltale calling card…"

Nadia smiled and rolled her eyes playfully. He continued. "cop was on the case. He was a rough-around-the-edges brooding cop. A broken marriage behind him, and an addiction hidden to all but one person. He will stop at nothing to catch the killer! Dun-dun-dun!"

Nadia slow-clapped him sarcastically. Her hands only making a quiet sound. "Who knows?"

He looked confused. "Who knows what?"

"About his addiction?"

He shrugged. "I dunno. A love interest maybe. His housekeeper?"

"Housekeeper? Where d'you think this is set? Hampshire in the 1930s?"

They both grinned and laughed.

Nadia then nodded. "Not bad," she said. "And you might be right, or close on a few of them but it's all about the variations on that style. I personally think this is a fine example of it!"

"I'll wait for the movie."

"Sometimes things are worth the wait," she said sliding over and putting her arms around him.

"I know," he replied and kissed her on the forehead.

"And sometimes there isn't a movie, so the wait is in vain." She winked.

Nadia met Robert long before the morning his son died. They were two very different people. He was tall and stocky, with a pale complexion that could flush red with emotion. She was short, skinny and mixed race. A small part Iranian, and a large part Indian, and so looked exotic. People often mistook her as being Mediterranean.

Nadia wrote children's books, so they both worked from home, hunched over, pecking at separate keyboards.

This weekend they escaped the rat-race for some time alone. They had driven down to the Devon and Cornwall border to look at houses. Moving was now a serious possibility. They loved both counties so either side of the border was fine.

They both wanted to escape their pasts and hidden away near the coast in the South-West seemed like a great idea. Life moved at a gentler pace around there.

Initially, they'd wanted to check out a house in Huntswood Cove, but when they arrived there was a huge police presence that wouldn't allow them anywhere near the house. It was such a shame. The house was on the South-coast, again up on the cliffs, but also buried deep within the woods. They decided against it then and headed straight to the north of Cornwall instead.

"That was strange earlier, wasn't it?" Nadia said. "What was going on do you think?"

"I've no idea." Robert had looked on his phone at the news but it was all very vague. The police were saying nothing other than there was a serious incident, and they had it under control.

"So, what about the place we're looking at tomorrow?"

A huge grin spread over Robert's face. "You're gonna love it. It's a large house. Probably larger than we need, and sat out on its own." He picked up his mobile and found the email with the pictures attached.

Nadia's eyes grew wide as she saw the front of the house, then swiped to see more pictures of the interior. "Why's it so cheap?"

He laughed, "It's hardly cheap! It's the top end of our budget."

"I know, but it looks too good to be true, don't you think?"

"Well, these are just pictures, the place could look completely different when we turn up to it." His gaze wandered outside towards the sea view.

"Are you sure about this, Rob?"

He looked back at her. She was serious, and he saw worry in her eyes. He smoothed her cheek with his hand.

"About what? Us? Or the house? I'm behind everything?"

Her hand covered his, but not to stop it, to feel his touch some more. "Moving away from your family? I don't want to take you away like that."

He was shaking his head before she'd even finished. "Don't be silly. We're both moving away from our families. We're both leaving because…"

And there it was hanging there. The elephant in the room of the small isolated house.

"The accident," she finished.

"Yes."

They had officially got together after the accident, but they'd already known each other. Intimately.

The day had been dark for both of them. For many separate reasons, and yet somehow through it all they'd found each other.

But Robert couldn't shake the pang of guilt he felt when he thought back to the days, months and years before that day. His life had been perfect for the most part. And then it was nudged off centre, before suddenly being blown completely out of the water.

After that day, everything changed.

Chapter 7 - Hudson

Hudson drove his ten-year-old BMW into the street to pick up his partner Jez. They'd been summoned into the station for a debrief on the previous day's arrest, and also to collect more case files to focus on. Hudson appreciated the heads up, but he also liked to choose his own cases. He felt he prioritised in a more efficient way, whereas the police — he felt — chose cases that pleased the hierarchy, the media, or the general public rather than cases more likely to be solved sooner, and with little or no casualties. Half of the cold cases were due to a lack of financial support and man-power, and a proportion, unfortunately, were down to incompetent police work.

Aside from his grief, these were all reasons why Hudson left the police. He hated the politics of it all. The weak reasons why detectives were pulled from cases in order to support a lesser crime. You cannot tell a victim, or a victim's relatives, that their case had now expired, and mumble through the red-tape that they were continuing to follow up all lines of enquiry. A standard stock lie.

Jim Ody

Jez was a tall and skinny guy who was a little odd-looking. He was an IT and gadget expert, but as if to offset this, Jez acted like he was still eighteen. He was far from that actually being deep within his forties, and with a habit of saying the first thing that came into his mind. More often than not, Hudson was left to smooth things over, apologise and keep the peace. It was also strange to know he was married. His wife Cass was a short firecracker who was relatively normal, and kept him in line. Despite her bark, she did have a playful side to her. The video of her that Jez had sent him was not the first. It was also the reason Hudson was picking him up on the curb like some cheap hooker rather than knocking on his door. He felt he'd seen Cass almost as much naked as he had fully clothed.

"Here he is!" Jez said, beaming as Hudson pulled up beside him. This morning Jez was wearing a white shirt with frills on it more commonly seen in an American rodeo.

"Morning, Cowboy!"

"Eh?" Jez looked confused as he opened the passenger door, and folded himself into the seat.

"Really?" Hudson grinned. "You wear that shirt, and don't think I'm going to mention it?"

Jez looked down at himself like he'd forgotten what he was wearing. "It was clean," he said like that was an acceptable answer.

"So are my swimming trunks, but I'm not wearing them."

Jez shrugged. "Too many people worry about what other people think."

"And they are people who wish to remain employed."

They were off to an official meeting with the people who contracted them, and Jez had decided to go in fancy dress. That was just like him.

Hudson had on a pressed shirt. He didn't like dressing up either, but you had to understand how things worked. If they had to look their best once in while in order to help right the wrongs in life then so be it. Not wishing to quote Elton John, it was no sacrifice, or little anyway, he conceded.

"Just remember our usual rules, okay?" Hudson said.

Jez tapped his knees that were almost under his chin. "Be polite and let you do the talking."

It sounded childish, but Jez had got them into a lot of hot water in the past.

"Remember the first time I met you?" Hudson grinned as they hit the duel carriageway that would take them to the police station.

"You tried to give me money," Jez said shaking his head. "You mumbled something about charity."

Hudson realised he had a goofy smile on. "I thought you were trying to look like Shaggy from Scooby Doo!"

Jez sighed like the mere memory was hurting his feelings. "I thought you were a bit simple in the head. I just happened to be wearing a green sweater with brown trousers."

"Bell-bottoms."

"They were just a bit baggy."

Hudson laughed at that. "Baggy?" He turned grinning. "Baggy is slightly more loose than normal, whereas those could've smuggled in at least four of Snow White's little stalkers!"

"I bet you don't joke like this when we see the sergeant."

That dropped the smile from Hudson's face, as he replied, "No, I won't, and you hadn't better either!"

"You think the sarge likes Miley Cyrus?" he grinned wiggling his phone in a threatening manner.

"Don't even joke."

The large police building stood large and domineering in front of them. They parked up, and made their way to the main entrance.

Pete met them at the door. "Gents… Jesus, Jez! The sergeant is in a foul mood as it is, what are you wearing?"

"It's my new shirt!"

"He's not a bloody bull!"

Jez gave him a look, and Pete lowered his voice a touch. "I know he can be a little bullish sometimes…but, you know? Come with the territory. But Jez? Why?"

Pete looked at Hudson, who rolled his eyes. "I apologise, as always for my son. He will miss a week of his favourite cartoons."

"Come on," Pete said, flashing a glance at his watch and shaking his head.

As they walked into the building, a stern-faced woman with a severe short, back and sides, looked visibly shocked at Jez, and bearing in mind the sort of people she dealt with on a daily basis, that was no mean feat.

"Case closed, Pete," she said, and remained deadpan when she continued. "Tell Roy Rogers we've found his shirt!"

Jez frowned like he didn't know what all the fuss was about. "Is that the football comic?"

"That's Roy of the Rovers," Hudson hissed.

The desk sergeant looked at Hudson and said, "I see you're the brains of the outfit."

Hudson nodded. "You got that right. He just plays with computers."

"Come on," Pete said nodding to the desk sergeant, and taking them through a secure door and to some stairs. Worried about the time, Pete quickened the pace as they went up some stairs towards an unmarked room.

"No comment!" Jez said as he walked in.

"Jez!" Hudson said under his breath. "Do you want to wait in the car?"

Jez held up his hands as a weak apology.

"I'll be right back," Pete said looking stressed. Jez had that effect on people. "Is he going to be alright?"

"I'm good!" Jez grinned. It was his way of maintaining some control. It was nothing to with power, just all to do with his immature stubborn nature.

Ten minutes later the tall and imposing figure of Sergeant Barnes walked in, Pete following behind clutching a folder. He was a big built black guy around Hudson's age of comfortably in their forties. Hudson had known him when he'd worked in the police, but had never had many dealings with him. He was tough, and diligent. He was ex-army, and his social skills suggested that feelings weren't worth the effort in combat. He had no interest in asking about the family, or going to social events — unless it was a competitive team-building exercise where he could bark orders, and belittle people in order to win. All that said and done, he wanted results too. Their motives differed greatly, but their goal remained the same.

"Right, I'll make this brief, as we're all extremely busy. Thanks for coming in, and all that," he waved that off as small talk, it was dutiful and without feeling. "I can confirm that we have charged Tristan Burns' parents Frankie and Sonya, with Tristan's murder. So great intel on that Hudson. I can also confirm paedophile Rodney Rhoades was arrested last night, and he has been charged with a number of offences. Once again, thank you both for your efforts." He paused and waited for a response.

"You're welcome," Hudson said, and glanced at Pete who was stood behind the sergeant grinning.

"The reason I brought you in here was the Darren Hughes case. I'm sure you're aware of it."

"We are," Hudson said nodding.

The Sergeant looked straight at Hudson. Eye-to-eye and man-to-man. He was stood straight, his chest out and his hands held behind his back. "The thing is we've hit a wall. We have to shift the man power, but we need…"

Hudson held up his hand. "Say no more. We'll get straight on to it."

The sergeant nodded like that was the correct response. He looked quickly at Jez, his eyes specifically glancing at his shirt. Jez responded by waving, and replying with, "All over it!" and winking.

"Hmmm, quite," The sergeant said slowly shaking his head in disappointment. Hudson could imagine the last man to wink at Barnes had probably been punched in the face, and Barnes was showing a huge amount of restraint.

Instead of unleashing an Anthony Joshua punch onto his side-kick's jaw, Barnes nodded to them both, and said, "Just keep Pete and me in the loop." Then disappeared from the room.

"He appreciates everything you two do," Pete said when the coast was clear. "He sees you as really important members of the team, in fact, Huds, he really wishes you were still a copper."

"I'll bet," Hudson said. He smelt the lies, and felt sorry for Pete. Hudson wasn't stupid, Sergeant Barnes preferred this arrangement. It was the perfect scenario for him. Hudson did the work, and if he was successful then the police took the credit, but if he made mistakes or failed then he was just an outside organisation of lower skill and quality. They both knew that if Hudson was still in the force, then by now he would outrank Barnes. It was just another reason he'd left. He wasn't interested in rank, titles, ladder-climbing, arse-kissing, or wage increases. These things didn't motivate him. What he wanted — and this seemed very comic-book-hero-esque — was justice. His whole being was based around keeping the peace, and living his life by the law. Justice for the good, and punishment for the bad. He longed for a society where good triumphed over evil.

"What about me?" Jez said.

Hudson and Pete looked at each other. Pete's response was less rehearsed. "Your work is appreciated too. It's… er, good to have skilled people in the background."

Jez made a face. "Hmmm, background? Personally, I think you're all missing a trick."

"I guess that's the risk they'll have to take, buddy," Hudson said, as Pete ushered them out.

As they walked out, the desk sergeant was booking in a dishevelled guy in baggy track-suit bottoms, a Liverpool shirt, and poor amateur tattoos on his face. He turned around and took in Jez.

"Look at this wanker!" he grinned, revealing blackened teeth and gaps where teeth used to be.

"Jealousy," Jez said.

"Don't engage," Hudson hissed.

The yob was wriggling, whilst the arresting officer was trying to keep him under control. "Listen to ya boyfriend!"

Hudson shrugged, "I'd have better taste than him."

This time it was Pete's turn to say, "Don't engage." But it was said in jest.

"Here you go," Pete said at the door, handing over the file to Hudson. "This is what we have."

"Cheers Pete."

So that was that. The police had handed over full responsibility of the case to them. It could be said that the big guns were on the case, but Hudson had a lot of cynicism to towards the police's actions. To him it felt like they were drawing the line under it. The one last chance for resolution before it was filed away in the vaults until the end of time.

Hudson looked at the file in his hands. It was thick. But this wasn't a burglary or a car theft, this was a missing child. A life that was in the balance. It was too soon to give up. Much too soon.

Hudson had to find Darren Hughes. That was the bottom line.

Chapter 8 - Hudson

Back at Hudson's flat, they sat around the dining room table in the lounge.

The table had the folder open with reports and photographs sprawled out. Then in the middle was a teapot, a jug of milk and two full teacups on saucers.

"Shouldn't we be drinking black coffee and complaining about the taste?" Jez said picking up his teacup, little finger extended as he lifted it to his lips and slurped.

"The British empire was built on tea, and if you think I'm starting a new case without one, then you're sadly mistaken!"

Jez pointed a finger at him. "You're quoting from movies again, aren't you!"

Hudson nodded, "Paraphrasing more like but yes, that was pretty much the line from the Guy Ritchie movie." Hudson was a huge tea drinker, but only when made properly. He didn't subscribe to the sloppy task of throwing a teabag into a mug like it was some fairground entertainment. Tea had to be made correctly, and that meant tea leaves measured into an already warmed teapot, a splash of milk into the teacups and specific brewing time adhered to.

"What have we got then?" Hudson said, as he looked at the contents of Darren Hughes' folder.

"It's sparse, Huds. The mother Sophie was at a job interview with Dice Commercials. They've confirmed that. The brother was seen the whole time at the park by a number of witnesses. It was confirmed he arrived, and then confirmed he called the police without leaving the area."

Hudson picked up his teacup. It was quite a dainty move, for such a strong looking guy. "And the father?"

"Currently doing a stretch in HMP Winchester. He's not seen Darren since his birth."

Hudson nodded and let all the detail sink in. That was how he worked. His mind was able to file away each fact into the correct place, and would continually move things around until something jumped out. It was why he was so successful. Solving crimes was all about evidence and details, and that was how the police worked, but Hudson could often see a motive, or could come up with a theory that would have them looking at things from a different angle.

"As I recall," Hudson said, his eyes half closed. "The park was busy that day. All of those witnesses."

"How did nobody see anything?" Jez said slurping again.

Hudson pulled a face and opened his eyes. "Do you have to do that?"

Jez looked apologetic but didn't say anything.

"What did you say?" Hudson then said.

"What? How? I thought I said it in my head!"

Hudson laughed. "No, before that."

"A lot of witnesses?"

Hudson nodded. "Exactly. What's better than no witnesses?"

Jez looked confused and shrugged. "Nothing is better?"

Hudson took another sip and placed the cup down. "Wrong. Lots of people is a perfect disguise. Hiding in plain sight. An adult wandering off with a crying child brings only sympathetic looks from other parents. They look away so as not to make the parent feel any worse."

Jez looked at the picture of Darren. "You think someone just walked into the playpark, grabbed him and walked out?"

"It's possible."

Jez had his tablet open on the table. He picked it up but stopped. It said everything about how they worked. Hudson looked through the file and hypothesised, while Jez straightaway looked to corroborate it with data, but even armed with his weapon of choice he was stuck. He still had nothing to look up.

"We have a list of witnesses. The other parents at the park," Jez said.

Hudson shook his head. "It's not them."

"How can you be so sure?"

"I can never be one hundred percent sure, but the witnesses are people who came forward in response to the appeal, or who were recognised by other parents. All of those recognised were there with their own children."

"So then easy to take another child?"

"Unlikely. You ever tried to make a child do something they didn't want to do? It's not easy. Try making your child leave the park, and abduct another child at the same time. Not easy."

"Like herding cats is what I've heard."

"Exactly."

"What about a couple? There were two on the witness list?"

"Both had two children, so again this could be even more unlikely."

Jez sat back on his seat and waved his hand at the information in front of him. "So you think the person responsible is not in this file?"

"I can't say that, Jez, but I think it's probably likely. But, that said, we need to go over these people again. No offence to the police, but sometimes it's the way you ask a question that can get a useful answer. We have to start with the mother first."

Jez suddenly looked serious. "Huds, you never talk about it," he began. "The incident… with Luke."

Hudson nodded slowly, and picked up his cup again. He looked past Jez and out of the window. "I don't like to talk about."

"Look, I'm not as… I don't know… as complex as you. I don't need much in my life, but Huds, I see you walking around with this huge cloud hanging over you. You're a good person. This thing is slowly killing you. You used to smile."

Hudson actually felt himself getting a bit emotional. He sipped his tea to help swallow down the lump in his throat. "I killed a boy, Jez. A beautiful little boy with the whole of his life ahead of him. His parents split up after that, no longer able to deal with the grief."

"You're being too hard on yourself. They split up because the father was having an affair. Which you know all about as it was your girlfriend he was doing it with!" Jez almost raised his voice. "They would've split up anyway. And you know what the strangest thing is?"

"Enlighten me."

"You're all about the how, what and why of things, and everything to do with that accident was not your fault. He ran out behind your car as you reversed from your driveway."

"I should've looked."

"You were racing to the scene of a crime, which proved to be your biggest case. Your work had caught one of the biggest criminals. You'd become obsessed with it."

"You don't know, mate." Hudson said quietly, almost as a warning. Tears were rolling down his cheeks.

"You're right, I don't. People were saying you were a machine. You worked the case all day every day, but I heard other whispers. The people that warned that a human couldn't maintain it."

"So what you're…"

"Shh, don't put words in my mouth, mate. You were one of the best coppers. Probably too good. I don't want to speak out of turn, but we're mates. That case is what killed Luke Southall. That case probably killed your relationship too. All I'm saying is, I go home to Cass. She does things to take my mind off the cases…" he waved his hands. "But, anyway, my point is you have no one, so you're here dwelling on the past, and working hard, but if you're not careful…" the words were left hanging.

Hudson wiped his cheeks. "I hear you. I'm going to the Grief Counselling sessions. I'm really trying." Hudson thought about Laura, but it was too early to mention her to Jez.

"You spend so long looking after others, but sometimes you have to look after yourself. We can't find Darren if you lose your grip on reality, mate."

"I appreciate it, mate. I really do."

Chapter 9 – Robert

A few years ago

It was situated a couple of miles from the main road. The sat nav on Nadia's mobile came through the speakers of the car. The technology of Bluetooth was such a wonderful thing, and soon told them they were close. Ahead they could see the faint line between the sky and the sea. A sea view would be the icing on the cake.

Then as they rounded a bend and headed up a long road to nowhere, there was a great reveal as they observed a driveway leading to a newly refurbished house. The *For Sale* sign leant over at a haphazard angle. It looked like it had been there a while. Next to it was another sign, but this one was heavily weather beaten and simply said, '*Seaview*'.

"Wow!" Nadia said in disbelief. "Are you sure there hasn't been some mistake? This place is gorgeous."

Robert had to agree. It was a little bit higher in price than the other houses, but it appeared to offer so much more. He'd tried without success to find the faults. It was a little out of the way, and a good five minutes before you saw another house, and ten before you came to a village, but surrounded by rolling farmland, and great views it offered solitude and tranquility. Or at least that's what the description had boasted. And looking at it, they were sure it must be true.

He pulled the Jaguar into the driveway glad it was the SUV model with better ground clearance. The crunching sound of the tyres on gravel was all that could be heard over the quiet hum of the electric powered engine.

Robert looked at his phone. It was a text from the estate agent. His heart sank, and he expected the worst. That would be about right after the wonderful carrot was still swinging in front of their faces.

"What's wrong?" Nadia ask sensing the change in him.

"The estate agent just sent me a text," he said opening it up. He then grinned in relief. "It's okay, she's been held up but has told me where the key is. We can go in and look around on our own!"

"Really?" Nadia said, her face lighting up. "Is it okay to just look around without the owners?"

Robert got out. "I'm not sure anyone lives here anymore."

The only sound was the faraway crashing of the sea on the rocks, and above them, the gulls that circled and called out.

The front of the house was in a cream cladding. It was large but simple. A double garage was off to the side, juxtaposed to the house, and a drystone wall framed the gravel area making it a courtyard. Some hanging baskets splashed an inviting colour either side of a dark blue front door.

"Under the mat," Robert said pointing down towards it.

"Really?"

As she stalled, he bent down and under the second corner he lifted, he came out with a fistful of keys.

He slipped the obvious front door key into the lock, turned it, and pushed it open.

There was a cold feeling to the wooden floor, that led them into a small dark area with a side table that had a vase of purple tulips on. The flowers appeared to be the only thing alive about the place, as an eerie silence fell upon them.

Still excited, they explored the house, both openly expressing their feelings with the appropriate sounds. Wide eyes and broad grins. They pictured what it would look like with their own furniture, already finding homes for things, and virtually moving in.

The front was the original part of the house, closed off and dark, whereas in contrast the back was a huge contemporary extension, light and open-plann, making full use of the sea view with a huge wall of glass that spanned the length of the kitchen, dining area and living room, that could roll back to bring the outside in, and inside out.

The views were stunning. There was a lawn with a small wooden house off to the side, that was also facing away and looking out towards the water.

On the other side there were steps leading down to an unfinished section that looked like it might be the beginning of a swimming pool. The area was cut away but it was obvious that construction had stopped. They got the feeling that something had happened to make the owners now want to just up sticks and move. Perhaps ghosts; a malevolent spirit driving them away, but soon they vanished. The house was so contemporary, it just didn't feel that way. Had it been a huge manor house, or a Georgian pub or hotel with dark Tudor beams, then you could easily be fooled into such thoughts.

"This house would be so much more if that pool was finished," Nadia commented, jogging down to the area. Her words were not said in disappointment, but with an edge of excitement that suggested she'd be the one to finish what had been started. A little project for her to get her teeth into.

"Would you want that completed?" Robert caught up with her. They were both caught up in a giddy feeling. Something about the place already made it feel like home.

"At some stage. How great would that be?" He had to agree. He thought about a child swimming in it. His heart weighed heavy for a second. He swallowed down the lump in his throat.

This would be such a wonderful family home. *Their* family home. He looked back at her and for

Jim Ody

a flash expected to see May stood next to him, his mind caught up in the past.

He shook it off the same way he did every time it happened, and took her hand.

They hadn't even looked upstairs and already in their minds they'd moved in and were thinking about parties they could throw for a whole new set of friends. Ones who knew nothing about their past.

The downside was that it was a few hours' drive from their current house in Wiltshire, and also, they would have to move things around financially. This would mean cutting back on luxury goods for a while before they would be financially stable. It was a slight risk, but the gain was great.

They stood, holding hands and danced into each other's eyes. Their smiles held back words of satisfaction that were unrequired; they knew what this meant to each other. Sealed with a kiss, they walked back up to the house. Each step gave them something new to look at, and only made them want the house more.

Upstairs was more of the same. There were a couple of good-sized spare rooms at opposite ends that both had sea views. A smaller bedroom, and another converted into some sort of study, that were both situated overlooking the front of the house. Then another staircase took them to a huge master bedroom and spacious *en suite*, that made up the whole of the converted attic. Windows in the room, and mostly glass along the wall looking out towards the sea made the master really light and airy.

"Oh my God!" Nadia said looking around at how large the room was. A big inviting bed with uniquely-carved wooden side-tables would easily draw you in to lie down and look out to sea.

The estate agent still hadn't arrived.

"I know." He pulled out his phone and shook it at her. "Shall I?"

"What? Take a picture, or make an offer?" She looked about ready to cry.

He grinned and saw a text. The estate agent was sending her apologies, as she'd had to head back to the office. He dialed her number.

Nadia grabbed him tightly. This was it. They couldn't lose it now.

"Hello?" The business voice said at the other end. She was polite, but always direct and to the point. "Robert?"

"Hi Sue." He couldn't keep the smile out of his voice.

"I'm really sorry about that. We had an emergency here!" she laughed but didn't elaborate further. "So, how do you like it? It has such great potential, don't you think?"

Robert could hardly contain himself any further. "Can we make an offer?" He blurted.

"Oh, yes, of course! Wonderful!"

And so he did. Nadia looked worried when he offered fifteen-thousand pounds under the asking price, but sometimes you had to do that, and considering the asking price, this wasn't a massive discount. Sue said she'd get straight back to them.

Jim Ody

"Why didn't you just offer the asking price?" She said when he put down the phone, disappointment creeping into her voice.

He kissed her forehead. "Don't worry. I will if it's turned down. If that can be knocked off then it will mean less scrimping over the coming months." He pointed outside. "Perhaps we could even look at getting the pool finished."

"God, I love you, Rob!" And she truly did.

"I love you too."

The house was well furnished, although it still seemed quite sparse and impersonal. Perhaps the agent had told the owners to keep it that way. There was enough to draw a buyer into seeing the beauty and practicality of each room, without being put off by someone else's clutter.

They walked back down to the floor below, briefly looking again at each of the rooms. With fingers crossed they hoped they would soon be able to call the place their own. The spare rooms looked out over the open plan rooms downstairs. They admired the large sofa which fitted the space so well. It was like something out of one of those celebrity homes programs. Where we get to see a snapshot of where they live, and question the authenticity of it all.

And then Robert's phone rang. It was Sue again. His heart rate shot up.

"Hi Sue!" He put her on speakerphone.

"Hello Robert. I've spoken to the vendor and they have accepted your offer!" Nadia screamed and felt her eyes fill up. Robert could hear Sue was talking but missed what she said.

"Sorry, Sue. We're really happy with that. Did you say something else?"

"Haha!" she laughed. "Yes, I said if you were interested in the furniture too, then the vendor would be happy to leave it all for another two-thousand pounds."

"All of it? For two grand?"

Nadia mouthed, "Wow!" grinned and nodded enthusiastically.

"Yes! We'll take it all too!"

"Congratulations then!"

And that was that. Robert and Nadia had bought their first house together. They could move away from the old life that held so many bad feelings, and move into this amazing place, ready to start their lives over again.

They walked hand in hand back down towards the edge of the garden and looked out to sea. It was a wonderful view. It was now *their* view!

"I can't believe this," Nadia said. "This is our time."

Robert nodded, and felt guilty. After everything he'd been through, his life had suddenly turned around for the best.

Nadia grabbed his hands and turned towards him.

"You're everything to me," she said. "I would do anything for you."

They turned and looked at their new house. It was large and spectacular.

"I know you would," he said. "I know."

Chapter 10 – Robert

They moved into the house a few months later. Robert put his work to the back of his mind as he pushed, chased and harassed the solicitors until the sale went through.

He was so glad he did. The house was perfect. As with upgraded new houses it still felt like they were on holiday. Robert was convinced someone would come down the road and demand they leave the premises immediately. But thankfully that never happened.

They'd rearranged the furniture at first, not because they didn't like the way it looked but to make it feel like it was their choice. However, they soon realised the previous owners had it right in the first place, and promptly move it back.

The surrounding area was quiet. For the most part it suited them both. They had found themselves venturing into the nearby towns and slowly integrating into social circles. It was natural and, if nothing else, healthy. The last thing either of them wanted was to grow tired of each other.

Robert was sat on the floor upstairs looking through an old box. It felt sneaky, although he didn't mean it to be. Nadia had gone into town on

A Lifetime Ago

an errand, and he was relaxing listening to old records in the spare room. This was his room; part study, and part chillout room, when he wanted to just reset.

The Beastie Boys were rhyming about stealing cars and general tomfoolery over a number of recognisable samples. The trio had stolen so many snippets of other musicians' music that they were one of the reasons behind the stricter sampling laws that came in by the 90s. The band, instead of being annoyed by this, picked up their instruments again, were joined by other musicians to jam. From these sessions, they sampled themselves for their next album proving their musical ability, not to mention showcasing how they could adapt.

But Robert wasn't pondering over these facts. He was lost in the past as he stared at the photo album deliberately placed in the back of the drawer. Nadia knew it was there. She'd seen it a few times before. It wasn't some dirty secret, but it captured moments of his past. The many years before he knew Nadia. The first time he was truly in love.

His fingers drew lines over the faces in the pictures. The feelings engulfed him, and he often wondered whether this was what a medium felt when being used to channel energy by a spirit. It was almost as if the very touch of his fingers took him back to those moments. Those times.

She was pretty. *Of course* she was pretty. He'd never say that to Nadia, but that was the truth. He never compared the two, because they were so different. He was riddled with guilt just admitting these things. Each glance was a betrayal. Should he be full of regrets? Would that make things any better? Should he hate her, and wish the two of them had never met? But for every ounce of regret, was a flash of her smile towards him. Intimate flashes that others would never share. The freckles on her breasts that he remembered so vividly, the unnatural noises she made when he touched her in those places.

But her fiery temper also dominated his memories. How she'd jump to conclusions and shout at the top of her lungs in anger, name calling and belittling, before calming down and being full of apologies.

He couldn't help it. His fingers screwed up into a fist and he felt the anger. But he'd never had anyone to direct that anger towards. He was just as guilty as her. He glanced at the other guy. Caught in the background at a BBQ, stood looking all rugged. Or just as guilty as him, he thought.

He turned the page. The child sat there with big beautiful eyes and the hopes of a huge world ahead of him. That innocent smile and the small and fragile body that cried for protection.

Parents have one major job to do for a child. Protect them at all costs. Do everything you can to ensure they are okay. At least until the time they can do it for themselves.

They'd both failed.

He didn't even know he was crying until he felt the tickle of tears down his cheeks. He closed the book but that face still remained. *Help me, Daddy.*

A Lifetime Ago

I miss you. The voice of the child and his own merged together.

He'd do anything to go back to that day. Maybe even the month before. Let's be completely honest with ourselves. That was when he first made the wrong decision. He allowed his selfish feelings to get in the way. He took his eye off the ball. Away from his family. He set the timebomb ticking, and now he was still dealing with the consequences.

He hadn't seen his ex-wife for a long while. He was empty in his feelings towards her. They vocally blamed each other, but silently blamed themselves. A once beautiful couple deep in a love turned toxic by circumstance.

Another album held honeymoon pictures. She hadn't wanted them. In fact, unless it had their son in it then she wanted nothing to do with it.

It was so sad. Snapshots depicting the newlyweds. Selfies at the airport, then later looking tired, but still in love in Fiji. As he turned the pages their skin got darker, and their smiles wider and happier.

He thought back to the months after, and then the pregnancy, and raising Luke. He couldn't put a finger on when things changed. At some stage they'd made decisions. Tiredness and boredom, senseless arguments. Little things that grew without them realising.

Nadia had been there, as a friend. Really, she was only meant to be a friend.

Right next door. The temptation a few steps away. A magnetic pull that he could no longer fight.

Last week, he'd received an email. It was from *him*. Mr Rough-and-rugged-at-the-BBQ. The other piece in the puzzle. Perhaps the true guilty party who deserved all of the blame. But Robert struggled to blame him. He may've exploded the bomb, but it was Robert who had originally set it.

The face of his baby boy appeared again. The smile and giggle from little Luke was almost audible from somewhere else in the house. Robert turned his head to listen.

But there was nothing.

The way his personality had formed and made him proud. He'd been become so independent. Maybe too independent.

Robert was sobbing now: curled up on the floor and letting it all out. A private and personal time.

He had just about composed himself, when he heard the car crunch the gravel outside. This gave him enough time to bury the book back into the drawer, and quickly splash some water on his face. He then rubbed his face hard on the towel, and made his way downstairs to see Nadia.

She came through the door and dropped her car keys down onto the kitchen counter with a little clatter. He walked over and swept her up without a word. They kissed hard. Love and guilt fusing into passion.

"Well that was a welcoming," she said as they pulled back from each other.

A Lifetime Ago

"I just wanted to tell you how much I love you," he sighed. It was as if the words would somehow cleanse the feelings he'd had a few minutes ago. "I'm a very lucky guy."

She took off her coat and went to hang it up on the hook but stopped. She turned around, clearly with something on her mind.

"Robert, I think you should sit down."

His heart immediately started racing, as his stomach hit the wall. Those words were never followed by anything good. They were used as a buffer. A safety net to let the person know they needed to brace themselves for bad news.

"What is it?" He sat down on one of the stools at the breakfast bar feeling suddenly tense and nervous.

"You know I love you," she began, but that was no better, it was a prelude to a sucker-punch.

He didn't trust his voice and so just nodded.

"Uhm. Shit, I don't know how to say this..." she was pacing. One hand on her hip and the other was nervously running her fingers through her hair. "I'm a... we're... pregnant! We're having a baby, Robert!"

"What?!" he said. He couldn't believe it. He jumped up with a huge smile on his face. "Really?"

Relieved, she smiled, and giggled. "You're happy?"

"Of course, I'm happy!"

They embraced, and kissed. "That's where I've been. I wanted to make sure before I said anything. I know what you've… you know… been through, and I wasn't sure…"

He kissed her again. "I'm over the moon! This is wonderful news!"

He grabbed her by the hand. "This calls for a back rub. You deserve it."

She giggled again. Another couple deeply in love.

"But they always end up…"

He winked at her before she could finish. "I know!"

Inside he wasn't sure how he felt.

He was happy. He was really happy. It was just…

A baby was great if it was your first. You were so happy that it was part of you. But it was only when they got bigger that you really saw the child they were. Just like Luke.

He couldn't forget.

At least momentarily, his worries were left in a crumpled heap with her clothes on the bedroom floor. When their naked flesh touched it was the last thing on his mind.

Chapter 11 – Hudson

The problem with a case like this was that you could easily stand there ready for action, and be frustrated, not knowing which direction to take.

Time was of the essence. A missing child was high priority, but the sad part was, once you got past a week or so, time was less important. Statistics suggested that a child abducted for sexual motives would either have been found alive and scared, or else dead. If the child was taken to be smuggled, or sold, then there was a greater chance of them still being alive.

Realistically, they were searching for a body, or a child that was probably no longer in the surrounding area, or even the country. Hudson knew the only way to find Darren — dead or alive — was to start the investigation again, and cover all bases.

Hudson and Jez had read the police reports. That was the point at which Hudson would often see something. A gap in the investigation, or a lead not followed up. And it was never about pointing fingers, but all about getting results. To be fair to the police, there was nothing that jumped out. A child taken in full view, the three main suspects all with alibis. The most common outcome for this type of scenario was accidental death by a parent. Distraught, they would get rid of the body and make out their child had been abducted. In the grand scheme of things this didn't happen very often.

The chances of a child being abducted were around one in three-hundred, but the majority of these were children of twelve and over. Despite popular belief, toddler abductions were quite rare.

Hudson and Jez were two people. They weren't a huge team, and the cases were time consuming. Interviews had to be done in person, while you could get information over the phone, nothing beat looking someone in the face as they responded. Body language was the key. Hudson had done a course on it and it often proved more telling than a person's answers.

Wednesday soon turned into Thursday, and in turn before they knew it Friday was there, and Hudson felt like the case was slipping away from them. Jez had spent a lot of time compiling data. He looked at Sophie and Steven, pulling together lists of mutual friends from various social media platforms. Then he did the same for all of the witnesses from the park. It was a long and arduous task, but important nevertheless. Again, more often than not abductions were done by people known to the victims.

Hudson had a meeting booked with Darren's mother, Sophie. It would be a hard meeting, but was incredibly important. He needed to get an understanding of her. She was also the best person to tell him all about Darren.

But Hudson was dreading it. He should've asked Jez to be there too. He wasn't sure whether he could handle it. He was going to talk to a woman who had lost her only child, and one that was the same age as the child he'd killed. It would be like speaking to the mother of that child.

He'd tried to reach out to Luke's mother, May. His phone calls and emails remained unanswered. He'd even tried to reach out to the father, Robert. The man who had taken his girlfriend. Hudson wondered whether it was their rejection that stopped him from healing, and ultimately moving on. Knowing he was still hated so much kept the cuts gaping wide open. Deep down, he couldn't allow the wounds to heal. If that happened, then it excused his actions, and how can killing a child ever be considered as okay?

He opened the cupboard in the kitchen, and pushed aside the tin of biscuits. There, at the back, hidden away like a dirty secret was a bottle of rum. He needed something to take the edge off the day. Something that would help him get through the next few hours.

Defeated, he grabbed the bottle and pulled it free.

And then his mobile went. It was Jez.

"Hi Jez," Hudson said with eyes fixed on the bottle in front of him.

"Mate, I just wanted to wish you luck, you know? I get that it will be… you know… with Darren being the same age an' all…"

Jim Ody

It was sweet of the guy. There were a lot of times that Hudson thought Jez was a complete lummox. A loping fool, who happened to be good on computers. But now he realised he had got it wrong. Jez may lack a filter on his mouth, but he did have a heart of gold, and deep down these were core attributes that Hudson admired.

"Thanks, Jez. I really appreciate it."

"You want to swing by when you're done? We could get some drinks, or something?"

Hudson felt a little overwhelmed, and found himself grinning from ear to ear.

"I'll do that," Hudson said, picking up the bottle.

They said their goodbyes, Hudson put the bottle back in the dark corner of the cupboard, and pushed the biscuit tin back in front of it.

He couldn't explain it, but relief washed over him.

Twenty minutes later and Hudson was parking his car outside of the terrace house, and walking up to the front door.

He went to press the bell, but the front door swung open to reveal a young woman in her twenties. Her eyes were bloodshot. Probably through lack of sleep or from crying. Or more than likely from both.

"Hudson?" she said, a weak smile did its best to appear, however briefly. Even in grief she maintained her politeness.

"Hi Sophie," he replied holding out a hand which she took weakly, barely squeezing.

"Please come in." She led him inside and directly into the lounge. Her arm gestured for him to take a seat.

Hudson sat down and immediately saw the photos arranged in a small shrine with a large half-melted candle in the middle. The pictures in the small frames showed Darren smiling, either on his own or with his mum. The many different angles, and ages of this small boy showed the love she had for him.

But that wasn't the thing that got him.

A small crudely drawn card sat on a shelf nearby. Made from paper, the weight of it bent over slightly as if any draft would see it falling off, and floating down to the carpet below. The words were bright, bold and shaky with a stencilled outline ghosted in the background. But the words were simple, and yet so powerful.

I love you mummy

Hudson had to clear his throat and pull himself together.

"Thank you for allowing me here," he began, his voice weak at first. "I'm not a policeman, but I work alongside the police. They have drafted me in to look at your case, and find what has happened to your son." Hudson would normally refer to Darren by his name, but today he couldn't. It was just too hard.

Sophie nodded as he spoke, and Hudson wondered whether she was listening to anything he was saying, or just going through the motions.

"I want to go over some things, is that okay?"

She nodded. "Will you find him?" She said almost ignoring his question. She was desperate for him to say yes. To give her some sort of guarantee.

Hudson had to play it a little like a politician. He would not focus on the chances, the hopes or the realities of the task in hand, but instead on what he could, and would achieve.

"I work with the police because I'm good at what I do. I've solved many cases with fewer details than this one. What I can promise you is that I will put my heart and soul into finding Darren. That is my goal…" she was nodding again, and he could see her eyes welling up. "I can assure you that he will be on my mind when I go to sleep each night, and he'll be the first person I think of in the morning."

She pulled out a tissue and dabbed her eyes. "Thank you," she said.

"Okay, I'll ask you some questions, but if it gets too much then please just let me know, okay?"

"Okay."

He paused a few beats to collect his thoughts. He looked at his pad as if analysing the data already collected. It was misdirection. He was taking in a deep breath. And then he began. "Do you know of anyone who might be interested in taking Darren? Anyone you know, or even anyone you've noticed hanging around the street?"

"No," she said after a second or so, and shook her head.

"What about other parents at school? Or neighbours?"

"No," she said again after a pause. It was a thoughtful response; she wasn't just saying it.

"What about friends? Anyone come over here and act strangely? Or any online friends?"

"No…" Hudson thought it was left at that but then she elaborated further. "Only a couple of friends ever come around. One has a daughter of about the same age, and the other has no kids, and to be honest she isn't interested in Darren at all."

"Do you find that unusual? Or was that typical of her?"

Something that may have been a smiled played on her lips. A memory causing the reaction. "Nah, that was Leesh. She likes to go out and drink. Having kids is just not on her radar." Hudson noted her full name down. He'd crosscheck it with Jez's data later on. It was surprising how some people could suddenly be influenced by a new partner.

"And online?"

"Nah. I speak to a couple of people but I've never mentioned that I have Darren."

"Are these men that you speak to?"

"Both," her eyes then widened. "I mean in groups and chatrooms, not like, dating sites."

"Do you use your real name, or have a nickname you use?"

"Sophie#1994. That's it."

Hudson nodded. "I take it you were born in 1994?" She nodded. "There are many times we give out information to people we don't know, and we don't even realise it. Like posts that say things like, *your spiritual animal is your birth month*, and *your movie forename is your mother's maiden name, and your new surname is your first car*. These are all things that can be used to steal your identity, or to find out things like your address."

She looked shocked. "Wow! I'd never realised. Those posts are usually put up by friends who I thought were just bored."

Hudson held up his hands. "Don't panic, most of the time these posts are put up for those exact reasons, but it's not always the people putting up the posts it's the lurkers. Those who don't comment. They may '*like*' a post, but they actually just lurk in the background, reading posts and judging. Sometimes these people have ulterior motives. My point is with the internet, it's not just the people we see who could have nefarious intentions."

"I didn't even think of things like that."

"Okay, so this might sound a little direct, but can you think of anyone who may be behind this? Any feelings, thoughts, anything at all?"

Sophie chewed the inside of her lip. Hudson imagined the faces flicking through her mind like pages in a book. Each being discounted. He also noticed how she was sat, and how she had responded to his questions. She was on edge, but not nervous. She was clearly upset and distraught. Her answers were thoughtful, but neither too quick, nor taking too long. She spoke directly, even when she looked a little upset. No eye movements off high when replying. Her hands were only holding her tissue. They sat naturally on her lap.

After a few more questions, Hudson was ready for the hard one. It was a very important question.

"So tell me about Darren? What is he like?"

This time, Sophie did pause for a time. The tears welled up in her eyes. She dabbed them and looked past him towards a picture on the side.

"He's a very special little boy," she began. "His smile is infectious… He hardly ever gets grumpy… I mean, other parents would talk about the terrible-twos, tantrums, or shouting and screaming, but Darren is never like that. Well, rarely anyway. He's just a happy little boy… Please find him. Please bring my baby back!" she then sobbed.

Hudson nodded. He was desperate to do exactly that. He got up. "I promise I will do my very best," he said.

She stood up too, as they both recognised the meeting was over. "I know you will," she said, and then caught him off guard by saying, "You have kind eyes."

Hudson smiled in acknowledgement, gave her his card, and said goodbye. He left, but when he sat in his car, he just stared out of the window for a good five minutes. He felt emotionally drained, but that was nothing compared to the way Sophie felt.

He could feel the pressure of the case.

Finally, he started the car and drove silently to Jez's house, ready to tell him what he'd learned, if nothing other than he knew Sophie had nothing to do with it.

Chapter 12 - May

It was easy to question what was right, and what was wrong. Everyone thinks they're an expert in feelings and how you deal with things until it happens to them. You cannot bring a child into the world, love and cherish them for four years only to see them die.

Was that better or worse? It was all in slow motion. Luke grinning and suddenly running. The reversing Ford Focus. The sound of the small head hitting the back of the car, and then the sound of his head hitting the tarmac. Instantly the life escaped the small body and went off somewhere else. And she'd been trying to follow him ever since.

She recalled the look of horror on other people's faces as she was bent down over her son. People shouted to her not to touch him, and a couple of people were already calling an ambulance. How could she not touch him? He was her son. Her baby.

And there was blood. Just so much blood. The head bleeds out like no other part of the body, but this was more than that. She could tell.

A mother could tell.

Jim Ody

His pale face with those vacant blue eyes. Those sweet blue eyes. The ones she looked into at night when they began to droop with tiredness. Then she'd kiss him on the cheek and tell him how much she loved him.

She did the same, as panic hit like a wave around her. The shockwave circle increasingly pulling closer the concerned and the downright nosy. Drama to fill the void in their mundane lives.

Then Robert holding her closely. His strong arms around her. The safe arms that should have been there to look after their son. It was the last time they embraced. And that last time was through tragedy.

Loneliness was an umbrella word. One grabbed and thrown into sentences without much thought. But try being a woman in your thirties. A family woman with a husband and a son. A life that was hectic, and constantly juggling work commitments, family time, chores and social events.

And then one day it was all gone.

Her beautiful boy taken from her. Her husband running off with another man's woman. Her work putting her on medical leave pending an evaluation after six months. And friends too scared to be happy around her, and so faded quickly into the past.

Back in the bedroom where she grew up. Her things in storage, and her house cleaned and on the market. She stared at her bookcase of battered paperbacks. The ones she'd read as a teenager, secretly hoping her life would mirror the mysteries that both entertained, and enthralled her. She never quite had a life like that, but that was okay. It was a manic family dynamic that suited her.

Until everything ended with her parents, with the huge argument.

And then for weeks, she just wanted to give up. Throw in the towel and start again. And if there was nothing after death, then so be it. She couldn't contemplate anything worse than what she was feeling right then.

She'd had her stomach pumped twice before she found out she was pregnant. And even then, she continued to self-medicate. The child growing inside of her seemed a constant strain on her mentally and physically. She was sure Luke had never been like that. She put on some weight. Not a lot, but enough to feel disappointed. Part of her wanted to terminate the pregnancy. A big part, if she was honest. She wasn't sure she had anything to offer a child anymore. A string of negative platitudes was hardly going to be motivating.

And the child would never be Luke.

She took long walks that ended up at schools or playgrounds. She sat and listened to the laughter, instantly transported back to when Luke was small. Of course, he was always small. At four, he died small too.

But he was a joy. That small loping run that looked like he'd lose balance at any second.

She wanted to go up to each of the mothers and tell them to watch their children closely.

Jim Ody

Especially those that gossiped, and completely ignored their kids. More interested in discussing television soaps, and fake celebrities rather than watching their children play. Anything could happen. What did it take?

She joined online groups for grieving parents. She needed the support. And soon she found it. Arguably at a time when she needed it the most.

And that's where she'd met Greg.

She'd been attracted to his avatar picture, assuming it to be a celebrity she didn't know until he posted another picture. He was a handsome guy. That also helped. He had a strong jawline, with a rough and rugged look. Then when they began to talk, she found he had a gentle and sweet side. There was a glimmer of something that might be hope. It might even be a fleeting attraction.

He'd lost a child.

She hated that phrase. People would say it to her. *I'm sorry to hear you lost your son,* they'd say. It made her seem careless. Like she'd misplaced him. *I didn't lose him,* she wanted to scream. *Some arsehole ran his car into him and killed him!* but of course she didn't say that, instead she just said, *Thanks.* The worse thing people could do was ignore it had happened, or feel too awkward to even speak to her again.

But Greg was happy to talk to her about Luke, and she about his son too, although he never called him by his name. He remained nameless, only known as his son.

A Lifetime Ago

Greg had a daughter who was slightly older, she'd been inside, a constant babble tumbling from her mouth, when Greg wondered where his boy was. The small lad had wandered outside, desperate to go in the family pool. Forgetting, or not understanding that he needed inflatables, he'd run out, and jumped into the pool. The family was deep in the house and nobody noticed the boy splashing around.

They thought he was in his bedroom. Greg found him in the pool – suspended there face down – just below the surface. The helpless feeling of another tragedy.

It was an awful story. She'd cried when she'd heard it. He'd typed it to her, and had thought she'd gone. She was there. Crying and unable to respond for a few minutes. She was sad for him. She was sad for herself. The circumstances may have been different, but the outcome and the pain would've been the same.

They'd shared so much over the past couple of weeks. He'd invited her to come and see him. Sonny too. She'd managed to put him off so far.

It wasn't that she didn't want to see him, she did. Of course, she did. She just had a few things she had to do first.

Perhaps he would be her future.

But before that could happen, she had to bury her past.

Chapter 13 – Robert

Two years ago

Walking around shops with the pushchair required an engineering degree. The designs of pushchairs varied, but mostly none suited going in and out of small shop doorways on a busy Saturday morning.

The door to Starbucks was large but stiff. Robert pushed it open, whilst Nadia manoeuvred the buggy through the doors, and through a chicane of chairs, and coffee-drinkers. They found a table in the corner away from the humdrum of people, and prepared to unload the bags of stuff that came with having a small child. Each trip felt like they were moving house.

Nadia fussed with baby Jacob, as she pulled levers here and there, and unclipped things, before pulling the baby out and onto her.

Robert queued up for coffees and for the bottle of water to be warmed. He smiled with pride as he looked back at the two of them. Nadia grinning to the little boy with the wonderful mix of her dark skin, and his lighter shade.

"Here's daddy!" Nadia said, as Robert came back with the second trip of drinks.

He sat down with his family, and blew on his coffee. This scene made him so happy. He still had the dark thoughts of his past, but he really felt things were getting better. Even his editor had begun to give him a hard time again, demanding more stories. He'd been treading water with rewrites, updates, and light-hearted stories, but he was being pushed to go back to where he was a couple of years ago before his loss. The big exposés.

"You don't realise how good you are," his editor said. "Or were at least. You were on the verge of something big. Now what? You're giving me nothing, Bobby." His editor liked to call him that. It was meant as a term of endearment, but somehow Robert always felt slightly offended by it. He thought it made him sound like a children's television presenter. He was sure CBeebies presenters didn't harass popstars, note drug deals, and escort transactions.

"Is that meant to be a motivational speech?" He responded.

His editor sighed. "How's this for motivation, huh? You want to continue to write for us, you give me something I can print. We're not a damn charity."

And that was how it had been left.

Robert knew it was time to dig deep.

Nadia added the milk powder to the six-ounces of water in the bottle, and vigorously shook it. Baby Jacob remained still, only his eyes looking at the bottle. Even when the rubber teat came near, he didn't move. But as a drop of milk touched his lips, in an animalistic move he suddenly clamped his mouth around it with a strong grip, and great suction.

The proud parents watched the liquid slosh around, and dabbed the milky dribbles away that ran like tiny white rivers down his chin.

Then a male voice, out of place with this family picture, spoke up from behind them.

"Robert?" At first a nervous question. He turned around to see a couple stood there, clutching bags of things they'd bought, and more than likely didn't need. The guy had grown an impressive beard in the years since Robert had last seen him, and the woman had put on an even spread of weight over her body – although her dress-sense was still immaculate and high-end.

"Hi," Robert said. "How are you?" It was a question said to buy time rather than a genuine wonder of their well-being. He'd not expected to see them, and was slightly lost for words. They were part of his old life. That life. The one he hoped to forget. A friendship he had no intention of rekindling.

"It's been a long time," the guy had started confidently, but now was struggling to know how to keep the conversation going. "You moved away?"

Robert glanced at Nadia. "Yes. After the... er... accident, I moved out. Uh, too many memories and all that." This was the reason they'd moved. It was bad enough having to go over things with his editor, let alone with someone he'd almost forgotten.

A Lifetime Ago

The woman looked awkward. She was happy to let the guy do the talking. She was probably desperate to update her Instagram account. A carefully positioned post of her takeaway coffee captioned with something inspirational.

The guy continued. "That was awful. I'm so sorry…" the words hung there in the air, nobody quite sure how they'd fall. Maybe the polite thing to do would be to invite the couple to sit down and join them. But Robert couldn't bring himself to say it. They were all thinking the same thing; the silence crept in and surrounded them like a fog. They were all thinking about the child. About Luke. They were noting the absence of Robert's wife, and the addition of Nadia.

"So, this is yours?" The guy said changing the subject and nodding towards the hungry baby.

Nadia jumped in, as most new mums do. "Yes, this is Jacob, our beautiful little boy."

"You two are together now?" The guy said, and then quickly added, "Sorry, of course you are."

Robert went to speak, but didn't feel the need to justify the situation. He didn't have to defend his actions or explain how the incident completely changed his world. In fact, these two could turn around in their matching *North Face* jackets, and get lost for all he really cared.

"Are you on holiday too? We're having a few days away before Tracy goes back to teaching." He was rambling now. Robert badly wanted to punch him in the face. He wondered how the beard would feel on his knuckles. Instead, Robert shook his head.

"We live here now. There's nothing for us in Thornhill. We wanted to get away from it all."

The guy took this in as the woman rustled her bags, and said, "I'll queue up for drinks." She looked briefly at them both and added a standard "Nice to see you again," but out of duty, and with a hand wave, left. She'd had enough. The guy, however, wasn't finished. "Not much has changed in Thornhill, or Swindon in general, if I'm honest." He flashed a smile, waiting for more to come back from Robert – who quite honestly couldn't give a shit. Fuck Thornhill. He was glad that Swindon was slowly swallowing it up.

He wished this idiot would get the hint.

Then Robert's phone rang. The happy melody rang out. He looked at it, and said, "Sorry, I have to take this. It's good to see you again."

The guy held up his hands and mouthed, "Sorry," before slinking off, appearing disappointed.

"Thank you," Robert said into the phone. He didn't need to as it was Nadia who like all good mothers had the ability to multi-task, and had slipped her hand into her pocket and rung him. "I thought they'd never go."

Robert hated being taken back to that time. The guy was called Sven. His parents were from some Scandinavian country. He was an okay guy, but there was the elephant in the room with him. He'd been the one to catch Robert coming out of Nadia's house when he'd still been married. He was the one who'd told his girlfriend Tracy, and she'd told his wife. On the face of it, you could argue that Robert was in the wrong, but things were much more complicated than that. The fact that Tracy didn't want to speak, nor engage, spoke volumes. She was clearly still Team May.

"That was awkward," Nadia said. "She didn't want to be here at all, did she?"

Robert took a sip of his drink. "I don't blame her, or him, but that doesn't mean I want to be friends either."

Robert and Sven had played 6-a-side football together for months before Robert's world fell apart. The guy was uber-fit. He was skilful and extremely social. He talked to everyone, and the couple went out to wine bars and restaurants all the time. She was deputy-head of a secondary school, and he was a consultant of some sort. But Robert was taken back to that night. He'd left the house Nadia shared with her boyfriend, buttoning up his shirt, ready to nip back next door to his own house when he looked up to see Sven stood by the lamppost, illuminated and smoking. To this day, Robert didn't know what the guy was doing there at that time of night, but they both clocked each other, and in the next few days everything exploded. Life was never the same again.

"D'you blame him," Nadia asked, as Jacob finished the last of the milk but continued to suck on air.

He shrugged. "Yes, and no." He held out his hands to take Jacob. He'd wind him whilst Nadia sipped her drink. "I don't care about the marriage.

You know that. It was already on the rocks, and we were always going to end up together. But, in regards to… you know… the accident? I don't know."

She nodded. He was sure she felt the same.

Cradling Jacob in one arm, Robert reached out and rubbed Nadia's leg. "We're a family. It's not worth thinking about how our lives could've been." He smiled. It was warm and reassuring. He was right.

"I know, but things just keep turning up from our past. I can't help having these weak moments once in a while."

"We all have them. It's why we moved, wasn't it? This is our new life now."

Nadia agreed, but he noticed she looked off to the other end of the coffee shop where he saw Tracy glaring over. He was sure she still blamed Nadia for Robert's marriage break up. She probably still met up with May and conspired on how to get back at them. Pentagrams and potions. That was probably the name of her blog.

He looked at Jacob. He was a perfect little thing, just like Luke had been.

If they wanted to hurt him, then that bundle of joy would be his weak spot. And that scared the hell out of him.

Chapter 14 – Hudson

It was Saturday, and as usual, Hudson had gone to see his dad.

It was only a five-minute walk to his dad's house. Hudson was desperate to move from his flat into a house, but he liked being close by to his dad.

His dad was his hero. He had made Hudson the man he was today, but the cruely of age had crept up on him. Hudson hadn't seen it, until he looked at some old photographs and realised his dad had visibly shrunk. It wasn't just in stature, either. He'd lost muscle mass, and that in itself had aged him. Thinner hair that was now almost resignation with life, whereas before he fought for everything, now he shrugged and let it pass.

His Mercedes sat in the driveway gleaming. Even the wheels had a showroom shine to them. Now his dad had retired, his time was divided between cleaning his car, gardening and complaining. The last being something he'd honed to perfection. It seemed when life became simpler, it meant you had to find other frustrations to make it appear more complicated. Often the things that annoyed him seemed so trivial and petty compared to missing children.

He let himself in the door, calling as he entered.

"Hel-lo!" he called.

His step-mum popped her head out of the kitchen. "Hello, love," she said by way of a greeting.

"Hi Lisa," he responded to the woman who was only a few years older than himself. She was bubbly, and always managed to add a giggle into almost everything she said. She was the sunshine tying to brighten up his dad's life.

"Your father is reading the paper," she said, although he thought that would be the case. He'd always loved routine. "I'll bring you in a tea."

"Thanks," he smiled warmly. Lisa was what his father would describe as sturdy. Most other people would say normal. She looked strong and did half a dozen separate fitness classes a week. She'd recently high-fived with fifty but she looked a lot younger. His father had done well for himself, having spent over ten years single after the divorce to Hudson's mum.

"Here he is," his dad, Richard said with pride.

"How's things, dad?"

"I can't complain," he began, which was itself a laugh as they both knew he could make it an Olympic sport.

His dad was still the tall alpha-male, who at one stage stopped just short of beating his chest, and threatening people with violence. He never did (that Hudson was aware of), but he had been imposing nevertheless. A couple of years back he'd had a heart bypass, and since then had shrunken into himself a little. He'd never admit it, but his perspective of the world had changed considerably from that point forward. He'd finally realised he was mortal.

"How's that group going?"

Hudson smiled and tried to make light of it. "Depressing, if I'm honest."

His dad let out a throaty cough, and laughed. The two seemed connected more and more nowadays. "You silly sod, that's the point of it!"

"What, to depress me?"

"No, but you have to listen. Son, you need to apply your work ethic to your personal life. Listen more, take advice, and take control again."

"Thanks for the pearls of wisdom, Dad."

"You work too much..." Hudson went to speak, but Richard held up a huge hand. "Let me finish, Son. I get it. You are dedicated. Jesus, I couldn't be any prouder of you. With everything you've had on your plate you've thrown yourself into your work. But you can't sustain it."

When he stopped for breath, Hudson jumped in. "You sound like Jez!"

Richard laughed again. "That guy is a hoot! But," he raised a finger. "Give him is due, he may look and act like a weird clown, but he's clever. He's got himself a lovely wife."

Then with some rattling of crockery, Lisa came in with a tray of cups, saucers, tea-pot and milk. She placed it down on a small wooden table that looked like it had been carved from one huge log.

"Speaking of lovely wives!" His dad winked at her.

"Only because I look after you," she giggled, and sat down on the sofa next to Hudson.

Richard then blurted out, "I told him he needs to get laid!"

Hudson turned to her. "That's wasn't exactly how the conversation went."

She giggled. "I'm sure. In a roundabout sort of way, he's probably right."

"I thought you were on my side?" Hudson said to her.

"I share a lot of his views on sex," she grinned knowing it made Hudson slightly uncomfortable.

"That's where your pal, Jez has got it right?"

Hudson was confused. "Come again?"

"He sent me a video of his wife naked and singing on an exercise ball. It was the funniest thing!"

"He sent you that too!" Hudson couldn't believe it. For a guy who was so good with IT, you'd think he'd know how to attach the proper file to an email.

They all laughed at that, but soon things got more serious.

"We're worried about you, Huds. This big case you've taken on. Do you really think it's wise?"

"Dad, you know I have to do it. That little boy is out there and he needs to be found."

"I don't mean to be blunt, but you realise you're probably just looking for a corpse now?" His dad spoke carefully, but there was no way to cushion it. Hudson knew that things would never be the same again. Even if they did find him, there was then a chance of physical damage, but worse was the psychological damage. He was young enough that he might get over it in the short-term, but the long-term damage could be massive.

"I know," Hudson said in response. "But he might also be alive. I have to hold on to that hope."

His dad nodded and looked over at the familiar picture on the bookcase. It was Hudson receiving an award. He'd gone into an old building where a father had taken his son. The father wasn't allowed custody, and it was obvious that the fight between parents was nothing to do with the small child, it was just about hurting each other. He was collateral damage.

The dad had grabbed the child from the boy's front garden. The mother had called it in. Hudson was the nearest policeman, and had taken the call. It was a Friday evening, a football match had been playing on the big screen of a pub, and the alcohol had turned the drinkers into idiots, like some zombie apocalypse. Most of Hudson's colleagues were there. Driving alone, he saw the suspect's car going the other way, so he turned and followed with flashing blues and twos.

They ended up in Cheney Manor Industrial estate. The car was there with the doors open. Hudson checked it was empty and called it in. He was told to wait for back up. He hesitated until he heard the ETA was another twenty minutes.

He ran into the building. Each footstep echoed loudly. He heard a noise, and a muffled scream. He couldn't understand why you'd want to cause your own child such distress.

Jim Ody

Slowly, he walked rolling his feet to remain as quiet as possible. In between row upon row of racks full of crates. It was an old logistics distribution centre. It was a vast sea of pallets and shadowed places to hide.

Hudson picked up a metal hinge that sat abandoned. With all his strength, he threw it as far away as possible.

And that's when he heard the gun go off.

A UK policeman was not meant to hear a gunshot. It was now very dangerous, and he was unarmed.

The armed man was in the next bay.

He remembered sweating hard. It was pouring out of him. Each of his steps now sounded loud. Too loud. Armed with only pepper spray and a baton, he tried to remain calm.

The child whimpered. Hudson followed the sound as they both got to the end of the aisle.

It was risky, but carefully Hudson pulled himself up onto a crate. The worst place to be was at the same level as someone with a gun. Below would trick them, but then you were a sitting duck. Up high was preferable.

The crate seemed to wobble. Hudson almost fell. Then from around the corner the dad came, one arm around the face of his son, and the other outstretched with the gun.

He only had one shot at it. It was risky. Very risky.

He leapt, bringing the baton down onto the hand holding the gun. That disarmed him, sending the weapon to the floor and skidding off, as all

A Lifetime Ago

three fell onto the hard concrete floor. The dad swung his arm wildly, and Hudson shot an arching stream of pepper spray into the general direction of the dad's eyes.

Hudson was on top of him and the dad was now shouting in pain. Despite his wriggling, Hudson was able to turned him over and with a knee on his lower back was able to cuff him. But what struck Hudson the most was how his son, seeing his dad in pain, slowly walked over to him and hugged him. Despite his dad's lack of care for his safety, this sweet little boy was still able to show compassion. Children never failed to surprise him.

He'd received congratulations from his team, and he still remembered the fear that ran his blood cold at the sound of the gunshot, but it was the look of the son hugging his dad that stuck with Hudson the most.

Hudson's dad nodded at the picture. "You were much braver than you admit that day. You deserved that award."

Hudson sighed, "I was only doing my job."

"Just slow down son. You need to take some time off."

"Maybe after this case I will."

"Yeah, and I'm going to play for Swindon Town!" His dad jested.

"You might score more goals," Hudson responded.

"Joking aside," Lisa said. "You do need to take it easy. If you have a heart attack," she glanced over at his dad." Like that old fool, then you're no good to anyone. Remember that." She was right. They were both right. He'd take a break after this case. Or the next one.

They watched the football, and later on had a takeaway. Hudson wanted to tell them that this was his break. This was him relaxing, thinking about them, but he knew they wouldn't accept it.

Chapter 15 – Hudson

Hudson woke up to no milk in the house. Not a big issue, but when you are in need of coffee, having been up late theorising about the case, then it was suddenly important.

Leaving his flat, he trotted down the stairs and was met with a sad sight. His young neighbour was propped up against her door, looking dishevelled and more than a little worse for wear. Her dress had ridden up to show a little too much of her, and in her hand was her front-door key.

"Alexis?" he whispered, not wanting to scare her. She murmured, as she came around.

She was a nineteen-year-old Lithuanian and had come to this country ten years ago with her parents. Now she was testing the waters of independence, and Hudson wasn't entirely sure how that was going. This wasn't the first Sunday morning he'd found her in her alternative bed. It probably wouldn't be the last.

"I'm just going to take your key, and open your door for you, okay?"

Her dainty fingers with sharp red nails touched her face, as her eyes twitched to open. Her make-up was smudged, and the smell of sweet alcohol lingered in the air.

"Where am I?" she said, her heavily-accented voice deeper than normal.

"Outside your flat. I'll help you inside, okay?"

She nodded, tried to smile but grabbed her head again as the hangover hit her with full force.

"I don't feel so good," she said, when she was finally on her feet. She shimmied her dress down her thighs too late to hide her dignity, and held on to Hudson as he walked her inside.

"You have to be careful, Alexis. I don't want to sound like your dad, but there are some bad people in this world, and a pretty vulnerable girl like you is easy pickings when you're that drunk."

She sat down. "I didn't drink much," she lied. They both knew it. Hudson wasn't there to argue, or lay down moral codes. He just wanted to get her safely inside.

He walked towards the kitchen and grabbed a glass from the side to fill up with water. If nothing else it would help the dehydration. He ran the tap until is was cold, and brought the full glass to her.

"Drink this," he said. "Why don't you go and shower? That'll make you feel better, yeah?"

"Thank you, Hudson," she said.

Hudson smiled at her and left her to it.

Outside the building the morning was fresh. There was the tail end of some fog in the distance, although the sun was doing it's best to burn through it. Only a few people were around. He jogged across the road, and then around the corner to his local Tesco Express.

There were a handful of people milling around the aisles not wanting to engage with each other.

A Lifetime Ago

This was the face of Britain nowadays. Fifty years ago, each person would've stopped and talked to one another, but now in the come-and-go age, people didn't feel the need to connect, happy to continue through their lives and knowing very little about their neighbours, despite living a wall's thickness away.

Hudson got his essentials, smiling at the lad on the till who looked even more tired than Hudson felt, and walked back out.

He stopped and looked down the road, it was a little walk but the McDonald's was only a few streets away. It would do him good to get some exercise, plus it gave him time to think.

Fifteen minutes later and he was clutching two brown bags of food, and a couple of hot drinks. He walked into his building and up the stairs. He stopped at Alexis's door and knocked.

It took a few minutes, but eventually her door opened slightly, then upon seeing it was Hudson she opened it up fully. She was wearing a dressing gown, and her hair was wet.

"Come in," she said, but instead Hudson held up the bag.

"I can't stay," he said. "But I brought you breakfast."

"For me?" she was surprised. She took the bag, and the hot drink. "Thank you, Hudson."

He said goodbye and turned to leave.

"You're not coming in?" she seemed disappointed.

"No, I've got a lot to do," he said. "Take care of yourself, yeah?"

"Thank you," she said again. She was still stood at her door as he went up the next flight of stairs. *This must be what it's like to be a father*, he thought.

When he got into his flat he threw his keys onto the counter and set about his food.

The rough-around-the-edges décor of his flat no longer just looked lived in, but tired and sloppy. He wondered whether he should clean the place up. It hardly seemed worth it before as no one visited him. Even the religious nuts and charity charlatans couldn't be bothered to tiptoe over needles and broken bottles to come up to him. Perhaps that said it all. Even God had given up on him. He was no longer worth saving.

Despite it all, and with the sudden spring in his step, he walked into the spare bedroom and looked at the wall. He did this often – in fact almost every time he entered the room. Fuck therapy, it was this that gave him something to live for.

The sunlight cut a path through half-tugged curtains, and diagonally across the room. The wall opposite held his attention. He walked up to each picture in his daily ritual, and wondered how he could possibly move each case on.

Up until the death of Luke Southall, Hudson had been a fine policeman. He'd received high praise from above and was told off the record that he would be fast tracked up the ranks. All he had to do was sit the exams and pass them. *It's just a formality*, he'd been assured.

A Lifetime Ago

Not only was he hard working, and proven in getting results, but he quickly gained the respect of his peers and was able to lead his team well.

From an early age he'd always wanted to bring justice to the world, but even once joining the police force, he realised all too quickly that it was an impossible task. The only thing you could do was steady the fires. Catch as many criminals as possible, and then later on, catch them again, when they were either let off with a warning, handed a reduced sentence, or witnesses suddenly refused to give evidence, developed amnesia or simply just disappeared.

Hudson believed in making the world a better place, and had sacrificed other things to do so. His long hours and dedication brought results but often his relationships suffered. His ex-girlfriend had been neglected, not deliberately, but he'd been consumed by the horrific killing of two children. It wasn't just the pressure from the press and his srgeant, but for himself. He had to catch the killer, and mundane things like relationships, eating and sleeping were no longer of importance to him. It was all he could do to drag himself into the shower each day.

And he did – catch the killer, that is. But following on from arresting, and convicting the person responsible, there was still a grieving family without children who, despite it all, would never fully feel the satisfaction of justice, just the pain where once there was joy.

And then the day the incident happened. His case was passed over to a colleague and he was put on leave. He never went back. After months of psychological examination, and update meetings with his Police Federation rep, and not to mention his own Chief Inspector, he was regrettably recommended for early retirement. His Chief Inspector did all he could to bring Hudson back in, but he knew he would never have that same focus.

The police like to look after their own, and the decision was put on hold whilst Hudson underwent further counselling. And later, when he still seemed lost, he was prescribed anti-depressants.

Staying at home alone is a dangerous thing for a vulnerable person. The cocktail of anti-depression drugs mixed with alcohol did nothing but keep him functioning. Months soon hit a year, and then another twelve months slipped by before his mate Jez contacted him, along with his colleagues, saying that they needed him.

At first, Hudson assumed it to be out of pity. Them trying to give him something to do; throw him a rope and try to pull him gently from the edge of an abyss.

The police gave him small cases to consult over. It helped him through the days, even if he still chewed down sleeping pills at night and awoke from dark nightmares in the small hours. But soon he recognised that he was wanted, and the set-up suited him. He could solve cases without the red-tape to get bound up in.

Finally, he was told about the grief support group, it was a way for him to get out of the house and know that others were going through the same thing. Which is what he'd unenthusiastically been doing.

In the meantime, more in-depth cases had come his way. His friend at the police shared more and more, and he unofficially threw himself in until he had each cold case file there in his room.

Each one of the children on his wall was just as important as the other. They had not deserved to be part of his gallery. In fact, he would love to have a room and just one wall for each. They deserved that at the very least. They all needed to either be reunited with loved ones, or taken away and put somewhere where they would receive love. The thing with children was statistically, a troubled childhood more often than not led them to either being a criminal, or a victim. Either way, they would become known to the police. Often, boys who were abused in childhood turned into abusers as men, whereas girls abused in childhood continued to find themselves being abused as women.

And now he had another motivation.

Maybe, just maybe, this might go some way to making him feel good about himself again. He was slowly realising that his corner was no longer empty, but he had Jez and if his wife Cass, his dad and Lisa, Pete and a whole host of police colleagues all willing him to clear the funk that had him close to the edge.

He pulled up a chair, sat down, and stared from innocent face to innocent face. Boys and girls of varying ages. Many of them from different walks of life, and from random areas.

He pulled out a plastic bottle, unscrewed the childproof cap, and dry-swallowed a couple of pills. He took a deep breath and moved to where his laptop was. He checked his email, and looked at the files. The problem was knowing which to focus on first. No one deserved to be at the bottom of the pile, and yet, someone invariably would be.

His mate Pete had sent him another one. He opened up the mail and glanced over at the wall. He was running out of space. Week after week more cases appeared than the ones that could be solved. It was a depressing fact.

Not wanting to miss a beat, he turned back and looked at the new case. That said everything about his life now. He was looking at a high-profile case on Darren Hughes, and still more cases came in.

A young girl called Tracy had been taken from a park a week earlier. She was twelve and hanging out on her own waiting for her friends when she disappeared.

He read the usual background details on the case and set about his own investigation. He was careful not to go over work already done by the police, and his speciality was to look into the people who lived with them, were related to them, or came within contact of the missing children. It was funny how many skeletons suddenly appeared if you dug deep enough. Despite what movies would have you believe, the abductors were more often than not known to the victim.

An hour later his mobile rang.

A Lifetime Ago

"Pete, hey," he said seeing his friend's name come up.

"Hudson, buddy! I've some great news!"

"Shoot."

"We've got him! The uncle in the Tina Barloff case. Your suspicions were correct, and the background intel helped us get the conviction!"

"Yes!" Hudson was so pleased. "There was something about him. How does the case against him look?"

"Airtight. Thanks to you we found him on CCTV minutes before she was murdered, and again coming away from the house with blood on him. We have a footprint, and more than a handful of holes in his alibi."

"You sure?" Hudson was too used to thinking everything was a slam dunk only to have the CPS throw it out for insufficient evidence. Correct procedure was so important.

"Yes, the CPS has given the nod and he's been charged."

"That's great. Well done!"

"It's thanks to you and Jez, mate. The brass know it too. They told me to pass on their thanks."

"It's good to be of some use."

"I know, mate. Did you see my email?" Pete knew the situation and let it drop.

"I did. I've spent the last hour looking at the parents and relatives. I've nothing so far. It's frustrating."

"I know. Tell me about it."

"Okay. Well, keep me updated." There was a pause at the other end.

"So… how are you, Hudson?" it was an awkward moment. They were both alpha males with no time for feelings, but they'd also been mates for a long time. Neither wanted to really admit it, but they appreciated each other.

"I'm okay. These cases keep me busy."

"That's good, mate. That's really good. Look, if you need a break…"

"That seems to be the popular advice."

"Huh?" Hudson realised Pete didn't know what he was on about.

"Sorry, mate. Everyone keeps telling me to take a break. Take some time off."

"Maybe you should start listening to them."

"Maybe." They left it at that.

Hudson got up and walked over to the wall, his eyes locked on the girl in the Peppa Pig T-shirt. He reached up, gave her a sad and muttered, "Rest in peace now, Tina. We've got him."

He didn't take the picture down but found the case file and placed it in a pending court pile. There were a few in there now. It made him happy, but far from satisfied. The open case files pile was huge and growing all the time.

"Another one down," he said to nobody but himself.

And then he looked up at the largest face. The granted pole-position. The sorry face of Darren Hughes.

"I'll find you," he said with hope rather than anything else. He had to understand that despite all endeavours, sometimes children were never found.

Chapter 16 – Hudson

Hudson got to the community centre late. This was a calculated move. He had no desire to make small talk with anyone. Especially when the very salutation of, "How are you?" could either lead into a downward spiral, or bend his ear for longer than he cared to engage. The meeting had been brought forward to Sunday night, which seemed even more inconvenient, and yet, here he was. Even if once again he'd left his enthusiasm at home.

It was ironic. The only time her felt really negative about himself and others was here. The exact opposite of what they were meant to get out of it. He probably just needed to relax and let himself go.

The whole reason they were in group therapy was to understand how they were feeling — maybe for those in charge to note suicide high risks too. Each person was given the opportunity — if they wanted it — to tell everyone either their story, or how they currently were feeling.

Often, the stories were filled with a bit more of a positive outlook, and whilst he didn't want to admit it, on some level he was becoming almost fond of some of them.

Jim Ody

He grabbed a coffee from one of the two large jugs, knowing that eyes were on him. If nothing else at least the coffee was worth turning up for. Strong and bitter, pretty much how he felt inside. As quietly as possible, he sat down at the back. A skinny looking woman was in the middle of her tale of woe. The audience lapping it up, and captivated by her wobbling voice and sniffing.

Hudson was a caring person at heart. He was a guy that had now dedicated his life to stopping pain by helping others, however, he was a doer. He was pragmatic, and not one to sit and soak up feelings for hours. Maybe this was seen as old school, but he had no time for sharing what he felt, and hugging strangers. He would rather they each gave him a list of things he could do to make them feel better, and he would be straight on to it. Instead, he was forced to sit and listen to them dwell on their troubles, almost drowning themselves in self-pity. It was emotionally treading water, when what they really needed to do was push forward, scoop back the water with their hands and kick for shore.

He knew it helped some of them. Maybe it helped most, if not all of them. Just not him.

Or that's what he continually told himself like a personal mantra.

His eyes wandered around, unable to focus on one thing for any amount of time. He ticked off the usual suspects with sideward glances, or recognising the backs of their heads. Each appeared to be in more clothing than required.

A Lifetime Ago

Everything was about comfort, and hiding within themselves.

A head turned in his direction and smiled weakly. It was Laura. Now she was someone he wondered about. He needed to stop messing around and get to know her.

He smiled back and held up his coffee in a form of greeting. Her smile grew larger.

He'd be lying if he said he hadn't been thinking about her. He had. It had been just under a week since they'd spoken, neither of them taking steps to offer, or ask for the other's mobile number. Maybe she was just being polite. Perhaps making a friend. He may have misread the signals. The irony of being so good at this on a professional level, but a complete failure in his personal life, was not lost on him. You only had to look at his last failed relationship. At some point his ex-girlfriend distanced herself from him, and had decided to swap pulling his duvet over her at night, with the heavier blanket of another man. He'd been oblivious.

He needed to kick himself up the arse. Who wanted to start a relationship with foundations built on woe? Women liked confidence, not needy men who required constant reinforcement of their feelings.

He looked back to where the skin and bones lass was coming to an end. After some sobbing, she'd talked herself into being in a better place, agreeing things were improving, and even went as far as thanking everyone in the room for their support. Hudson thought this to be a bold statement as most had just remained tight-lipped and allowed her to talk. Half of them were probably just daydreaming.

The room fell quiet. No one wanted to speak first. The moderator thanked her and eagerly looked around the room for another speaker. His eyes stopped at Hudson, and smiled encouragingly.

"Hudson, is it?" he started, and Hudson wanted the floor to give way under him, or for something bad to happen to the man. Mainly the latter.

Hudson nodded, and held up defensive hands. "I've nothing at this time," he said hoping that was enough. It suggested that at some stage he would open up. Hudson knew this was about as likely as receiving a lap-dance at the session, but kept that, and every other comment he'd thought, locked away inside his head.

The guy nodded and understood, and he moved on to a woman who looked permanently stunned. This was potentially another car-crash of waterworks. She'd not spoken before. Hudson knew she was one of those that a single word would open the floodgates.

"Penelope, would you like to speak?"

She nodded, and took a deep breath. "It's been so hard since it happened," she began looking around at the nodding heads and reassuring smiles.

Jesus, here we go, Hudson thought and made himself comfortable. This was going to be a long one, he could tell by the way she stumbled over her words, and corrected herself over irrelevant details. At one stage he looked over to Laura. She had a blank look on her face. Hudson wondered where she was. There was no way she was still in the vortex of depression listening to this. If she'd used her head, she'd have taken herself virtually off somewhere better too.

A further twenty minutes and he got to ask her that very question. She'd made her way over to him. He played it cool and let her take a seat next to him. ahead of them, people were hugging, and crying, whilst others had gone for a toilet break, cigarette or coffee. The moderator kept a keen eye out just in case it all got too much, and someone tried to top themselves. Hudson amused himself by thinking about starting a sweepstake. His money was on a pale guy who sat with a permanent shellshocked look on his face and visibly shook.

"And here he sits," she said. "All alone in the back, not wanting to be here. The rebel of the session."

He smiled at her. She looked good. She'd painted her lips and added make up since the last time. Or perhaps it was now a shade that was more noticeable.

"And yet she joins me. So where were you for the past half hour or so?"

"Just there." She frowned pointing to the now discarded seat.

He shook his head and grinned. "I know your body was there. I was looking over at you but don't tell me you were listening to it all."

Jim Ody

She nodded at that. He'd known her better than she'd thought.

"Bournemouth. A night out with friends, if you must know."

"An actual memory or a fantasy?"

She laughed. "You think my fantasies are in a Bournemouth nightclub? Wow, and I thought you got me!"

"You had taken yourself off to another place though."

She ignored him. "So, why d'you come if you don't want to be here?"

"Why d'you think? The uplifting discussions."

"The company? The discussions help some people."

"Okay, you tell me why you come here?" He pushed. He figured it was all part of once being a cop. You could answer a question with a question. With a little pressing you could get people to open up.

"My therapist thought it would be a good idea," she ran her hand through her hair then held them both up as if unconvinced.

"And you don't?"

"I don't know. I do know I'd rather be somewhere else rather than here on a Sunday night!"

"Like a Bournemouth nightclub."

"Exactly like a Bournemouth nightclub. What about you?"

Hudson looked around noticing the moderator had come back to his chair and was checking his watch, and then counting people.

"Same. My therapist. Some obligation I agreed to in a moment of weakness. I was a policeman once and you see all kinds of horrors… but sometimes it's only when things get personal that they take their toll."

"I wouldn't have you pegged as a copper."

"Does that disappoint you?" Hudson had said the words before he could filter them. They suggested more than a hint of flirtation.

"Not at all."

Then the moderator was up clapping his hands.

"Okay, guys! What I'd like is for everyone to split into groups and talk about one thing they'd like to improve in the future. Okay? Maybe groups of threes?" Hudson hated this part. It was bad enough sitting and listening without being forced to contribute and engage.

There was the sudden noise of movement as people scraped chair legs across the floor. Hudson and Laura looked at each other, and then both painted on their best fake smiles as a shy looking overweight woman looked at them expectantly. She'd found herself on her own and by default would be in their group.

"I guess I'm with you two?" She asked in a question, her voice going up an octave at the end of the sentence. It was either that or she was Australian.

"Sure, come on over," Laura said.

"What's your name?" Hudson asked her, but instantly felt awkward. It was mechanical. And written on her sticker.

"Chanel." She held out her hand but only intended to touch the other persons hand with her thumb and forefinger. And even then, it was weak and without feeling.

"So, Chanel, why don't you start?" Laura said, but instead of the positives, Chanel took them back to why she was there. Each word sucked the life out of them as they listened, nodded and expressed empathy.

Chanel carried with her a lot of guilt. A misguided trust in men had opened up her door to an abusive guy. As usual, the guy was charming to start off with. Loving, caring and got on well with her kids. But soon he'd become demanding, his temper shortened, and the kids began to get in the way. Chanel loved him. Despite everything she cared so much for him. Maybe those feelings were false, and she was misinterpreting a safe haven from a father figure previously missing from her twenty-two-year-old life. She made excuses for him, and defended him against her own children.

Hudson already knew this. The problem with being a policeman.

He'd been sent a file all about her; or rather about her boyfriend and the threat to her child.

Wearing a false beard and a cap he'd called by to look at the boiler. Chanel had let him in herself, and he'd installed a couple of hidden cameras. A neighbour had raised the alarm but there was nothing the police could do. There was no evidence and the family weren't talking.

A Lifetime Ago

The video from the camera convicted the boyfriend Lance Stockton for abuse, but not before beating to death six-year-old Maggie.

Maggie and her sister had been pictures on Hudson's wall. The sister was still not back with the mother. Chanel concluded her story that this was what she really wanted in the future. Laura smiled, and patted her on the back reassuringly, whilst Hudson could only picture the broken body of Maggie, smeared in dried blood and with an arm broken in the wrong position. He knew that some parents could be oblivious to the obvious dangers surrounding their children with new boyfriends and girlfriends. But Hudson wasn't so sure that these tears now were about the disappointment of not knowing; or the residual guilt of not doing something.

He sat back in his chair. Completely disengaged. He was angry at her for allowing it to happen.

And then the lump formed in his throat, and tears began to flow. He could no longer continue like this. It wasn't Chanel he was angry at. It was no longer her child that he was crying for.

He was angry at himself. At *that* morning when everything was great in his life.

And then the accident happened. He was careless. Too busy looking into the future, without concentrating on the now.

And then everything in his world went black. Hudson went out like a light, and crashed to the floor.

When he opened his eyes, Laura was leant over him.

"What happened?" He asked and instantly felt the wetness on his cheeks.

"You fainted," she said quietly. "You'll be fine."

"When I opened my eyes, I thought you were about to kiss me."

"Had you still been out cold then perhaps I would've."

"What, taken advantage of me?" he weakly smiled.

"That or your wallet."

He couldn't keep a straight face to that. "I think I need some fresh air."

"You need water," Laura said taking charge.

Chapter 17 – Hudson

Once outside Hudson and Laura just kept walking. Neither looking to go their separate ways. Maybe that was an unspoken agreement they shared. No excuses, or talk of tiredness, just two people enjoying each other's company.

They walked in an awkward silence along the street to a bar called Capers. The place was popular in the town, and had live entertainment as well as an American-style diner all under one roof.

"That was good to see, Hudson," Laura said as they opened the door. "You had it all bottled up."

She walked in first and added. "Don't feel bad. I know you feel silly, but don't."

Hudson was beyond embarrassed. He'd spent the last few minutes trying to start a sentence, but given up every time. Had she not been so friendly, he may well have disappeared never to return to the group. But back at the meeting, she'd helped him back to his feet as Chanel got him a glass of water, and despite the humiliation, everyone was supportive, and accepting of it. Roger, the moderator was quick on the scene and reassured Hudson this sort of thing happened regularly.

Jim Ody

"You want alcohol, or food?" Hudson managed. He was half-ignoring her comment.

"Let's start with food."

He liked that. She wasn't rushing away from him. She also smiled a lot. He considered that to be a good thing.

They slipped into one of the booths. This was the first time they'd sat face-to-face, and it all seemed more intimate now. They quickly looked over the menus, using them as a distraction. Peeking out above them every now and then.

Then without warning, Laura put the menu down, and dropped a bombshell. "I have a confession," she said. She looked worried.

Hudson was sure it couldn't be too bad. "Go on."

"You know how much you hate the group? You don't see the point of it?"

"I'm not sure I used those exact words," Hudson said, and went to argue otherwise, but he'd already said enough to suggest otherwise. What was the point? Instead he shrugged.

"Well, I'm not there just because of my therapist…" She let the words hang in the air for a while. She tried to study his face and gain a reaction, but his was built of stone. She struggled to gauge his emotions. "Well, I am, sort of, but not for the same reason as you. I help run the sessions with Roger."

Hudson's eyebrows rose in surprise, and he couldn't control the flash of his eyes going wide for a split second, and then he smiled. "No?!" it seemed almost unbelievable. "Really?"

She nodded. "They like to have two people just in case things get out of hand. I'm a trained counsellor, but Roger is more of a man upfront. The senior. He loves to lead the groups."

"I didn't know." He felt deceived.

Idly, she placed a hand on his. "Why would you? That's the point. The second person should try to blend in as much as possible."

Hudson felt disappointed. He was self-conscious about being the basket case of the group. The one that therapy wasn't working for so needed special one-to-one tuition.

"Let me ask you something?" Hudson said.

"Sure. Anything."

"Are you here with me now, because you want to be, or because Roger thought it was a good idea?"

Her hand was still on his. Her forefinger moved gently over the back of his hand. "D'you think Roger would approve of this?" She lifted his hand and kissed the back of it. "Or this?"

"No. I suppose not."

They both looked over the menu again, re-reading items they'd already seen. Letting that conversation sink in.

Hudson lost himself in the menu. With his work he was used to grabbing food, and his diet was nothing short of awful. So, when he came to a place like this, he liked to dive in and treat himself. He'd enjoyed the burgers on previous occasions, but he wondered whether it was time for something a little sugary. Maybe a stack of sweet pancakes. His mind wandered away from what she'd said like a defence mechanism. Somewhere deep in his brain he was processing it. He didn't really care that she was part of the group in an official capacity. Did it really make a difference to him?

"Anything you fancy?" he said, suddenly conscious he wasn't looking at her.

"It all looks good," she said.

"Good?" he put down the menu, using this to inject some humour. "Everything's great here!"

She was amused by that. They locked eyes, and both gave small smiles that accepted the situation.

Laura then spotted a fresh order that had just been cooked, and was awaiting delivery to a table. A large hotdog bursting out of its bun, and smothered in onion relish, and cheese.

"Wow!" She said. "I want one of those!"

Hudson turned and looked. A grin spread over his face. "Capers' Big Dog. They're great! I can personally recommend them."

"I'm sold!"

Nodding, Hudson got up and ordered the food at the counter.

The girl who served him was friendly, and courteous. Her face was round, and her hair was pulled back. She had a name badge that read Nelly. She was new, but you'd never know. She oozed confidence and loved to speak to people. Which was good, as Capers was always buzzing.

Back at the table, they sat in an awkward silence again. Both wrestling opening lines, but not being able to go through with them. That is until Laura asked, "So honestly, you not getting anything out of the meetings?"

Hudson wasn't sure what to say. It was far from his thing, but he'd met Laura. He decided to just be honest.

"I'm getting out of my flat and meeting people that have nothing to do with my work. So that's a good thing. I might not want to share, but I do listen. You learn so much from other people."

She nodded. "I know. The stories are so sad. It's not just a job for me either. I genuinely feel we do a good job."

"That's easy to see. Those that want to share, get a lot out of it."

"So why don't you share your story some time? Especially if you know it helps?"

He knew she was right. "I'm just not ready to speak out loud. I admire those that do. And d'you know what? Sometimes I feel like a fraud. Others have stories so much worse than mine."

She held out her hand and took his. "It's not a competition. You don't have to prove your worth at being there."

Then Nelly arrived with their drinks, and Laura quickly pulled her hand away.

"Anything else?" Laura asked when Nelly had gone.

"I met someone, so it's not all bad."

"Really?" she said, sipping at the coffee. "And what's she like?"

Hudson supressed a smile. "She's okay. Nice to look at."

"Just okay?"

"Okay is good. I don't know enough about her to decide further." He looked out of the window. He wasn't used to this. His last relationship had ended badly. Since then he'd been too self-absorbed with work and depression to even think about meeting someone new.

Deep down he didn't think he deserved it.

Nor did he trust anyone.

She was holding onto her cards. Perhaps she'd been burnt too. Her eyes danced from the other patrons to him, and then away again. Metaphoric fingers brushed her cards ready to tip them before moving away again.

Just then a tall, strange and familiar looking guy walked in. He was wearing dark glasses and a leather biker-jacket, even though the sun had gone down. He looked around the tables and then noticed Hudson. He headed over.

Jez.

"Detective!" he said loudly. Not that this was out of character for him, he was unable to be quiet. He winked and fired off a shot from his finger-pistol.

"It's the Terminator," Hudson said, and then added with a sigh. "I'm retired now."

Jez liked the initial comment. "I'll be back!" He tried an Arnie impression. It sounded Spanish. Then he added, "You're still working for the police? Strange retirement."

Hudson liked the guy, but he was one of the last people you wanted to meet whilst with a woman you were trying to impress.

"But on my own terms now. Anyway, how're you? And why are you wearing shades?"

Jez nodded, grinned and kept looking at Laura. "Low sun out there. It goes straight into your eyes."

Hudson glanced outside. It was dark. Street lights now illuminated the street. "There is no sun."

"Just details," he waved it off. Everything Jez did he was able to justify. He looked back at Hudson and Laura, and winked again. "What's this? A date?"

Hudson couldn't feel any more uncomfortable at that point. He was also worried that Jez might want to join them. The cop in him took over.

"This look like a date to you, Jez?"

For a second that stumped him. He even frowned. "Sorta," he confessed. "She'd pretty, and you've brushed your hair."

Laura giggled, and then made an overexaggerated, "Phew!" sound, and wiped her brow. "That's good 'cause it is a sorta date!"

Jez went all out Cheshire cat and nodded. "Thought so. I'll leave you two love birds be then." He started to walk away, but stopped suddenly, a sure sign he'd just remembered something. That was bad.

"Oh," he said turning around. "We need to schedule a meeting." He gave a nudge-nudge to thin air.

Hudson held up his hands. "Tomorrow."
"When?"
"Whenever."

"Roger that!" Jez held up his hand and was off testing the patience of poor Nelly.

"What a strange guy," Laura remarked.

That made Hudson laugh. "Really, you don't know the half of it!"

Their food arrived which slowed the small talk. They offered up sneaky glances but both had walls built up. They talked about TV, music and sports. When their food was eaten, they went next door into the bar and grabbed a quick drink. The music was louder so not as easy to talk, and eventually they found themselves stood outside. The cool air now whipped around.

"I'm off this way," she said reluctantly. They held hands and acknowledged this was that anxious part.

They hugged, Hudson bending slightly to go down to her level, and Laura planted a gentle kiss on his cheek.

Neither wanted the evening to end, but they were busy people. And whilst neither admitted it, they both needed to take things slowly.

Chapter 18 - May

May packed up the car. She didn't have much in all honesty. They didn't need much. It was just her and Sonny off on a road trip.

She strapped him in next to her. He looked lost and vacant. She struggled to hide her disappointment. Not for the first time she wished he was Luke. But he wasn't. She knew she should stop comparing them. Sonny was different. He was withdrawn, his speech was well below expectation for his age. He looked at her but didn't seem to take her in.

It made her angry, she knew it shouldn't. She was his mother! For God's sake, he should be able to show something toward his mother!

She gritted her teeth, forcing a smile to try and hide her frustration. She would continue to call him Luke. He *would* grow into his name. He *would* become what Luke was, he just needed time, she thought, and a little encouragement.

Yes, he just needed time.

A final glance back, and May pulled her car out of the driveway and off they went.

Strangers went about their day. Faceless folk anonymous and without a care. Driving in the opposite direction, they whizzed by her in a blur. Their vehicles quickly forgotten.

Another bead of sweat trickled down the side of her face, testing her expensive makeup against its marketing claims. She'd applied it an hour ago. Touched it up barely a few minutes back, but paranoia was already whispering lies into her mind. Planting seeds that only prescription pills could stop from growing. Numbing reality to take the edge off her life.

Her car was large. Possibly considered heavy machinery, and she, the dazed operator. Inside she shrugged. She felt okay. You have to listen to your body, right?

It was a blazing hot summer. Her hands gripped the steering wheel as best they could, and a small smile played upon her lips. Despite everything — makeup and sweat notwithstanding — she was happy. Slightly giddy, but she felt alive.

She flipped the air-con and immediately felt the blast of cool air. The control at her fingertips. Empowered by technology.

In the distance, the heat wobbled and distorted the horizon. In the foreground, the world bounced and juddered with each bump. She eased off the accelerator; the well-built car suddenly felt smooth with the drop in speed.

"It's a beautiful day now, isn't it?" she said to Luke next to her. He nodded, used to answering to another boy's name, and when he felt like she wanted more he looked over, wanting to please. He wasn't much of a talker. A lot like his father.

A Lifetime Ago

Although *that* man was good with his hands, *and* knew his way around a woman. He didn't always care who she was either. Or where she'd been for that matter. This would go a long way to explain his absence today.

"You're awfully quiet today, Luke? You holding out for some ice-cream?"

The boy's smile was all big and toothy. One of his front teeth was missing and he now looked more like his uncle Del than ever before. Add in a black eye and tinge his teeth brown, and they'd be like two peas in a pod. Del was a side of the family she stayed away from. No good would ever come of associating with him or his kind. They lived in the poor area of town. She couldn't understand why they didn't want to escape from it. He'd taken the silver spoon he'd been born with and sold it for the excitement he was still chasing.

May was the wrong side of forty. She'd done her very best to still look pretty, but by supressing her appetite with fags and gin, had only resulted in her looking gaunt and gone-to-seed. Foundation and the odd Botox injections did their best to smooth out the cracks, but reality was beginning to show. The sands of time only went one way.

She glanced in her rear-view mirror. This was the fourth or fifth time. Maybe it was her anxieties, but it felt like she was being followed. A dark vehicle seemed to hang back a little out of the way. She sighed to herself and looked at that sweet little child next to her. Her wonderful boy.

He was everything to her. It was just… she couldn't think like that.

A few miles further, she turned off the dual carriageway. The road was winding, and the hedges grew higher making her feel like she was lost in a maze. She followed signs towards the little town of Sandy Cove in North Devon. She didn't know a thing about it other than it more than likely had a place that sold ice-cream. *What place near the coast didn't?*

And it was where Greg lived.

She looked over at the boy again. Her Luke was looking out of the window lost in his little world. She couldn't explain the love she had for him. A mother and child had a bond so strong it literally hurt to be apart.

She could hear the faint sounds of Joan Jett on the radio, shouting about feeding dimes into a jukebox. May liked it as background noise rather as entertainment. She was too worried about getting lost and losing concentration. She was all about safety. And not drawing attention to herself.

She wondered when she'd be able to take another pill. Just a little something to take the edge off. Already she wondered whether this was a bad idea.

"You enjoying your birthday trip, Luke?" she said looking across at him. It was a game, she'd told him. It wasn't his birthday, but Luke's. So let's pretend it was.

He shrugged in a way that could break a mother's heart if she didn't know him. Some days it was like his enthusiasm was a yo-yo, continually going up and down. He was happy in his own little way. She guessed he could be dismissive like his dad. She hoped he wouldn't grow up to be a prick like him too. And decide to have sex with a neighbour.

"Let's get that ice-cream," she said pulling into the car park. The worn tarmac was covered in sand blown in from the beach. The untidiness of nature evident for all to see.

May got out of the car, and glanced at the building. Its faded colours spoke of better days. Sun-bleached happiness and age-old patina. The cyber-generation preferring to Facetime, rather than meet in person. Hiding their feelings behind laptop screens and vague emojis. Passive-aggressive attacks with keyboard strokes and damning memes.

She smoothed down her dress and walked around the front of the car to meet her Luke. As usual he had his head down. Overwhelmed by the new surroundings, and change in his schedule, he was silently panicking. He wasn't a fan of social interaction, but he did love ice-cream so something had to give. Each day brought forth its own battles for him. Her too, if anyone asked.

They walked along the side of the building, and May rested a maternal hand on his shoulder as they pushed open the door to the large café. He visibly stiffened as they hit a wall of noise. A cacophony of merged conversations and kitchen sounds. All new and unfamiliar, he was full of anxiety.

There were splashes of red and white, and a humdrum of chatter in the place that seemed to be quite a social hub of the community. The inside spoke louder of success than the outside did.

Oasis was coming out of the speakers. The snarling vocals of Liam Gallagher took May back to when that particular song had been a hit.

Her Luke snuggled into her side a little more, as a heavy-set woman with too many buttons undone called over to them.

"Be with you in a minute!" She smiled and made a frantic grab for a pen and paper.

May and Luke vinyl-surfed squeakily into a booth and grabbed the sticky menu. The lack of cleanliness disgusted May. She could only wonder what they would do to their food whilst preparing it, although there were infectious smiles on the faces of the staff.

"You want a Coke?" May asked, but the boy shook his head. His eyes were darting all around.

"Milk, then?" He smiled at that. "And ice-cream?" He put the menu down satisfied with the order.

"You're gonna be all dairied out, Luke. You're going to get allergies. Don't you want any chips, or a burger?"

Luke shook his head but it was evident that he was uncomfortable. Perhaps he figured they'd be up and out sooner if he didn't order something that needed to be cooked. He'd be locked back in the safety of the car. He tried not to look uncomfortable. That didn't come easily. He was a sensitive child. His little fingers silently drummed

A Lifetime Ago

on the table. A sign of him trying his best to control his feelings. All his energy poured into the quiet rhythm.

The waitress walked over with a slight waddle and a larger-than-life grin on her face. May was sure the woman had never attended a yoga class, or juiced in her life. Such a shame. She was literally dying in front of them.

"Well, aren't you just the cutest pair," she said with a local burr, which May assumed was part of her sales patter. The last person to call her cute had later held his hand on her throat and ejaculated on her tits. Her last view was him pulling up his trousers over a hairy arse, and disappearing into a cloud of nicotine smoke. This was certainly a more preferable scenario. She'd knocked internet dating on the head after that.

Greg was different. For a start, they were online friends. And she'd been working out every day since they first spoke just in case they ever met.

"What can I get you?" she asked, slightly more down to business. Perhaps she was fishing for tips.

"I'll have a portion of chips, and a tea, and Luke here will have a glass of milk and some ice-cream, please?" She was hungry. She'd do squats and press ups later to burn it off.

The waitress turned to Luke and bent over, "What flavour ice-cream, would you like, m'dear?"

Jim Ody

He shrugged and looked at May for help. He was more than likely worried that the waitress's huge breasts would tumble out and smother him.

"He doesn't speak very much," May said to the waitress before addressing Luke. "Chocolate?"

He nodded.

"The strong silent type, huh?" she winked to him. "Well, okey-dokey then, I'll get straight to it!" she grinned and then she was gone. Wobbling her way back to the kitchen. Probably testing its wares whilst out the back there.

There was a lot to be seen in a place like that. Lorry drivers, business men, children, pensioners, families, and teens on dates. All of these different people drawn into this one area for the sole purpose of sustenance. The counter had a great array of homemade cakes, and the place seemed so good they even sold their own merchandise. Although the quality was questionable.

May looked around and wondered just what stories these working-class walls could tell. Small towns were held together by tales. Lies and gossip mostly, but also truths that would drop your jaw.

Chapter 19 - May

Along with the general chatter from the other patrons, some pop song from the 80s and 90s was playing through long-end speakers. For May it sparked memories from her youth. She was dressed up like Cindy Lauper. All back-brushed hair piled high and hard with Ozone-killing CFCs, and on her face, she wore bright coloured eye-shadow and lipstick. Her skinny arms tried to control chunky bangles, as hooped earrings swayed with her dance moves. Her clothes were a mix of stone-wash denim, and bright polka dots. It was as if in the 80s, bright garish colours were discovered for the first time.

Her parents would throw weekly parties at their large Hampshire home, and she would walk around the men, enjoying the attention as she grew into a woman. Those days without responsibility were times she hankered after. It wasn't as if she didn't like her life now, but to her it almost felt like it was over and she was living out her remaining years.

Up until a few years back, everything had been going fine. She'd replaced her husband with painkillers. Ones that dulled her emotions, but never cheated on her.

Jim Ody

A couple of teens were singing along to the old pop song, unaware of what life was like around the time it was originally released; one of them was recording it on her phone. Within minutes a mass of strangers from all over the world would share the same moment, but without the full experience. Most would scroll past it, preferring to find a funny cat video instead. May wondered to herself why she never used to fill her spare time laughing at animals. Was this really life moving forward?

And that's when she was brought back to reality.

"You new? Or holidaying?" A gravelly voice from behind her said. It was more of a demand than a question.

She turned, wondering why the guy was being so loud. She then realised he was talking to her. She hated that. If she was to be hit on, then she preferred them to not look like some worn-out lorry driver.

"I'm sorry?" she said politely. It was never good to rile up those types of people. She knew she'd done rough men before back in uni. Sometimes, these blue-collars understood what a woman wanted. Of course, other times they couldn't give two hoots and she'd be left sore, aching and making an appointment at the clinic. They high-fived at the thought of sex with a posh woman. She ticked a box.

It hadn't always been like this. At one time she had hopes and dreams. Back with Robert, she'd had a huge house, a career and a rich man who loved her. But true romance often lasts as long as the movie. The credits roll all too quickly in real life, and the sequel is too ugly and honest to ever make it to the big screen.

The guy was looking at her like she was a potential victim. His eyes bore into her and lingered for too long on her chest. It was past uncomfortable and was extremely awkward. His hair was receding, and his stubble had flecks of white in it. He may have been a looker in his day, but it seemed to May that his day had come and gone, and now he was a has-been who drank too much and tried his luck wherever possible. The look in his eyes suggested he figured Lady-Luck had had a change of heart.

"I said, are you new 'round here?" He repeated, not pleased he had to repeat himself.

She paused for a second not really wanting to engage, but this guy didn't look the sort to give up easily. He was licking his lips and checking her out, specifically her small cleavage, like he was a hungry baby.

"We're just passing," she said trying to dismiss him. Sometimes they gave up, and other times they assumed she was playing hard to get. You never could tell with men. A lot of them only heard what they wanted to hear.

He laughed deep from his flabby belly, and judging by his jiggling chest that was more than likely a little soft too. "No one just passes through Sandy Cove! You have to have a purpose to stop here!"

"I guess ours was hunger then," she added matter-of-factly. She couldn't hide her frustration.

He got up and made his way around. "Ya mind if I join ya?"

"Look, we're just trying to have a quiet meal here, so I guess we do mind?" May began to get a little anxious. Her heart was beating hard. Her mind flashing back. She didn't need this goon invading her space.

He did indeed look like he might have been an athlete back in his prime. He was probably some rugby player, but now years on he'd hit the booze and fish & chips, and the muscle had softened up. His eyes were wide like he might be high. Or perhaps he was just desperate and in lust.

She wanted to pop a pill herself, but in front of this guy, it didn't seem like a wise move.

"I won't say anything. I'm just tryin' to be friendly," he said making a move to try and squeeze in the booth. May slid over on the red vinyl to stop him, and noticed at once the fear in Luke's eyes. He hated confrontation too.

He'd been through enough already.

"Please just leave us!" May said with all of her courage, and a little louder than she expected. A couple of people nearby looked over at the commotion.

"Look, I ain't…" he began, but a deep voice shouted out.

"Martin! Why don't you just leave her alone like she told you."

The guy whipped his head around and scowled at the cook, who was a big old tub of lard with a shiny head and evidence of the full menu down his apron.

The guy then fixed his eyes on Luke, and then moved accusingly to May before muttering, "Uptight bitch!" and sitting back down at his table.

May flipped a glance behind her noticing that the balding head was now sipping at a coffee and looking out of the window, but more importantly minding his own bloody business. She didn't buy his ignoring her crap for a second.

But now she couldn't relax. She reached into her handbag and pulled out a small blister pack of pills. She popped out a red pill and quickly swallowed it down.

Then the waitress came back and placed their orders on the table. She grinned like this was their competition winnings.

"Can I get you anything else?" she said, and then threw a glance at the guy.

"No, thank you," May replied and pushed the spoon over to Luke for him to attack his ice-cream.

She felt the seat behind her wobble as the guy got up, he turned to her, "We'll meet again," he said menacingly. "I'll show you a real man." And then he left.

May let out a deep breath in relief.

"That looks great, doesn't it?" she said to Luke hoping he didn't pick up on her discomfort.

He nodded and stuck a spoonful greedily into his mouth. He smiled large and bright as the full explosion of dairy and sugar hit his taste buds. It was the sort of delight that vegetables just couldn't hold a candle to no matter how you dressed them up.

She proudly looked at him. His blond hair was perhaps a little long, but it fell into place and made him look cute. She'd combed it over, but it didn't quite sit like the *real* Luke's did. And his roots were beginning to show. It would have to do. And of course, he had those eyes.

Those sweet little eyes.

Chapter 20 – May

She glanced at her phone and then went on to the app. There was nothing from Greg. It had only been two days, but she was worried he was ghosting her. Unless he was busy, then they usually spoke every day. She wanted to see him in person and knew his house was nearby.

It was that, rather than the need for ice-cream, that was behind the reason for having taken this detour.

She wanted to just casually drop by. Maybe park up outside his house and grab a glimpse of him. Perhaps knock on the door to surprise him.

Luke was looking like he was okay now. Still sat in the café he was hardly comfortable, but now that he was eating something, his anxiety was lessened. She hated it when she heard him cry. The sound that breaks a mother's heart.

"Okay?" she said to him when he was done and they were ready to make a move.

He nodded. She didn't expect to hear words from his lips. She paid the bill, and they made their way outside.

"I knew you'd want some chips too!" May laughed, as the waitress smiled and waved as they left. May had ended up sharing her chips with him when he finished his ice-cream and was fixated on her meal. She didn't need all of those carbs anyway. She had to keep trim.

They walked down the outside of the café, May holding his hand tightly, and round to where she'd parked the car.

She unlocked the SUV and helped Luke in. A small breeze playfully whipped up her dress making her suddenly smooth it down to keep her dignity. That said, she hoped somewhere someone was watching, and hoping to glimpse more than they should. She missed that now she was getting older. She wanted to be desired again. The object of somebody's fantasy.

There was still a hunger in her belly. She hated it, so pulled out her e-cigarette from the glove box and took a long drag. She exhaled a huge cloud of vapour into the atmosphere. Just like her hopes and dreams it floated off and away from her.

The first drag tasted so satisfying. She sucked it in like oxygen, and let out another cloud. It might not be the healthiest way to suppress your appetite, but along with her little pills it did the job.

Suddenly a familiar voice from behind them sent chills up and down her spine.

"You ready for me now?" he said pulling out a knife. Barely looking at its size but inside all she could think about was how sharp it was. It didn't have to be huge to scare her. No one wants to be stabbed.

"Look, what is it you want…?"

A Lifetime Ago

"Shut the fuck up and do as I say. I swear to god I'll cut your boy!" He hissed, clearly unprepared and acting completely crazy. He was subtle enough that if anyone was to look over, they wouldn't notice his knife, and may only think it was a couple having a disagreement.

She tried to lock the doors, but he was already there yanking open the passenger side.

"Try something like that again, and he gets it!" he gestured to Luke. "Now get out!"

She was panicking now. It put her recent feelings into perspective.

"What? No! Leave us alone!"

Without a warning, he slapped her hard. It hurt, but she was more shocked than in pain. She'd been with some rough men in uni, but they'd never hit her. Her eyes darted out at the car park, but they were parked in the corner away from the road.

"I said, get out! If I have to repeat myself then it will be a fist!"

May looked over at Luke. He was stunned. His eyes wide.

"Now!" The guy demanded.

May slowly got out. She always thought she was a strong woman, but now when it came down to it, she was that weak woman in the movies that you wanted to shout at.

He stood behind her. His strong body pressed up against her back. The knife at her side, his other arm groping her.

"Now, slowly and naturally, we're going to walk over to my van."

"I need to get Luke," she said, the word *van* echoing in her head.

"He doesn't need to watch."

"What!?" Her voice was shaky. Her legs now jelly. She thought she was going to pass out.

She turned around resigned to her fate.

And then there was another man.

He swung something that made contact with the other man's head, and knocked him over.

It had to be the stress of the situation, but the guy looked remarkably like Greg.

"May?" he said shocked. "Is that you?" It was him! She couldn't believe it. Relief washed over her. She nodded, unable to speak. The emotion of the situation overwhelmed her.

"Get back in your car. Drive out and wait for me. I have a black Range Rover. I live close by."

The words scattered around her. She was already sat in her car, nodding and trying to remember the keywords.

She started up her car, automatically locked all of the doors, and drove out of the car park.

"It's okay, Luke," she said, now just shaking. "Greg's here now."

She saw the Range Rover coming up the road behind her. He pulled up next to her.

"Are you okay? Not hurt?" he said in a concerned voice.

She was left nodding and shaking her head in response. "Thank you," she managed.

"You okay to follow me?"

She smiled. "Yes, if that's okay."

"I think it's the least I can offer."

A Lifetime Ago

May slowly followed the expensive looking Range Rover. The handsome man she'd been speaking to online was in front of her. He wasn't ghosting her. He was here and in person!

She couldn't decide whether she was really lucky, or really unlucky.

The trip had already been full of adventure.

Chapter 21 – Hudson

It wasn't even twenty-four hours before he received a text from Laura. Hudson was around Jez's house when his phone vibrated.

"There's something here," Jez was saying whilst bouncing around on a chair that squeaked far too much. It sounded like bedsprings in a cheap hotel. It had been a long time since he'd experience that.

They were looking into the background of a guy who they suspected of grooming children. Until today, everything had been hearsay, rumours and hunches. Like a lot of cases, you could see a crime. You could have a suspect that looked good for it. A sloppy detective could go as far as making that suspect fit the crime, but that wasn't enough. You had to have an airtight case, or else the CPS would throw it out. And then all too often the suspect would escape and go to ground.

"We have him on CCTV in five different locations. All around the same time as the victim." Jez was grinning. There was a reason he was kept away from the public. He was great at his job, but often misunderstood the seriousness of the crime. It wasn't that he was devoid of sympathy, just that he loved the cat and mouse of the chase that his immature streak saw as a game. He was desensitised to what was actually happening and in place of feeling horror, he was fist-pumping and high-fiving from catching a suspect red-handed.

"Great work, Jez!" Hudson said patting him on the back. He looked at his phone.

Laura had simply written:

Hi! Are you free later? We need to talk. Laura

For a first text message between them it was shit. It was all serious, and a million miles away from being romantic.

That first kiss looked destined to be a missed opportunity.

"Your date?" Jez said, not taking his eyes off the screen.

Hudson nodded. "I guess."

"You guess?" Jez spun around. "Laura, right? She wants to meet and talk."

Hudson frowned. "How'd you know?"

Jez beamed a huge grin that showed off his dental work and spun around to his monitor. He clicked a button and the text message appeared.

Hudson was shocked. "How the…?"

"It's a program I'm working on," he said and gave an over exaggerated wink. "It picks up messages within the vicinity."

Jez was a clever guy. Sometimes too clever. And unfortunately, lacking in common sense. He could come up with all kinds of computerised inventions, but often failed to understand the legal implications, and social or moral impact. He needed strict guidance. Hudson assumed that was his unofficial role.

"I'm not sure how that sits with GDPR, mate. You know, General Data Protection Rights."

Jez blew a raspberry. "I know what it means! Anyway, it's a prototype."

"It's still illegal."

He waved that away like it wasn't important. "So, you meeting up with her then? Your hot date?"

"You read the text, Jez. Did that sound like the prelude to a hot date?"

"She wants to meet up and talk, so what? You can't go jumping her bones straight away. Even I know that!" Jez let out a noise like a walrus being attacked, but Hudson knew this to be his laugh.

"Jez, whenever a woman says, *we need to talk*, then the outcome is rarely good."

"*Really?*" This confused Jez. Most women confused Jez — his wife included.

"Trust me, it's the same as telling me that she wants to meet up, but to manage my expectations, she will be doing all of the talking, I will be nodding and feeling awkward, before she leaves and I never see her again."

"Jesus, your date must've sucked last night!"

And that was just it, Hudson thought it had gone well. At least that's the way he'd seen it. They'd talked, and eaten. It was all friendly and they both seemed comfortable. The ending was awkward, hugging in public, a kiss on the cheek, and they'd gone their separate ways.

Jez clicked his fingers again, and Hudson wished he was talking to anyone other than Jez about this. In fact, he wasn't sure why he was still talking about it.

"Friendzone. She got that feeling with you like you were her brother or some such shit. I've seen it in loads of rom-coms. It's not your fault. It's just you give off the wrong scent or something."

"Right." Jez was the last person on the face of the earth he'd ask for advice on women. Granted he was married, and by all accounts they fought most days. Jez spoke of his wife in two ways: either as an evil woman looking to kill him; or as a sex beast whose sexual appetite would send him to an early grave. There didn't seem to be any middle ground, and all roads led to death. Apparently.

"Don't be hard on yourself, mate."

"Okay. Um… thanks."

Jez nodded in a knowing way. "You're welcome. I don't know much, but I do know all about computers and women!" He laughed again. Hudson agreed on one of those points.

He hit reply:

Sure. Why don't you pop over to mine? 6pm?

Hudson hit send, and as he looked up, he saw Jez reading on the screen.

"Nice," Jez said, not even trying to hide the fact he was reading it.

"Now what?"

Jez turned around with both hands on his lap. He looked like a father about to lecture his son before a date.

"I see what you did there. You could've met her anywhere, but instead you asked her back to yours. *Good move.* She sees you in your own environment." He nodded in approval, and then held up a finger. "Still, a slightly risky move, may I say. But bold, and ballsy. She'll like that."

Hudson was frowning; he'd not considered any of that. "I just thought we'd be free to talk without being in earshot of anyone else."

"Indeed," Jez continued, and again with the nodding. "Invite her in, offer a drink. This is my place. Let me show you my bedroom. Bang! Homerun! Dude, you're good!" He was pointing now although it wasn't clear at what.

"*Dude*, you're not American! I have no intention of anything like that. She wants to talk, and there we can talk."

"*O-kay*," Jez grinned, and winked knowingly. "We'll play it like that."

Hudson's phone vibrated again.

Great! Send me your address, and I'll see you then! X

They both read the response at the same time.

"It means nothing!" Hudson said just as quickly as Jez was saying: "You got a kiss!"

"Right, well, I've got to go. You okay with the surveillance?"

"Sure am, boss!"

"Okay, well I'll see you tomorrow, Jez."

"You go get the girl, mate!" Hudson went to respond to that but instead said, "I've got an interview first."

"What?" Jez spun around in his chair.

A Lifetime Ago

"With Darren Hughes's uncle, Simon."

Jez frowned. He was confused as Hudson had forgotten to tell him earlier.

"For a job?"

Hudson could only stare at his partner in absolute shock. "Sometimes I think you need medicating, mate. No, not for a job, for the case we're working on."

Jez looked almost relieved. "Ah, right. That makes more sense."

"You think?" Hudson's sarcasm was thick, and of course lost on Jez.

"Yeah. You'll want to get his side of things, just in case he's tellin' porkies, right."

Hudson raised a hand as a parting gesture. "Now he's gone cockney," he mumbled under his breath.

Chapter 22 – Hudson

Simon Hughes was a well-dressed guy. He wasn't twenty until the next month, and he was handsome in a fresh-faced kind of way. He clearly cared about his appearance, and Hudson thought he looked like the cleanest man he'd ever met, although against Jez and his own father, that wasn't such a glowing accolade.

Simon lived in the same area as his sister and nephew. His house was an immaculate coach-house that was as tall and skinny as the lad standing before Hudson.

"Hi," Simon said, reaching out and pumping Hudson's hand. It wasn't macho, but in a polite manner. He wore a branded T-shirt that would see little change from a hundred pounds, and skinny jeans with carefully designed holes in the knees. In Hudson's day, this look was born of necessity rather than high-end fashion.

"Thanks for agreeing to speak to me, Simon," Hudson said. "I know this is an awful time for you."

Simon nodded, and understandably looked forlorn. He showed Hudson to a lounge that was immaculate, and nothing like the bachelor pad he was expecting.

A Lifetime Ago

"I just want him found," he said looking at the ground. It was a shame how the aftershock of these awful incidents affected so many people. He nodded to Simon, but his mind was already going back to that fateful morning. Perhaps that was the kinship he suddenly felt with this lad.

"Of course," Hudson responded to his original comment. "I'm sorry to have to make you go over the details again, but…"

"I know. I just want him found," he repeated.

Hudson paused, and allowed a buffer of silence. He knew you never wanted to suddenly fire out questions to people. You may have a couple of questions, or you may have a whole list, it didn't matter it wasn't a quick-fire round of a TV gameshow. You weren't shouting them out, noting the answer and moving on. These were human beings. Sensitive and fragile, it was often a long process. It had to be.

"I know it's hard, but please take me back to that day. Did you see anyone when you left the house?"

Simon was thoughtful. He may have been asked this before, but he was thinking about it again, possibly racking his brains for something he'd noticed, but not noticed. An inconsequential detail his mind hadn't thought relevant, but now he might conjure up, dragging it to the forefront.

He sighed when he admitted, "No, not that I can remember." He turned to Hudson, looking him directly in the eyes, and said, "You know when you do something a hundred times, and then you have to think of a single specific time, they all merge together." He knew only too well. That was the problem with witnesses. They became confused with too many details in their memories, and that often muddied the waters.

Hudson nodded. "I know. It might be there is nothing new you can tell me, but in my experience, things can suddenly jump into your mind when you're least expecting them.

"And you were at your sister's place, correct?"

Again, he nodded, "Yes." He began to wring his hands slightly. "We went along the path by the side of the house, down the alleyway, and from there it opens up to where the park is."

"And you didn't see anyone?"

"There were people around. You know, this place always has people walking around. Either with dogs, jogging, or towards the shops over the way."

"Anyone in particular? Anyone you spoke to, or smiled at?"

"I saw a guy walking a huge Alsatian. I know him, but don't know him, you know?" Hudson did. The people you politely say hello to but never know anything further about them. Most of the people in his block of flats were like that.

"D'you know his name?"

"No. He's older than you and often wears a cap like the sort in *Peaky Blinders*."

"And he lives around here?"

"Yeah, I don't know where exactly. He nodded to me, and I nodded back. That's normal for us."

Hudson was jotting it all down. "Anyone else?"

"No, not until I got to the park." Simon looked up at the corner of the room and he suddenly looked devastated. His face lost colour, and his eyes welled up. Hudson followed his gaze and saw he was looking at a picture of his nephew.

The same one his sister had been looking at when he'd interviewed her at her house.

"Your sister has the same picture," Hudson commented, deliberately lowering his tone. "It's a wonderful photo."

Simon's Adam's apple bobbed as he swallowed, and his head nodded slowly and gently. A light movement rapt in thoughts of the delicate child in question.

"I took it," he said, the words were almost like a confession. He turned, smiling at the memory, and added, "It took us a few minutes to get him to stay still. He just wanted to play. He was so happy — *so* very happy."

It was hard. Hudson knew it was, but he had to get back on track.

"And you recognised the people at the park?"

Simon swallowed again, cleared his throat and said, "Yes. Katie and her daughter were already there, and her friend Sandra was over with her little Ruby on the swings… there were a handful of other parents that I knew by sight, but no one suspicious."

"And all had children there?"

"Sure. I mean why…" and he suddenly stopped dead still. It was like he'd been paused.

"What is it?" Hudson pressed. "Anything could help."

He half-shrugged, and said, "There was a woman. I mean, it wasn't anything strange. She just walked by a couple of times."

"D'you remember what she looked like?"

"I don't," he said, but was clearly giving it some thought. "She had red hair. Like ginger but lighter."

"Almost blonde?"

"Yeah, but definitely a redhead. Shoulder length."

"Build?"

He puffed out his cheeks. "Normal, I guess. I mean, she wasn't like big, nor was she skinny."

"D'you remember what she was wearing?" Hudson had everything crossed.

"Jeans and a top." Unfortunately, it was quite generic.

"When you say top, was it a hoodie? A jacket? A jumper?"

"A hoodie, I think. Sort of dark. It might've been blue."

"Age?"

He pulled a face. At nineteen, most adults look older. Even thirty seemed middle-aged.

"Thirty-odd, I guess. Hard to tell. She was pushing a pushchair."

Hudson sat up. "With a child?"

"I didn't see one, but I don't remember the seat being empty."

"But it might've been?"

"It's possible. You don't think…" He didn't want to say it.

"I don't know. We'll check it all out though."

Hudson tapped the notepad with his pencil, and then realised it was quite loud and abruptly stopped. "What type of pushchair was it?" He asked.

Simon looked like he'd just been asked about the laws of physics. "I don't know. Regular, I guess."

"I mean," Hudson started, "Was it a small fold away one, or one with the big off-road-type of wheels?"

"I think it had three wheels. One in the front; that sort." Hudson knew every detail was important.

"Whereabouts did she come from?"

Simon looked even more shellshocked. "She walked along the path by the playpark. First towards us, and then later on back the other way."

"Pushing the pushchair?"

Simon nodded.

"Could she have just been taking a walk, or going to the shops?"

"I have no idea." The truth was Hudson hadn't meant to say the line out loud, he was saying it to himself.

Hudson readied himself for the hard part. The details of when Darren disappeared.

"What happened next?" Hudson asked the line he'd said hundreds of times before. Each time as a prompt to push the story on.

"I was talking to Katie. She was telling me about getting an extension to her kitchen. She's nice, but she's a little…erm…"

Jim Ody

"Self-centred?" Hudson finished, then chided himself. It wasn't good practise to put words in people's mouths. Not good practise at all.

"Yes. She doesn't mean to, but... I guess her family is..." he swallowed again. "Everything to her."

"And Darren? Where was he?"

"He was over by the little car. Well, it's a climbing thing, but underneath is a little seat with a steering wheel."

"Was he on his own?"

Simon shook his head. "No, it was suddenly really busy. I think a pre-school had just finished. Sandra came over, and her daughter was still playing with Darren in the car."

"And when you say busy. What are we talking? Another... how many people?"

Simon was deep in thought thinking back to that fateful day. "At least another five or six adults, and at least that many kids. It was suddenly really loud. I went over to check on Darren. He was giggling with Ruby and another lad. That's went Soph rang."

Hudson had the call details. He knew the time and length of the call. He also had statements from Katie and Sandra. Everything matched Simon's story.

"And it was after the call you noticed Darren was gone?"

Simon's head moved slightly in an attempt at a nod. His hands were visibly moving. It was a slight tremor. The sort that can't be faked.

"I thought it was his jacket," he almost pleaded. "But… when I went to tell him it was time to go, it was another child."

"We'll do our best, Simon. This isn't your fault."

"I know but…" he puffed out his cheeks.

Hudson quickly jumped in. "Seriously, mate. Don't blame yourself. You cannot help the actions of others, okay?"

"I know…" he began again.

"No, don't torture yourself. Look, if you need someone to talk to then give me a call. Anytime, okay?" Hudson pulled out his card and passed it over. "I also know a good support group."

"No, no, I'm fine." Simon almost seemed offended.

"Don't suffer on your own, mate. It's not a weakness. Trust me, I know."

Simon was moving the card between his fingers. His hands were happy to have something to do. "Okay."

Hudson left him to it. He was happy to rule Simon out of any involvement.

Outside, he took the short walk to the park. When he arrived, he saw it had a small fence around it. It wasn't big, and designed more to keep toddlers in than anyone else out. An adult could easily step over it if they needed to.

The path led off left and right. The left took you out onto the road towards some shops, whereas the path to the right took you out in the direction of a residential street.

Jim Ody

Hudson looked behind him to where there was a metal bench. The brother had been sat there, but admitted that whilst on the phone had got up and walked around. He'd lost sight of Darren, too busy with a call from his sister.

A mother was fussing over two small children and paid him no mind. In a way it was sad. He could be anyone. A single man stood outside a playground and turning in circles immersing himself fully within the environment.

He had a feeling. A niggling feeling in the pit of his stomach that this was an unusual case. He felt it. The pull of something he couldn't explain.

He completed another circle and looked into the bushes and hedges all around.

This time when he glanced over the woman had called her children over and was looking at him with suspicion.

"Are you okay?" she called.

He held up a hand. "I'm fine. Sorry, I'm looking into the disappearance of the missing child," he said walking over.

She looked down at her two children, smoothing their heads. They could only have been two or three. "That was awful," she said.

Hudson nodded in encouragement. "I don't suppose you saw anything?"

She was well presented. Her make up and hair were immaculate. Hudson got the impression she was in casual, even though she was dressed smartly for a corporate job.

"I don't know," she said, suddenly clamming up.

"Anything could help," Hudson pressed. Normally in these areas people would happily talk, however, further over in the less affluent areas nobody ever saw a thing. Snitching was a huge social crime there.

"I saw a woman and child, but I don't know. They were acting… erm, unusual."

"How so?"

"The child looked scared. Not upset, but petrified, you know?" He did. He'd seen too many little faces looking like that to not know.

Instead he nodded. "Where were they? Walking?"

She pointed towards the alleyway. "It was through there, and then down the road a touch. They were getting into a car. Well, she was forcing the child in."

"And what sort of car was it?" This was the important question.

"I don't know, but it looked old. It was red. Not a big people-carrier thing, not an estate. Just small." On the plus side red was better than it being black or silver.

"And what did she look like?" Hudson was hoping that she had a good description.

"She was about my height. She had reddish hair pulled back and a darkish top."

"Did you recognise her? I mean, have you seen her before?"

The woman shook her head. "I don't think so. I mean, I might have done, but she didn't look familiar."

"I'm assuming you didn't get the registration number?"

She gave a weak smile that said it all. "I'm afraid not."

Hudson took down her details, said good bye, and walked off. When he got to his car, he sent a text over to Jez with the vague vehicle details. You just never knew.

Chapter 23 – May

May puffed out her cheeks. It hadn't quite sunk in yet as to the situation she'd just escaped from.

"What're we doing, Luke?" May said albeit rhetorically. She glanced towards him but he still had that emotionless look on his face. He tried to smile although she could see it was forced. Things were still laying heavy on his mind. Of course, he couldn't fully comprehend what had just happened, but then any sort of disruption to his routine filled him with fear. He was just glad to see her again. She was sure of it.

"He's a good man," she said aloud, perhaps more to reassure herself than Luke. Luke had nothing to add to that.

The black Range Rover drove at a steady pace in front of them. The sun was shining high in the sky, and as they drove along the main road, the sea was in view to their right. It was a beautiful view, and helped calm her a little.

May was now feeling nervous. This was Greg! *Her* Greg!

She pulled down the sun-visor, and slid open the plastic section to reveal the vanity mirror. She carefully glanced into it. She knew she'd never be completely happy with her reflection but what could she do? Besides, he'd already seen her now.

They turned off the road, and headed down quite a steep gradient. After a couple of bends, they turned into a lane where the roofs of a couple of houses could be seen. Both of which looked to have the sea at the back and within walking distance.

The Range Rover pulled in to a drive that expanded to reveal the large house. It was picturesque. The garden was well-maintained, and the house was a mixture of contemporary white cladding and flashes of huge glass panes. There was a large wooden door, and windows in the roof. The whole scene was something out of a movie.

Greg rushed over to their car.

"Are you alright?" he said with real concern. "I should really call the police. I know that guy, he can't get away with that!" Greg was suddenly all worked up. It had been scary. May realised then just how scary it had been, but was relieved that Greg had been there.

"No, no," she said. There was no way she was going to the police. The mere image of a policeman only brought her back to that morning. She couldn't go through it all again.

"But you don't have to go there, I could get them to come here. It would be just a quick statement…" he clicked his fingers. "The café will have CCTV. It will all be there. You'll just have to outline what happened, and that's it. All done."

She was already shaking her head and gesturing with her hands, before he'd even finished.

"No, Greg, please. Look at Luke, he doesn't like the police. It would all be too much for him. I want to just drop it." Really, she was thinking about herself.

"Are you sure?"

She nodded. "Look, how about I think about it. Look…" she held up her hand. "I'm still shaking."

"Come on in then," Greg said. "You've had an awful ordeal." He smiled and she couldn't help but be drawn in by him. He was a little taller and more handsome than his picture. Well, perhaps not more handsome, just that in real-life he was more, well real.

"Hello, by the way," he grinned, standing back and taking her all in. She felt a little embarrassed that his eyes were looking at her.

"You look good," she said and flushed with embarrassment, and instantly touched her hair. "Sorry, I sound like a teenager."

"I don't mind," he replied. "My teenage years are a long and distant memory. And any compliments were last sent my way about the same time!"

"That's hard to believe."

May walked around and opened up the door for Luke to get out.

"Ahh, and this is…" Greg said clicking his fingers.

"Luke," May finished. "I call him Luke."

The child looked up at Greg. His eyes questioning everything he saw.

There was a flash of something in Greg's eyes. Something he wanted to say. She knew what it was.

"I know," she began, as Luke got out. "Luke was the name of my first son. I… *you know*… I like the name."

Greg held up his hands, and looked apologetic. "Oh, I'm not saying anything, nor judging. I was just a little surprised, I suppose. Yes, that's it. Anyway, come, come!"

He led them up the steps, and he unlocked the door and ushered them in.

The place was immaculate. May had never seen anything quite like it in her life.

"Wow! This place is gorgeous!" she turned to her son. "Isn't it, Luke"

The little boy stood and looked around but avoided the question. He was feeling uncomfortable. His senses had been overloaded already with too many new sights and sounds; once again she wondered whether it was all too much for him.

"Please, just make yourself at home." Greg stood back and took her in again. "Wow! I can't believe it's you!"

May shuffled her weight from one foot to the other, and blushed again. It had been a long time since she'd felt like this.

"I know, talk about fate!" she agreed.

"Serendipity," he said in a way that was slightly poetic. Drawn out and playful.

"Let me get you a drink. Hot or cold?"

Like all mothers, May looked to Luke first. "You want a drink, Luke?" He was shaking his head vehemently like she'd asked him whether he wanted to eat worms.

"Cold for me," she said.

"I have lemonade, or even some wine?"

May looked at Luke. He sat down on the sofa and was swinging his legs gently. He did this to calm himself. He was trying, which was a good sign.

"I'll have a small glass of wine, if I may."

"You may, May!" They grinned like kids as he moved off quickly through a door to where the kitchen must have been.

May looked around at the white walls with splashes of colour. The place looked like it had been professionally staged after a refurbishment, and before a sale. There were splashes of green that popped out. Paintings adorned the walls. She was no expert but they looked expensive. It was minimalist, with strategically placed items that spoke of wealth and taste. An artist's eye and a banker's wage.

"You okay?" she glanced at Luke, saying the familiar line again. It was such a shame. He would always be in his brother's shadow. She knew she had to try and accept that the two were separate people. But it helped her cope. So how could that be so wrong?

He just looked back at her. The fact he wasn't shaking his head and covering his ears with his hands was a good sign. He was coping.

Jim Ody

Greg soon returned looking eager to please her. He handed over the glass of white wine to her, and was also holding one for himself.

"Is white, okay?"

She grinned, "White wine is perfect." She then made a show of glancing around.

"Your house is amazing! God, I'd love to own a house like this!"

"You're very kind. I'd love to say I worked my butt off for it but I was lucky to come from rich parents!" He threw her an expensive smile. He was modest in his wealth, just like her. They shared a similar background.

A small smile crept over May's mouth, and she smoothed her hair. She took in the small entrance hall, and then how the whole room just opened up with a small piano in the corner. A staircase that dominated the area to the side, as it wound around up into who-knew-where.

"Most men would pretend they were something they weren't," she said.

"I'm not most men." But of course, that was obvious. Most men didn't spot trouble and follow into the eye of a storm, less burst in and save a woman from violence.

May took in the clean white décor. Her tastes were very similar, even if her house could fit inside this one twice over.

"Let me show you the pool," he said standing up.

May paused. "Are you sure?"

He nodded. "Yes. I don't blame the pool," he said, which was a strange way of putting it. He wasn't as scared by the tragedy as she was.

"You want to see the swimming pool?" May said to Luke. He nodded, but it was more out of duty, and in response to her hopeful tone, rather than because it was what he wanted.

Greg gave them a brief tour as they went, leading through a large and spacious kitchen/diner, and then out to a beautiful kidney shaped pool. May took it all in. It was nothing like she'd ever seen before. She'd had friends with large indoor pools, and she'd been green with envy. It's what she'd always wanted. She'd worked so hard and built a life, but then everything had been snatched away.

Had the accident not happened, she wondered, would she be living in a place like this now?

Life could be so unfair. But she knew that.

"You want to take a dip?" Greg asked, innocently gesturing towards the pool.

May nodded before adding, "Well, we would, but we don't have any swimming stuff."

"No problem. He can swim in his underwear, and I can get you one of my wife's swimsuits, if you like?"

"You still have her stuff?" May said. "Your wife, I mean?"

Greg nodded, and shrugged it off like it was nothing. "She still has some of her stuff to pick up."

"And you're separated?"

"Yes," he said. "It's funny, isn't it? You get married and think that person is the one and then…" he made a dismissive gesture. "You grow apart." *Or your husband has an affair, and runs of with some floosy*, she thought.

Luke was looking at the pool like it was an amazing thing. How could she say *No*?

"Your boy looks like he wants a dip." He turned to Luke. "You want to go in?"

Luke looked at May for approval.

"You want to go in?" She echoed towards him. He nodded. She smiled and looked again at the pool.

"Okay, but stay in the shallow end, yeah?" She turned to Greg, not wanting to upset him. "He can't really swim."

"You want me to get you a swimsuit?" Greg pressed.

"I don't know. Would she mind?"

"She'd have picked it up by now if she'd been that bothered. Give me a minute."

He trotted off with an added spring in his step and May walked around the pool, looking at the faux-bamboo hut that housed what appeared to be a bar. The smell of chlorine was now thick in the air. She held onto Luke. He couldn't stop grinning. He loved the water. She couldn't believe they'd forgotten to bring swimming stuff. Okay, *she'd* forgotten to pack it. She felt guilty again. As her obsession increased, her neglect of him did too. She really didn't want to admit it, but deep down she knew it to be true.

A Lifetime Ago

"You okay?" she asked him once again. It was a question she asked every hour or so. It reassured them both.

He nodded, and pointed to the pool. He then began to take his T-shirt off, and his trousers soon followed. They were quickly discarded into a crumpled pile on the stone slabs, his scrawny little body so fragile it almost made her cry.

"Sure, in you go." He walked over to the steps at the side of the pool. He giggled as he stepped forward and the water engulfed him. One of the first sounds to come out of his mouth in hours. Again, that was his way.

She sat down on a wooden chair and watched as Luke splashed around enjoying the feeling of the water washing over him. It was liberating to see him at ease. The water looked so good to May that when Greg came back, she thought nothing of taking the swimsuit from him.

"You can change in the room there, if you like?" he said pointing to the laundry room.

She nodded, and glanced at Luke. She didn't like leaving him, but from the room she'd hear him, and run to him if he needed her. It was then that she looked and saw he'd brought her a bikini. It made sense as both sections had ties, so on the plus side, it would fit. But it did seem like it just consisted of three small pieces of material to cover her intimate parts, so for the first time in many years she was glad she had small breasts.

"Stay in the shallow end," she said to Luke. He looked at her with a blank expression, then grinned, and bounced in the water again.

Splashing around like a creature in the sea caught by a predator.

"I'll keep my eye on him," Greg reassured her.

It didn't take May long to get changed. She'd not normally wear a bikini, and with it now on she suddenly felt slightly sexy. Still exposed — in fact very exposed — but a little liberated too. She returned quickly to the pool not wanting to leave Luke there on his own. She could still hear him splashing and giggling the whole time, and that had put her at ease.

It was amazing how quickly she felt at home there. She could picture her and Greg as a couple whilst Luke swam in the pool. She even allowed herself a small fantasy to tumble to more erotic thoughts. Massages, candles and their naked bodies intertwining. It had been a long time since she'd felt any sort of romance. Of late, it had been drunken fumbling, quickly turning to being flipped over and penetrated from behind for a couple of minutes. By the time she turned around and wiped her back, they were dressed and making excuses to leave.

Robert had been a lot of things, but at least he'd been attentive. Until he wasn't. That was near the end. When he was being attentive to someone else.

It was still raw. Very, very raw. The anger built up inside her and threatened to make her explode. Or do something incredibly stupid.

She thought about the pictures of him with her.

And with their child. The replacement for Luke. She gritted her teeth, and felt her jaw tense.

She looked over at her own replacement, the hypocrisy of it never once registering.

She was here now. There could be no turning back.

But just as quickly she looked down at herself. The sun warm on her light skin, and the thin material of another woman's clothes pressed against her naked body. Instead of silently thanking the woman, she was thinking about replacing her, and indulging in carnal activities with the woman's husband. Ex-husband, she reminded herself.

After a while, the heat had her looking at the water and wanting to take a dip.

The feeling of the cool water washed over her warm body as she slipped in, and was incredibly satisfying. She'd not done this outside of an expensive spa in a long time. And it was even longer since she'd swum in a small pool outside on holiday.

Chapter 24 – May

This was definitely something she could get used to. Luke was enjoying the pool, and she sat out in the sun looking at where the beach trailed off to the sea. Their own private hideaway.

May and Greg had each danced around it. Small talk quickly got deeper, but May would only say so much. Her past embarrassed her. She felt deceived, and was determined never to let another man do it again.

"Can I get you another drink?" Greg asked from the side. The wine had been finished a long time ago "I was going to do margaritas?"

May nodded, and he smiled at her and turned away. Part of her wished he'd stripped off and slipped in to the water with her too. Instead, he remained on the side watching. Perhaps the tragedy stopped him from enjoying the pool.

The truth was, she didn't know how she felt. Greg was now real. He'd been a fantasy for weeks A perfect man. When lonely, and late at night, her idle fingers wandered below the waistband of her underwear. And now, she didn't know. He was handsome, and witty, but he wasn't Robert. She just wasn't sure what was going on with her feelings. Perhaps the pills had numbed her.

She watched him walk away all the while comparing him to the perfect man she'd never have.

She looked over the house, smoothed her now wet red hair and for a second fantasised that this was all hers. The garden flowed out down to a wooded area. She could see neighbours but the houses were a few hundred yards away. This was what she wanted. This was a place that she could live. She once again thought about her situation. Almost swinging between lives. Harking back to her past and not wanting to fully move on.

A few minutes later, Greg walked back wearing only swimming shorts and holding two drinks. She looked over the muscles of his chest. Not too defined but beneath a small amount of hair was a body that worked out, even just a little.

"You okay?" he asked as he got nearer.

She felt herself go red although with the heat and her complexion she knew it was easily disguised. Lustful needs knew no boundaries, and were shallow in their desires. Perhaps he was someone she could work with.

"Yeah," she replied. "It's been a strange day."

He raised his eyebrows and tilted his head to the side in a slight shrug.

"I get that… I'll put your drink on the side."

Just then his mobile began to ring. He slipped it out of his shorts.

"Hello?" His face lit up. "Sindy! How are you? Ah-ha… good… and Bee? Great! Hey, I've got someone here with me. Two people in fact…" He went on to explain the scene at the carpark. Was it his wife? May wondered. They seemed very friendly for a couple who were estranged.

Greg looked over and smiled at May. "Yes, that's what I said… Uh-huh… yeah, that's where they are right now!" He laughed and walked over.

"Hey May, it's my wife Sindy, she wants a word."

May's eyes widened, and her heart beat faster. What did his wife want? She got out of the pool, wrapped a towel around herself, and took the phone.

"Hello?"

"Hi, you poor thing! Did he hurt you?" A sweet voice said on the other end of the phone. It was almost enough to make her cry.

"No, not really… but if your husband hadn't shown up then it could've been so much worse."

"I know. I know, Honey… Look, our house is your house for as long as you want, okay?"

"I… I don't want to intrude…" May said fighting back the lump in her throat. If they were estranged, then why be so accommodating. She couldn't quite get to grips with their relationship.

"Rubbish, you're not. Now, Bee and I are not there, poor Greg gets lonely. Enjoy the pool and the food. Relax, okay?"

"If you're sure? We can leave if it's a problem… you know, us being here?"

"Of course it's not a problem! Hang on, Bee wants to have a word!"

"O-kay." This was all very weird. Now their daughter wanted to speak to her.

Suddenly an excited higher-pitched voice came on the phone.

"Hel-lo?"

"Hello."

"Did that bad man get you?" the voice said very matter-of-factly.

Through nerves it only made May giggle as she replied, "No, your daddy saved me."

"He's great! He didn't save Mamma though. That bad man had sex with her…" She heard Sindy nervously laugh.

"Uh…" May didn't know what to say but she heard the sound of the phone being handed over again.

"Sorry about that," Sindy said, the embarrassment evident in her voice.

"That's okay… I'm… Look I didn't know," May said stumbling over her words. The air on her wet body giving her goosebumps.

"Okay. Look you got away. You… you just look after Greg, yeah?"

"Sure."

"Okay, can you put him back on? Take care, May."

"Good bye." She handed the phone back to Greg, and then grabbed her drink. She really needed it now. Greg hadn't mentioned anything about his wife having been attacked. Was that the reason for their relationship failing? She had so many questions now. Things had begun to get extremely complicated.

He finished his call and grabbed his drink too. He looked off into the distance for a moment, his mind clearly somewhere else.

"Yes, it was a bad time," he said still looking off out into the trees. "We've not been the same since."

"I'm sorry," she said. She knew even when a crime is over the effects can last for years. Sometimes forever.

"It's not your fault," he said, but there wasn't a whole lot of emotion behind it.

"I got away. I feel guilty."

He grabbed her arm. Not hard but enough to know he was serious with his words.

"Don't ever feel guilty for getting away from that arsehole, May! He'll get what's coming to him one day." The statement was weighted with words not spoken. Was it a threat? Something he had planned? Part of her was too scared to continue with the subject.

Instead, May tried to relax into one of the chairs. They were comfortable. May assumed a lot of money had probably been spent on the furniture in the garden.

"I sometimes want to just go over and tie him up. Get something," he shrugged as if racking his brains for ideas. "A blowtorch, or a knife or something. I'd love to make him really pay."

"But you don't."

He shook his head, and took a deep breath. "No, I don't. It's a weakness I suppose. I was raised to be better. I've a wife and kid, and that would just land me in a heap of trouble. Even if they don't live here anymore… I don't know."

She gave him a consolation smile. It told him she understood, even if deep down she didn't. She thought she'd have no problems in tying that man to a chair and drilling holes in his kneecaps. But whilst she'd been raised with money too, she'd also had a father who didn't take any messing. An alpha male, who was strong and overpowering, and thought nothing of puffing out his chest and swinging his fists when the need arose.

Silence fell upon them. The sun had moved around slightly, and Luke was now floating face down, every once in a while, suddenly bursting his head out and blowing water from his mouth.

"You not got someone back waiting for you?" Greg asked. He knew she'd had dates. He was fishing, wondering whether there were holes in her truths about her relationship status.

She shook her head. "Nope. They seem to come and go from my life. I guess I never seem to get my claws in to them!" She said it deadpan but he laughed loudly at that.

"You're funny!" he said. "And beautiful." The last word was said as he turned away. It was said as a compliment rather than in some flirtatious manner.

"Tragic, is what I am. I'm the wrong side of forty with a kid, and still looking for a guy who'll stick around in the morning."

He laughed again. "That is a bit tragic!"

"Exactly."

"That bikini looks good on you."

"Thanks..." she paused, not quite sure how to respond. Then suddenly humour kicked in. "Usually if a guy's seen this much of me then he's naked, and thinking of an excuse to leave."

"Haha! I think you're seeing the wrong guys!"

"I get told that a lot."

"There you go."

She took another quick dip when she got hot, whilst Greg sat and watched her every move. Then he made some more drinks a few more times and their tongues got looser. May was just happy to be outside relaxing. To tell the truth she was no longer bothered that Greg could see her nipples, or even be self-conscious of her body at all, she hadn't been expecting to be sat in a bikini anytime soon. Her stubbly legs hadn't put him off yet. He was a fit guy. And this was a good time. She'd even venture to say this was the best she'd felt since the incident.

But he still wasn't Robert. Her Robert.

"You okay, Luke?" she asked but the constant smile on his face was already enough of an answer. He nodded his head and even managed a fist pump.

"You're from Wiltshire then?" Greg stated after a while. It was almost in a slightly excusing way.

She shrugged. "Thornhill. Near Swindon." She always did that. Nobody had ever heard of Thornhill. Not many people had heard of Swindon either, if she was honest. It was one of the lesser known towns off the M4, somewhere between

Bristol and Reading. Americans assumed it to be just outside of London.

"You like it there?"

She pulled a face. "I did. Now, I think we could do with a change."

He took another sip from his margarita. "Interesting," was all he muttered, and she really wanted to know what he was thinking.

The sun had moved around the side of the house and begun to drop but the heat still felt the same.

"You hungry?" he asked.

Nodding, she replied. "Yes."

He got up and with a smile said, "I'm not much of a cook, so how about we order a take-away?"

"Sounds great!"

He held her gaze for a second and she was sure there was something there. That dangerous spark between two people who had no business being together.

"Maybe later we could all walk down to the beach. What d'you say?"

"I'd like that," she replied, and wondered just how long she could put her plans on hold for.

Chapter 25 – Hudson

When Hudson got back to his flat the enormous task ahead of him hit home. He'd not had a woman there for a while. He'd grown comfortable, and lazy. He had an hour to work a miracle. He quickly made a list of the important areas to focus on.

The bathroom and the kitchen. These were areas that insisted on appearing clean and hygienic. They were far from the biohazard zones of his friends' places, but they were hardly free of germs either. They had a definite *lived-in* feel and smell about them.

He figured he'd then set about the general appearance of the place. All the things that looked like they'd just been dumped. That included mugs and plates, and of course he did the male thing of filling up the sink with hot soapy water and dumping them all in there. They could soak, and later he could pull them out, dry them off and put them away. At the end of the day he was known for solving cold cases, not as a cleaning sensation. He would lose sleep over that.

It was almost amusing the effort he was going to. She wanted to talk, and the subject matter would neither improve, nor go south depending on the cleanliness levels of his humble abode. But still, good impressions and all that.

He found an air freshener and sprayed the curtains. It was an old trick he'd used in his previous relationship when his girlfriend had gone out and left him to clean the house. He'd always had good intentions, but these were often put down and forgotten once the football kicked off on the television.

He glanced at his watch and saw he had about twenty minutes. Catching a glimpse of himself in the mirror, he knew he had just enough time to jump in the shower. He wouldn't wash his hair as that would be obvious, but he'd scrub every part of himself until he was sure that he would smell clean.

You never know. Like cooking, preparation was key.

He threw on a shirt, which of course meant he tried on three before deciding on one, just before he heard a knock at the door. He'd not felt that sudden sense of panic in a long time.

He puffed out his cheeks, kicked a rogue sock under the bed and headed for the door.

She was all smiles as he opened it. She had on a plain jacket, T-shirt and jeans, and her hair had been pulled back into a messy ponytail. He felt foolish for the effort he'd gone to.

"Hey," he said.
"Hi Hudson."
"Come in. Can I get you a drink?"
"That would be nice."

Jim Ody

He showed her to the sofa in the lounge, and set about making the drinks.

"Is everything alright?" He called, and then realised it probably wasn't the best thing to do. She didn't come around to shout through the archway at him.

"Yes, I…" she paused, and he walked back in. "I just wanted to be honest with you."

"Oh, sounds ominous."

She looked concerned. He sat down next to her. Not too close. Just enough. He thought about what Jez had said – "Friendzone."

"I know you're a policeman…"

"Was a policeman," he corrected.

"Was. But I also know what you do now."

Hudson tried to inject a little humour. "What, wallow in self-pity and indulge in a poor diet?"

She gave a half smile. "It's more than that. I know people who speak very highly of you. You help people. You find people."

Hudson rubbed his hand on his chin. He didn't like talking about it with civilians. This was not something he should be doing, even though he was still working with the police, technically, he was still retired. But he couldn't escape the thrill of the tracking, surveillance, hacking, filming and use of government property. It pulled him back into the action, and he went from cheering on the side-lines, to making the deciding moves.

"I do," he said to the question, as he stood up.

She stood too, and placed a hand on his arm. "I know… It's just… there's a little boy called Darren. Darren Hughes."

His heart sank at the mention of the name. And then the penny dropped. The talks. The bar. The date. It was all to get him to do something for her. The classic female spider spinning the web to catch him in.

"You said it yourself, I'm not a policeman anymore. I'm already looking into the case so don't feel like you have to do this…" He let the words float in the room, as he turned his back and walked out to the kitchen. He continued going through the motions of making tea, but he didn't know whether she'd be there long enough to drink it.

She appeared in the kitchen. "Hudson, please. I didn't go to the bar with you last night because of a missing child. I honestly went because I thought we…" Her words trailed off. She was worried her mouth would spill words before her brain had a chance to validate them. "I like you," she decided, and even added. "I like you a lot."

Hudson poured the hot water into the teapot. "I get it," he sighed and added milk to a small jug, unaware that what he was doing was now considered old fashioned. "I know this case." He sighed. "It's my main focus." The words now soft as he no longer cared about what he should, or shouldn't be divulging.

"What do you know?" She suddenly pressed. "We're frustrated. The police have nothing. Darren comes from a good family in a good area. He just vanished."

"I know. I know the case inside out. I'm currently living and breathing it." He nibbled his lip in thought. What he was about to do had certainly not been in his plan for the evening. But then first dates often went like that, didn't they?

"Come with me," Hudson said walking out of the kitchen and towards the door down the hall. Laura followed.

He opened the door to his spare room and hit the lights. She gasped as she saw the pictures all over the walls. The sweet innocent faces staring back with hope.

"Jesus." She gasped. Her hand was on her mouth. "There are so many of them."

Hudson nodded. "I'm sinking, Laura. Look, whether or not you came here to hand me another case, or whatever, the truth is I'm already on it. Look at all these kids. Some are missing, some are in a bad place, but all of them are in danger. I can't begin to tell you how frustrating it is for me trying to help them within the confines of the law. I want to save them, and I want to bring the accused to justice, but do you know the percentage of cases that we successfully do that are?"

She shrugged, looking at him briefly before her eyes were drawn back to the innocent faces.

"Twenty percent. So for over a hundred cases I've been looking at, only twenty we've saved the children and brought criminal charges against someone. I have a further twenty or so I've not even looked at yet."

"I don't want to push you but if you just hear me out, then I'll drop it." She walked up to one of the pictures; it was of a teenager holding a cigarette. "Is she from a good background?" she pointed towards another teen with a shaved head. "Or him?" He didn't like what she was insinuating, and he could easily take offense, but she was also right. Some cases were about who they were, and where they came from.

"It's not like that for me, Laura. I can't make a decision on who I'm going to save over another. I'm not the detective here anymore. I'm helping them. A consulting role, if you like… it's just not that easy!"

"So how do you choose? You said that you've not even looked at twenty of the cases."

Hudson held up his hand almost in despair. "I don't know. I glance over them. I make a judgement call. I try to see which I can save, or find first. Really, the priority is more about when I receive them. A missing child would receive a little more time, and a higher priority, especially if it was completely out of character."

"It was. Darren was..." The words trailed off as she noticed the picture. The one of Darren Hughes staring back at her.

"Oh," she said walking up to it.

"Like I said, Laura. I'm familiar with the case. He comes from a modestly affluent family. He was being looked after by his uncle when his mum, Sophie rang whilst they were out in the park. She was happy about having had a successful job interview, he was pleased for her and distracted, he didn't notice him disappear.

"The uncle was questioned at length. I questioned him too. There were witnesses that said he was there with Darren, and was on his phone. The park was busy, and they were there in the park the whole time. Even when he was taken."

"Oh," she said again.

"Come on," he said. "Let's get our drinks and you can tell me more. But Laura, please, trust me. I'm doing all I can with the time and resources I have."

She looked slightly embarrassed. "I'm sorry," she said. "I didn't mean to imply you were not working hard on this…" He held up his hand.

"You're right to question."

"Thank you."

"I can't promise you, the family, the police or the press anything. All I can do is my best. But if you have more information, then sometimes that's all it takes."

They sat down on the sofa. Hudson placed the tray with the teapot, milk, sugar and cups onto a small table. Laura smiled, clearly wanting to say something, and looked around the room taking it all in for the first time.

Hudson was mixed in his feelings. It was like he was fighting against a strong tide of evil. Laura was now wanting this case solved too, and there was no way he could ignore it. Even without her he was obsessed. Despite what the movies would have you believe, children from affluent families rarely went missing or were kidnapped. Kidnappings more often than not consisted of custody disputes from estranged parents, or family members. It was very rare for strangers to be involved. The risks were just far too great.

"You're traditional?" she said looking at the cup, and then picking it up. He nodded, and neither wished to continue with the subject. It was a conversation for another time.

Laura pulled out her phone, and emailed some more pictures and data over to him. Hudson pulled them up and studied the details, but he already knew this was a tough one. He was forwarding the stuff on to Jez at the same time.

"The parents?" He asked, even though he had their background. "Anything you can tell me?"

It was all well and good having the words in front of you, but those were lists of facts, what he was interested in was much deeper than that. Their personalities. Their secrets. The people around them. He'd met Sophie and Simon and they were the picture of innocence.

"I know the mother, Sophie. She loves Darren deeply. The father is in prison, but I guess you already knew that." She paused, and the emotion was there for all to see. She swallowed, and wiped her eyes. "Sophie was desperate to get a new job. She wanted more for them both. The interview came out of the blue, and her brother Simon stepped in. He's brilliant."

"Does Sophie have any other men in her life?"

Laura shook her head slowly. "No. She's lonely, I know that, but with Darren still being young it's so hard to meet someone when you have a small child."

"Not even dates? People online?" He knew he'd already asked Sophie the same questions, but sometimes people lie, even when they don't think it's important.

"I don't know. She's never mentioned it. I guess it's always possible."

Hudson nodded. "Okay, let me make a quick call."

Hudson tapped the face of Jez on his phone. It rang a few times before it was answered.

"Jesus, mate, you pick your times," an out of breath Jez said. A strange noise of a muffled voice was shouting in the background.

"What's that noise?" Hudson asked worried.

"Cass. She's gagged and tied to the bed, I was just…"

"Whoa! I don't need to know. Look, I'm just sending you a file. Er, finish what you're doing and then if you could take a look that would be good. I want your opinion."

"Okay, mate. Gotta go, I'm starting to go soft!"

Hudson pulled the phone away from his ear and cut the call. "Jesus," he muttered.

"Everything okay?" Laura asked.

"That's my expert – the one you met at Capers. Unfortunately, for every brilliant thing he does, he feels the need to compensate and do some strange things too."

"What was he doing?"

"Having sex with his wife by the sounds of things."

"At least it was his wife." She half smiled and looked away as she added. "That sounds quite a natural thing to be doing too."

"You don't know, Jez!" That shot her eyes open with shock. The subject was dropped; it was very early in their relationship to be discussing sex, even between two other people.

They talked some more but Hudson felt the pressure there. At the meetings they were able to bounce off each other with friendly banter, but the importance of this new scenario made it hard. He was trying too hard. He knew, and perhaps she knew it too.

There still seemed a lot that both were holding back on. Risky discussions that might end a relationship before it started. Hudson glanced at her long sleeves remembering the scar below, but again it wasn't something he wanted to bring up.

After a couple of hours Laura yawned, and checked her watch. "Oh, I'd better make a move," she sounded disappointed, but Hudson wasn't sure. Maybe it was what she did when dates got boring.

"Okay," he said, trying to mix politeness with a hint of disappointment. He had no idea whether he'd pulled it off.

"Sorry," she said. "I have an early start."

"So do I," Hudson agreed. "I'm going to find Darren."

She smiled at that, and began to walk towards the door. They hit that awkward stage again.

Jim Ody

The evening had not had any touching. It was all eye contact and positive body language. Subtleties easily misinterpreted.

"I've enjoyed tonight," she said turning to him.

"So have I." Again, he felt like he was just copying her.

She opened the door, then stopped and turned back to him. She quickly reached up and kissed his cheek. "Can we do this again?"

"Of course," he said, his hand smoothed her arm. She waved, winked and walked down the stairs.

He stood there. The residual feeling of the kiss still lingering on his cheek, and a huge grin on his face, but a longing for those lips to be on his.

Chapter 26 – May

It had been an interesting time. Luke sat playing video games, and Greg and she were talking like old friends. She felt so comfortable with him. Maybe it was something to do with the fact they had spoken at length online. They already had a few inside jokes from things they'd said over the previous weeks. Both had emotional baggage, but they'd swapped and shared the gruesome details a long time ago. Neither scared off by what they'd learnt. There was little flirting now, just a comfortable developing friendship. She liked him. Of course, she did, and she got the feeling he liked her too.

Luke seemed at ease which was completely out of character. He loved to play games on these consoles, it was another way he could escape the world, transporting him to somewhere else. No more was he a shy and awkward child, but often a hero killing whatever came into his path. He was empowered.

An hour later and they were sat around the dining table eating pizza. Luke picked the cheese off first before setting about the pizza crust. He had a unique way of eating it.

Jim Ody

"Don't you like the cheese?" Greg grinned, pointing his own triangular food towards him.

Luke looked worried, and his eyes shot to May.

She tapped his hand reassuringly, before saying, "No, he loves cheese. So much so that he saves it until last. My Luke has his funny little ways, don't you?"

Luke looked back down at his food, and continued with the deconstruction process. He set about it like it was of great importance.

"This is great!" May said through mouthfuls careful to cover her mouth as she spoke. "You're so kind to take us in like this."

Luke nibbled at a bit but he never ate much. Food wasn't of huge importance to him. His small skinny frame was evidence of that.

"Don't be ridiculous. It's my pleasure. Anyway, my wife would never forgive me if I'd just let you two head off."

"Ex-wife," she corrected.

"Yes, ex-wife."

"But you didn't have to. We'll finish this and then be out of your hair."

Greg was already waving this away, taking a last bite. "Don't be silly. Stay overnight and see how you feel tomorrow, yeah?" He said swigging a bottle of beer. "Let you get some bearing on this situation, yeah?"

"Okay."

"Sorry, did you have other plans?"

May shook her head. "No, we were going to head to a cheap chain hotel for a couple of nights. That's all."

"And you've nothing booked?"

"No."

"Perfect. It'll save you some cash." He looked over to Luke. "You can buy the little man something with the money you save?"

May nodded. "I guess it wouldn't hurt if you don't mind."

"Not at all."

She didn't really fancy trying to find a hotel to stay at now. She was also quite comfortable here. It had been a strange day. Nothing quite like how May had envisaged it. She assumed they'd be sat in some generic hotel. The sort that all looked the same and had no food, just a pub next door that served all day.

She fell silent, her mind taking her back to the attack. She felt vulnerable. It wasn't a feeling she was used to. In fact, not since that morning.

Well, she didn't need to go back to then.

Greg noticed the quiet, and saw that Luke was now playing with his food rather than eating it.

"Shall we have a walk down to the beach?" Greg said, standing up and beginning to clear the table.

May instantly glanced at Luke, who made a half-hearted smile. She knew he was getting tired, but the walk would mean he would fall straight to sleep when they returned.

She would be alone with Greg.

"Yes," she said. "Let's do that."

They quickly cleared away the pizza boxes, plating up a couple of remaining pieces, and then they headed outside.

The moon was high in the sky, and they had put on hoodies and jumpers to cover their arms. A cool breeze danced around.

There was a small path behind the house; there was a small sandpit in the lawn as they got near a little gate. Beyond, the grass gave way to sand. To the left were some dunes, and to the right it flattened out.

"You're so lucky," May said without thinking.

"Not with everything," Greg sighed. He gazed out towards the sea.

"I'm sorry, I didn't…"

"I know," Greg said. "Don't apologise."

Luke ran ahead. His energy had retuned.

"Careful, Luke!" She called. "You'll get stitch!"

The sun was dropping. There was nobody else on the beach.

"You never mentioned your wife getting attacked?"

Greg stopped still. "I know… It was a really bad time. It was weeks after… er, our little boy drowned. She was in a daze. That man," his face scrunched up with anger. "He took advantage of her. He attacked her."

"Raped her?" She remembered the words his daughter had said on the phone. Ugly words spoken in such a beautiful sing-song way.

He nodded.

"Why's he not locked up?" May was confused by it. She was surprised Greg hadn't gone completely crazy with the guy. He'd shown a great deal of self-control.

"There was no evidence. It was his word against hers."

"That's awful. Who is he?"

Greg looked deep into her eyes. He was searching to understand how much he should say. How much he wanted to say.

"He was her work colleague." He sighed and looked away. "I accused her of having an affair. I got the whole situation wrong."

"Oh," she said. It slipped out.

"I know. I got the whole situation wrong. Very wrong. Ultimately, it's what finished us. It was the final nail."

"You seem okay now though? On the telephone call…" she struggled to finish the sentence. She started strong but forgot where she was going with it.

"We're friends. Great friends. We still care about each other, it's just… we can't go back to the way it was."

May nodded and looked out at Luke splashing in the puddles of tiny rockpools. Sometimes children helped awkward discussions. They were a distraction, and a way to quickly change the subject if needed.

May looked back and that's when she saw something. A flash. Then next to it a figure stood still. It wasn't unusual to see other people on a beach, but whilst the figure was small, she was sure it was a man. And he was looking directly at them.

"We should head back," Greg said, and as he said that, Luke ran back to them looking tired out.

May agreed, then when she looked back where the man was, he had gone.

They laughed together as they walked back to the house. It looked even more impressive from the beach. There were a couple of houses either side but neither had any lights on.

"Let me show you to your rooms. If you don't like them, then you don't have to stay!" Greg grinned as they got back in the house. He spoke in jest. They all knew they were there for the night.

They went to Greg's daughter's room first. This would be where Luke would sleep.

It wasn't quite as pink and girlie as May thought it would be. The girl had a sickly-sweet voice which she assumed would mean fairies and dolls. The room, however, was a light beige wash of colour. A boy band was pouting on the wall, her favourite member then alone in another poster. His look was sexy bad-boy. Covered in tattoos, but with piercing blue eyes, his look helped his generic vocals over a corporate-manufactured sound. She had a large mirror with make-up on the side. Perhaps to stare into and dream of going on a date with the popstar. Having never had a girl May didn't know at what age girls became obsessed with their looks, but clearly Bee was at that stage.

Luke had been swimming all afternoon so was tired out. He wasn't used to the fresh air and was exhausted. He was more than ready for bed.

"I'll leave you to it," Greg said retreating from the room. "Come and get me and I'll show you to your room too."

"Thanks again," she replied.

Luke looked up at her, and then his eyes darted all around the room. She read the anxiety behind those baby-blues. He would never be a bad-boy in a teenage girl's fantasy. Not because he wouldn't ever be desirable, but because she wouldn't let him. Women can be cruel. But men could be evil. Really evil.

"You're okay, yeah?" she said to him. "You can do some more swimming tomorrow, or we can go off, just the two of us. What d'you say?"

Luke shrugged. He knew his words meant nothing. He just wanted to please her.

"You want me to sing you a song?" May asked tucking him up. She'd done that a few times before when they were in strange places. They stayed in strange places a lot. Adventure moulded you into something unique.

He yawned and shook his head.

"Good night, sweetie!" she whispered, kissed her fingers and touched them to his forehead.

He wiggled some fingers but there was something so vulnerable and sad about him that it almost broke her heart.

So close to his birthday too. Well, the real Luke's birthday she remembered.

"Good night, my beautiful Luke."

She turned away not noticing the tear escaping from his eyes.

Chapter 27 – May

May joined Greg in the living room, where he was sat lounging on the sofa. The TV was on with some BBC period drama playing. It was another world to the one she knew.

Greg glanced over with a smile. He'd poured red wine for them both. His glass was half as full.

She sat down with a comfortable space between them, and without words both had accepted her decision to stay up a bit longer.

"This is nice," he said. "It can get quite lonely here." He gestured towards her glass.

She picked it up from the table, took a sip and asked, "How long have you been on your own?"

He shrugged. "It's been nearly 6 months. I know I should've got used to it by now, but… I dunno." He shrugged. "I think I've just found it hard to move on."

"I know how that it is," she agreed, but left it at that. Did he need to know how it still ate her up inside each night. How her whole marriage had just been a great big lie. The times she'd stood at the bathroom mirror trying to guess what it was about her that had driven Robert away into the arms of another woman.

"Of course," he added. "You were married too." He must've sensed that she had floated off for a second.

She took another large gulp of wine. The liquid slipped down nicely. "I was," she confirmed, and left it at that.

"But you don't want to talk about it." He was fishing but trying not to appear so. She felt her jaw tense. Why were men so manipulative? Sometimes it was a full-time job to read between the lines and try to understand what it was they weren't saying.

"I've nothing to add, I guess." Her words finally came out, and she hoped it would defuse the situation. "Tell me what happened with you."

He waved this off. "You don't want to hear my tales of woe. It will just bring you down." He was trying to do the same thing she had.

"Try me. Tell me about your wife."

Greg sat back into the sofa. With his glass on the side, he laced his fingers behind the back of his head.

"I met Sindy at university. We fooled around and fell in love." He paused looking out to the other side of the room. Perhaps he was just wondering what to say. "I dunno. It wasn't all roses, you know? We had our ups and downs… We split up, and I moved away. Then a few years later we reconnected."

"Wow," May said, and felt more interested than she would ever have thought. There was a small amount of healthy jealousy, but to know it was never perfection helped.

Jim Ody

"Maybe I'd grown up? Or we'd both calmed down. I mean, Sindy wasn't a shy innocent girl, and of course neither was I. The girl part anyway!" He grinned at his joke. May smiled, acknowledged it, but encouraged him to continue.

He waved his hand a little, almost flicking pages of his past forward a few years as he said, "Then we got married, and Bee came along. I thought that was it. Then my little boy arrived and I thought my world was complete." He bit his lip. There was a lot behind his eyes.

"And then the accident," May said. She'd noted how he refused to say his son's name, as if not saying it might somehow keep him alive.

Greg took a deep breath, and sighed. "It happened before that. Sindy started going out. At first it was once a month, then quickly it became once a week… I didn't think anything of it. My work schedule was busy. When I was home, I enjoyed the family. If Sindy needed a break then that seemed okay."

"But?" She was intrigued to find out the sordid details.

"Then she stayed out all night. I found a text from that guy. The one who attacked you…" he reached for his wine, took a sip and rested the lip of the glass against his cheek whilst he looked away. He was looking up at a painting on the wall. It depicted the Eiffel Tower, surrounded by hundreds of people. The beauty of the painting was in the detail of all of the people rather than the iconic tower. But also, you could focus on the tower, and the people became a blur. A very clever composition.

May thought he was close to tears.

He turned to her, and instead just looked blank, and devoid of emotion. "We had a fight. Then the accident happened. It forced us together again, if only to grieve together. But the gap between us was growing each day. Bee was being neglected by quarrelling parents, and this whole house…" he raised his arms (even the one holding his wine glass). "Was toxic. Then I came home to Sindy and that guy." He shook his head at the memory.

"You caught them?"

"He was leaving. I passed his car and he grinned at me. I was home early and Sindy was there laying naked in our bed. She was crying but it felt false."

"Did he rape her? Or did she…" May didn't want to finish her mild accusation.

"That's what she said, but she wouldn't press charges. I'd had enough. We tried for almost a week before Sindy packed her stuff up and moved herself and Bee away into town."

"What about the guy?"

"What about him? She spoke to the police and then dropped the charges. I don't know, I mean he's clearly not a nice guy…"

May didn't know what to say. Nothing added up. Was his wife having an affair and got caught? Was he blinkered to it all?

"Why did he attack me?" she said out loud, but it was as much a thought in her head than something she meant to verbalise.

"I guess that's what he does. It's what men do when they can't control themselves."

Silence fell upon them. He'd shared a lot. But then when he looked at her again, it was in a deep and penetrating way. She was mesmerised by his eyes. There were a few seconds of silence before he spoke again.

"The one thing I really miss," he began, his words almost a whisper. "Is the touch of a woman." his words dropped off as they leaned in together, and their lips touched.

May suddenly pulled away. She was flustered, and embarrassed. She felt like she'd somehow instigated it. "I'm sorry. That shouldn't've happened."

Greg looked surprised. He touched his lips as if remembering the kiss. "But it did," he said in a whisper. "And I think it did for a reason."

May was taken back by this. "I just don't want us to move too quickly. We're both emotionally vulnerable. We've only just met."

"Hardly May. Physically, yes, but we've spoken online for weeks. This is hardly a one-night-stand." He then held his finger to her lips. "Don't over think things." May was already shaking her head, and moving to get up.

"I know. I just don't want to mess things up between us, you know?"

She thought back to how she'd felt when she'd found out about her ex-husband. The wind was smashed out of her sails. Betrayal taunted her, as did the smirks from the people around her. And the one thing that was at the forefront of her mind was that it was wrong. She was cheating.

Even though her husband had since divorced her, their dead son would always bind them together.

For a second Greg sat back, the flash of a petulant child evident, and then he smiled. Acceptance finally given.

"I know. I apologise, do you want more wine?"

"No, I'm fine," she said. "I've drunk more today than I normally do in a month!"

"Nothing wrong with that. So what are your plans? For the next few days, I mean?"

May glanced up to the ceiling as if she could see Luke asleep. "I don't know. Maybe drive to Cornwall, take in the sights. A little road trip. Just the two of us."

"You could always stay here. Or pop in on your way back."

She looked into his eyes. The alcohol was making it harder to not kiss him again. Late nights and alcohol had a way with her. She tried to bury her thoughts of Robert deep into the furthest corner of her mind.

Greg put his glass down, stood up, and held out his hand to May. She took it and stood up too.

An energy had begun to flow in the room. The alcohol again devious in its intentions.

They kissed and embraced tightly. Hands roamed over each other's bodies. May took a gulp of breath as Greg's hand slid up her thigh. With all the willpower she had she pulled away. She just couldn't do it. Part of her was disappointed.

"I'm so sorry, Greg. I can't do this."

He looked confused. "You don't want to do this?"

"I didn't say that. It's just..." she shrugged. "It's too soon."

For a second, he looked like he was going to explode, and then suddenly he visibly calmed. "Okay," he managed. He went to say something else but stopped himself. He intrigued her.

She rubbed a muscular arm and said, "Look it's getting late, so maybe we should call it a night."

He nodded but it was only a little after 9pm. He looked confused by the situation.

Reluctantly he got up and took her hand. It was friendly and without passion. Just functional. He flashed a quick smile, and showed May to the spare room. He opened the door and pulled his hand away.

"This okay?" His words slightly clipped.

"Perfect," she said, feeling like she'd done something wrong. Men could be such children sometimes when it came to sex.

Before she closed the door, she called out to him, "Greg? Thank you for everything today."

He smiled, nodded and replied, "You're welcome. Sleep tight, May."

She closed the door, and sat down on the bed. The room was bland with nothing much there. She opened a drawer and found a battered paperback. Some old horror. Then behind it she noticed something else.

Handcuffs. They were pink and fluffy. The sort bought in sex shops and taken on hen-dos. She wasn't sure what to make of them.

Yawning, she slipped under the covers in her vest and pants. It was a while before she dropped off to sleep. She kept wondering whether Greg would come in. She allowed herself to fantasise about him slipping under the covers naked, as she finally allowed him to do what he clearly wanted to do.

She was aching for him to do it too. Maybe use those handcuffs and ravish her body.

If only the circumstances were different.

Tomorrow was a new day.

Chapter 28 – Hudson

Hudson was awake early. He couldn't help it and despite stifling a yawn, he swung his legs around and got out of bed. He was still used to the structure of the police. The early policeman catches the crim.

He made himself a tea. It was a little quaint, but he saw nothing wrong with making himself a pot, and drinking from a cup and saucer. Perhaps this was a throwback to when he was younger. When his mother was still in his life and insisted on tea being drunk this way. "Mugs are so uncouth," she was fond of saying. It was one of the few things that linked him to her. She'd disappeared abroad chasing a fallacy many years ago, and never returned. When she had time, she'd send an email. It was a few vague lines, mostly to make sure he was still alive. He guessed she was happy.

Hudson noticed a text message. It was a simple thanks from Laura. His new case. He responded back with a simple: ***You're welcome***, before sipping his tea, and eating his scrambled eggs on toast. Protein helped to stop crime; he was sure of it.

He thought about adding more to the text. Asking her on an actual date, rather than another get together. After ten minutes he realised he was overthinking things and left it.

His phone rang.

"Yo, Huds!" It was Jez.

"Jez. I assume you're clothed now."

There was the sound of a walrus roaring, which of course was Jez's laughter. "Sure am. What about you? You on your own?"

"Yep."

"How was it? You scare her off?"

"It was good. She brought up Darren's case. She knows the mother."

"Sophie?"

"Yes. She wanted me to look into it."

"We already are. You could get some extra Brownie points for that, if you know what I mean?" He was laughing again. That awful wounded animal sound.

"Hmm, I think I'll pass on that."

"Ah well, missed opportunity in my book! You'll be pleased to know I've been up for the past couple of hours looking over this case."

"Uh-huh. You got anything."

There was the sound of Jez blowing out his cheeks, before he answered, "Not a lot."

"Wow, Sherlock. Is that it, then? The reason for your call this morning?"

"And to check on your hot date."

"Thanks," Hudson said. "Anything else?"

Hudson could hear the excitement in Jez's voice. It had gone up an octave, and his words came out quickly. "I think it's one of two things. Either circumstance, or premeditated."

"What other reason was there? Come on Jez, give me something." Hudson liked to get Jez to use his head more. Jez relied on data but wasn't so good at hunches or body language.

"Well, I think the perp is not known to the family. They were either walking by, or had been watching the family."

"Okay. And you don't have to say 'perp'." Hudson smiled. Jez thought he was on CSI or some such programme some days.

"We have a list of people seen in the area. I'm in the process of getting some security surveillance footage." Jez continued ignoring the dig.

"From the police?" Hudson asked.

"Yes, and no. There are a couple of CCTV cameras, but not in and around the park. The police have sent them to me, but they've already been through them, and noted down the details. Nothing much doing there.

"And no, as in I have a list of locals with cameras on their houses. Some are only pointing to the front door, but others show the whole front of the house. There are a couple of shops too. A child doesn't just disappear into thin air."

"Okay, good stuff. Send me anything too. We can cut down the time if we're both looking through things."

There was a moment of silence which always worried Hudson. "I had a good night last night," Jez suddenly said.

Hudson rolled his eyes. He was happy for Jez, but really, he didn't want to start talking about it.

"I'm pleased for you, but I don't need details, nor do I want to see any pictures."

"You're funny!" Jez said. "Anyway, I can't talk all day about my sex life, so stop asking!"

Hudson was left looking at his phone. How had that suddenly changed so quickly.

He got up and went into his office. He glanced at the hopeful faces pinned to the wall. It was these that motivated him each day. To some of them he was their last hope. Their only hope.

He opened up his laptop and went over the notes on Darren's disappearance again cross-referencing with the notes from his interviews. He stared at the little boy's smiling face. The whole thing was different to the cases he was used to. Everyone spoke of how happy he was. A little boy with big dreams. Everything pointed to a happy childhood, and only reinforced his feelings that it was nothing to do with the family.

So far all they had was a vague sighting by a local resident. Her name was Beryl, and she was an elderly woman in her late 80s. Not always the most reliable of witnesses, but sometimes you had to work with what you've got. Every once in a while, you'd get a good quality curtain-twitcher. The type who notices everything, and marks down the registration number of vehicles they don't recognise. A good old fashioned busy-body.

The problem here was that if a child wasn't in distress then it was quite normal to see an adult walking along with a child, or wheeling them along in a pushchair. Darren was four, an age where they were still trusting.

Hudson knew he had to go to where he'd been abducted from. You could read reports and look at crime scene photographs but it was never the same. You had to go there, stand and survey the area. Sometimes it was almost like he had a sixth sense. He would stand and look around trying to channel an energy that would give him ideas about what might have happened.

It was a horrible world when you could no longer take your eyes off a child in a play park.

Hudson took one last look at the boy. He wasn't religious but found himself sending up a silent prayer. He shut the lid of his laptop, and grabbed his keys.

Chapter 29 – May

May was awoken by a noise. She jumped out of bed and was suddenly disorientated with the unknown layout. She forgot where she was.

She was both cross and embarrassed with herself. The alcohol and her sexual frustration had got the better of her again. One of these days it might kill her. Maybe she should really consider finding someone to settle down with. A man who was not married, and she could do whatever she desired with him without guilt. Or the walk of shame the morning after.

She got out of bed, conscious that she only had vest and knickers on, and made for the door. She hurried to Luke's room and found his bed empty. With a sudden panic she stood on the large landing, checked the bathroom and then ran down the stairs. She was equally worried about him, and cross with herself for not having him in the room with her.

"Hey!" she called as she saw him at the door. She couldn't believe it. In the excitement, she'd forgotten his tablets. He got like this. He wandered.

He stopped, turned and looked back at her. Eyes vacant and void of emotion. Almost disappointed.

"Where're you going? You lost?" She said, her voice full of heavy breaths. Her heart still pounding.

At first, he didn't move probably now only understanding what was happening. Then he nodded, turned and walked back towards her. Not looking her in the face, he clung tightly to her waist. His complicated world confused him. Again, she was cross at herself for putting him in a separate room. His needs overshadowed by her own. She'd ignored him on the whim of some stupid schoolgirl fantasy. Guilt washed over her. A feeling that was becoming regular to her.

She couldn't help it but inside she was frustrated. How old would he be before she could trust him not to wander off? What if she'd not woken up? Where would he have disappeared to? What would have happened? It didn't bear thinking about.

As they headed back up the winding staircase Greg appeared. He wore pyjama trousers but was bare-chested. His body strong and welcoming to her. Almost taking her breath away.

"Is everything okay?" he said scratching himself on the stomach and looking half asleep.

"Yeah, he was sleepwalking, weren't you, Luke?" she said holding his shoulders. The boy nodded but refused to look up. Who knew whether or not he understood what was happening?

A Lifetime Ago

"Okay," Greg said, threw up a half-hearted wave and headed back off to bed. May was almost disappointed. She glanced down at herself wearing next to nothing.

May looked down at Luke. "How about you come in with me?" It wasn't a question.

He nodded and followed her back to her room. She rooted in her bag for his tablets, and with a sip of water he gulped them down.

Eventually, whilst everything swirled around her brain, Luke was snoring evenly. He was deep asleep. Dark shapes moved around the room, as her mind struggled to switch off. She held Luke tightly until she drifted back to sleep.

In the morning she was awoken by the smell of bacon. Sunlight bullied its way through a gap in the curtains. Her head was a bit fuzzy from the alcohol, but she'd woken up in worse states. She looked across at Luke whose eyes blinked open. He looked worried.

"You're okay. Remember where we are?" He half sat up and surveyed the room. It was hard to tell with him whether or not recognition had kicked in. Sometimes his face looked scared, even when she knew him to be calm.

She got up and pulled on her dress. They both used the bathroom before heading down to the kitchen.

"Good morning!" Greg sang out as they appeared. The dining room table was laid out with coffee and juice. He had on a tight T-shirt that showed off his muscles. Her mind flashed back to the night before.

"I poured you a coffee. Sit down let's get some food inside you both!"

"Wow! Thanks Greg," May said, and even Luke managed a smile.

"You like bacon sandwiches, buddy?" He asked Luke, nodding towards a plate with a huge doorstep of a sandwich on.

Luke looked at it and his eyes grew wide. He nodded slowly.

"Well dig in then!"

They added their sauces of choice. Without a word, Luke attacked the sandwich like he'd not eaten in days.

"Slow down, honey," May said tapping his arm. He nodded, but still took the biggest mouthful ever.

"What shall we do today?" Greg asked. "We could go for a drive? I could show you around the area."

May wasn't sure what she felt like doing. Part of her didn't want this to end. It was Luke's birthday tomorrow so she should get some sort of cake organised. She needed to get him a present.

"We should get out of your hair, Greg. We've taken up too much of your time already."

Whilst chewing, Greg shook his head instantly dismissing the idea as foolish. He took a gulp of coffee, and said, "Don't be daft. Stay another night at least." He held her gaze. His eyes seemed soft and dreamy. She was nodding before she even realised.

A Lifetime Ago

"One more night, I guess. Okay Luke?" She looked over at him. He'd already cleared his plate and drunk a glass of milk.

Luke stretched out his arm and pointed out towards the pool.

"Ah-ha! You want to swim?" Greg said with a grin.

"He did enjoy it," May agreed. "Perhaps we can go out later?"

Luke nodded and Greg gave them the thumbs up.

"Have a sit down first," May said to Luke. "You can't swim on a full stomach or you'll get stomach ache."

May drank a couple of cups of coffee. It was just what she needed. The bitter taste mixed well with the saltiness of the bacon. She almost felt a little self-conscious as her stomach felt like it would burst. She felt cross with herself, knowing she'd look bloated in the bikini. Why hadn't she thought of that earlier?

Just then Luke started to wriggle, and pointed upstairs. May was aware of his signals. He was in need of the call of nature.

"You need the bathroom?"

He flashed a glance at Greg, and then began to nod when he looked at her.

"A man's gotta do what a man's gotta do, buddy!" he said and got up to clear the table.

Luke got up, and jiggled on the spot.

"Go on up, I'll check on you in a minute," May said. He left the table and headed upstairs to the bathroom. He'd eaten a lot and sometimes food went straight through him. Especially when he was anxious.

Within a few minutes, May was stood looking in the full-length mirror in her temporary room. She'd put on the bikini bottoms and she held the top in her hands. She stared at herself, a feeling of disappointment there in the pit of her stomach. There had been times when she'd hated her body. She'd wished that her breasts were huge and not these tiny little things barely bigger than her areolas. She wanted to look more like a woman and less like a boy. So many things she felt held her back. She ran her left hand through her red hair. It had a wave she could do nothing about. She even wondered whether it would look better when she was fully grey.

She turned to the side. Her skinny frame meant she had no bum. Did men dislike that? She didn't know, but she did see a lot about women wanting bigger butts now. She turned back in defeat.

She was about to put her top on when a voice from behind startled her.

"Don't," he said. She turned around and saw Greg standing there.

"What?" she said, covering her breasts as a habit, but she could tell by the way he was looking at her what he meant.

"I know that nothing is going to happen… but I just wanted another look… *that okay?*"

She stopped, dropped her hands to her sides, and turned to face him. There didn't really seem to be any harm in it, did there? And for a second, she lost herself. She pretended he was the new

A Lifetime Ago

man in her life, and those large hands of his would soon touch her intimately.

"Why are you so sad?" He commented taking a step towards her.

"I'm not," she argued but without conviction.

"I like what I see, but I get the feeling you don't."

She glanced out of the door.

"He's fine."

"I don't know," she admitted. "I'm a single woman with a child. I miss having a man to love me."

"Don't ever put yourself down."

He was taking in her body from her breasts, down to the slight stretchmarks on her abdomen, and the cellulite of her legs. All of her insecurities.

But like a switch had been clicked, his head snapped to the side and out of the door.

Suddenly he turned quickly and was gone.

At first, she was completely offended and then she pulled on her dress over the bikini bottoms.

What if it was Luke trying to leave again? Then she heard Greg's angry voice. "Don't ever go in there!" he was shouting as she came out of the room. Greg was waggling a finger at Luke who looked like he was about to cry.

"What happened?" she asked. "Luke?"

"He was in there!" Greg said and then taking in a deep breath, he composed himself. He took in a huge breath, and said, "I'm sorry I shouted… but…"

Luke looked up at May, his eyes darting all around. His fingers fidgeted.

"Stay out of there, Luke, *yeah?*" May said, but who knew whether or not he would listen. He was wired differently. He did whatever appealed to him, sometimes without reason. "Greg's our host, so we must do what he says, okay?"

Luke nodded.

She turned to Greg. "What's in there?"

He struggled to get any words out at first, and then he said, "Stuff… from before…*his* stuff."

He looked really uncomfortable. It was the first time she'd ever seen her hero rattled. She guessed it was his son's room. No wonder he acted the way he did. She felt mortified that Luke had just barged in there. It was so out of character for him.

"I'm sorry," May said. "Luke won't go in there again." She turned to Luke. "*Will you?*"

Luke shook his head, but couldn't look at Greg.

Greg took a breath. "I'm sorry for shouting. It's just… things come flooding back."

She nodded and then turned to Luke. "No more, Luke. You know better than that. Why don't you go in the pool?"

Luke nodded and walked away. He headed down the stairs.

"Stay in the shallow end!" she called after him.

"I'm sorry," Greg said again. He looked her up and down again. "I was enjoying the view."

She blushed. Her pale complexion betraying her as she knew a ruddy rash had appeared on her neck and chest.

He hugged her tightly. It felt good.

She glanced at the door and wondered just what was in there.

A Lifetime Ago

Jim Ody

A Lifetime Ago

Chapter 30 – Hudson

The sky was slightly overcast and threatening rain. It was only a few streets away from Simon's house where he'd been the day before. A nice area. You could tell by the lack of litter, and the well-maintained gardens. Couples walked hand-in-hand, children smiled politely and dog-walkers looked proud of pets they considered to be smaller family members. The cars in the driveways — apart from the odd one — were mostly less than five years old. Not a rust-bucket in sight.

There were no kids hanging around the corners, mouthing obscenities, and the bus shelters had all their glass panels intact, with graffiti being non-existent. The local shops consisted of a farm shop that sold local produce, rather than a betting shop, or boarded up windows of an off-license. It was basically a nice slice of suburbia. But go a few streets over and it was like stepping into a different world.

Hudson pulled in behind a new BMW. Next door an expensive Tesla sat as shiny as a trophy.

He unhitched the small gate, and walked up a pathway that had a number of well-maintained

A Lifetime Ago

rose bushes proudly on show. A bright spray of yellows, pinks, whites and reds.

The door was pristine. He'd not so much as moved to reach for the door-knocker before the door opened up, and a small lady with a thatch of curls stood there, squinting with suspicion. Her make-up was overdone, like a child playing on a doll's head for the first time.

"Are you the policeman?" she asked accusingly. He didn't want to correct her. She'd more than likely clam up and refuse to speak. Instead, he nodded and replied, "We spoke on the phone." His smile was as warm as he could muster. She looked like she would attack him at any moment if she didn't like what he had to say.

"You'd better come in then," she beckoned him over the threshold, before glancing left and right outside to see what horrors might be lurking around.

The house was tidy, but lived in. The décor was surprisingly contemporary. The odd picture of smiling children in their school uniforms sat on bookshelves, and tables. Memories to keep her alive.

"I've just made a pot of tea, if you're interested? Take a seat." She didn't wait for a response as she shuffled off into where he presumed the kitchen to be.

"Yes, please," he called. She didn't respond, so he sat back on the sofa and tried to make himself at home. Try as you might, you never quite could in someone else's house. He loved a good pot of tea, and clichéd or not, old ladies were often the best at making them. At some stage they must get whisked off and trained in a covert operation that nobody ever talked about.

Hudson looked at the many smiling faces in each framed photo, and saw that it was the same two boys but over a number of years. This suggested Beryl wasn't in contact with the boys that often. Perhaps they lived far away, and this was the only contact she had. Of course, there could always be another explanation, and he might be jumping to conclusions, but he'd been a policeman for long enough. Your first feeling was often the correct one.

Beryl soon returned, the sound of crockery tapping each other as she walked. He made a move to stand with an intention of helping, but she was quick to scowl, clearly taking offense.

"It's alright," she scolded. "I'm quite able."

He gave a consolation smile, as she placed the cup and saucer on a table next to him.

"Thank you," he said, and then pointed to one of the pictures. "Grandchildren?"

She picked up the teapot, and poured into the teacup, and nodded.

"Yes. My son's. He whisked them off to Southampton a few years back. Some fancy job. I'm sure he could've got something similar here." The bitterness was evident. She missed them and resented the loss just as much.

"You miss them."

She shot a look towards him. "Of course, I do. What mother, and grandmother wouldn't?"

"It must be hard." Of course, he was desperate to ask his questions, but experienced enough to be patient. It was like trying to get into a jewellery box. You could either smash it open and hope you didn't break anything, or spend a bit of time picking the lock in order to guarantee you get everything inside.

"Of course, but what can I do? I can't travel like I used to."

"Do they visit often?"

She poured her own cup. "I see them once or twice a year. When they can be bothered" She looked up at the photos. "At least I have these."

Hudson nodded and smiled at her. "I was admiring them. Some handsome lads." But it was also apparent there were no photos of her son. The absence spoke of another silent hurt.

"They are in their photos," she said and let the words hang there. It wasn't obvious whether in person they were little devils, or she was having a dig at an absent son.

Hudson smiled in acknowledgement before looking to press on with the reason he was there.

"So, Beryl? Can you tell me what you saw on that day?"

She looked off into the corner of the room, and when she spoke, she was careful with her words. "I saw a woman pushing a child…"

"Darren?"

She nodded. "It just didn't look right. She was hushing him, and he was wriggling to get out."

"Are you sure?"

She nodded; her hands shook slightly on the cup. "The child just didn't look comfortable. His eyes were everywhere, and he looked really distressed."

"Please don't take offense, but could the child not just have been having a tantrum?"

"Like I say, Officer, I'm a grandmother, and a mother. I know the difference." Again, he didn't try to correct her. This could be promising.

"What did the woman look like?"

Beryl made a face. Inside she was trying to grab the right words. "She looked cross. She had red hair, and wore a dark top."

"Was she looking around, or just focused on the child?"

"She was definitely looking around, and telling the child to be quiet. I think that was what I found most strange. She was less bothered about the child than she was about people seeing and hearing them."

Hudson placed his cup down and got up. "So looking out of the window, which way did she go? Left to right, or right to left?"

Beryl lifted an arm and pointed a crooked finger. "Left, and moving towards the right."

"Is there anything else of note that you remember?"

Beryl nodded. "She had a slight limp. The woman, I mean. And a tattoo on her hand down the side. Some sort of writing."

"Really?"

Beryl nodded. "I noticed because I thought it all strange. She didn't look like she came from around here." It sounded like a dig at her social class. Beryl was still of the generation that saw tattoos only on the working class.

"And at what time was this?"

"Just after two in the afternoon. I know because I was all ready to watch *Countdown* on Channel Four. I love that show. That Nick Hewer is so dreamy!"

Hudson smiled at that. Nick looked like an old man to him. He got his phone out and pulled up a picture of Darren. "Was this the little boy you saw?"

Beryl squinted behind thick-rimmed glasses. She went quiet but the recognition was there for him to see. She couldn't take her eyes off the picture. "Yes," she said finally. "That's the poor child."

"Are you sure?"

"Of course," she said. "I'm neither blind nor senile."

"Of course not. Thank you, Beryl," Hudson said. "You've been a great help."

Hudson finished his tea whilst indulging her in more small talk. Beryl clearly enjoyed the company, and he wondered how good a witness she would be.

Another ten minutes and he was outside, He'd updated Jez with a description of the woman, which matched the witness from the day before.

Where are you? Hudson thought. *Where the hell are you?*

Chapter 31 – Jez

This was what Jez lived for. The excitement of the chase. The puzzle that he could solve. Well, that and having sex in different ways with his wife. For all of her bite, she was putty in his hands when she was feeling frisky! All he had to do was put on some Tom Hardy movie and she'd agree to do almost anything. He'd never understand women as long as he lived.

Back to business. Hudson had given him a detailed description of the woman with the pushchair. He had a number of CCTV clips narrowed down to around fifteen minutes of when it was thought Darren went missing. Hudson had confirmed the time the old woman had thought she'd seen her, so that was a good starting point. As long as she wasn't senile. The war did that to people. Some women even burnt their bras, though he wasn't sure what the point of that had been.

The first house was like watching a still picture. Literally nothing happened for two minutes. Jez grew bored easily. But then suddenly a woman could be seen striding along, pushing a pushchair with one hand and almost wrestling

A Lifetime Ago

with the child in the seat with the other. Unfortunately, they were the other side of the road, and the camera was grainy. This would serve as confirmation of time and direction rather than as identification, and cut and dried evidence. It was like looking through a dirty window. Not that he'd admit to having done that.

Next was a camera sitting up high on the front of a small store that sold healthy stuff. Jez didn't trust those places. He liked proper labels and brands he knew, not handwritten labels and weird shit he'd never seen before.

The manager admitted he'd only purchased the camera to bring down the insurance premium on the building. They'd never had a cause to look at it. In fact, the manager had been a little nervous as to whether it was recording at all. Thankfully it was.

Again, into the frame about ten seconds later was the woman wrestling the child. Just like before, the child with blond hair looked to be agitated, trying to get out, and the woman was looking all around suspiciously. Most people Jez knew didn't care about others when shouting at their child. In fact, most seemed to enjoy it. This woman looked to be hissing at the child, but didn't let up on her grip. Once more, the picture was fine up close, but they were the other side of the road, so it was hard to tell actual features.

They went out of view.

The next house was further down the road. It was a better-quality camera. In fact, so good it could pick up a blue tit on a chewed chip. Jez made that line up. He thought it was funny. He wrote it down on a notepad. He'd tweet it on Twitter later.

He watched intently but saw no one. A car drove past, but the pair never made an appearance. Typical. He checked the clock. It was almost twenty-past-two. They'd either gone into a house, or got into a car.

The car!

He rewound the clip. He paused it as the car went by. The red car. He zoomed in on the driver. A woman with red hair. In the back was someone moving around.

The car was a red VW Golf but he couldn't see the registration plate. The adrenaline was released into his bloodstream. His tongue poked out with concentration.

Next, Jez pulled up his map app. It was like Google Maps but showed him all the CCTV cameras around the area. Each one given a specific code. The direction of the car told him that it would pass two cameras, both on traffic lights.

He logged into a government website, and entered the first CCTV code. He clicked the right direction of the camera and watched for the car.

At first the car shot by, but when he took it back, he was able to stop the film frame by frame until he was able to get the full registration number.

"Got you!" he said triumphantly, and logged into another website. This was owned by the

DVLA, and he was authorised to access the full registered details of the owner.

He popped in the reg, and was happy to see that it was indeed a 2012 red VW Golf. It was registered to a Colin McGill with an address only a few streets away from where the child had been taken. It was across an invisible line to a poorer area of the town.

But it didn't end there. He pulled up Facebook and searched for Colin McGill in Thornhill.

There was only one. This showed a picture of a guy missing teeth and holding up a can of beer like it was trophy. Jez clicked into his profile. It was lacking any educational details, but had a number of recent pictures of a party. Or a drunken gathering of broken Britain, more like.

Jez clicked into it to see a group of anti-socials wafting cigarette smoke around, and generally larking about. They were flashing underwear, and flipping V-signs, with tongues waggling out in some false over-exaggerated idea of a mating ritual. It didn't seem to matter whether they were same sex, or same parentage.

Colin looked to be anywhere between twenty and forty. Cigarettes had not been kind to him. Judging by his eyes he'd been high on something other than cigarettes and alcohol at the time. He glanced over the photos, and saw a number of people. Most of them, he hoped to God he'd never meet in person.

And then he found her. Grinning at the back in a black hoodie, then behind drunken friends in another one, and then kissing Colin, and part of a group-hug in a third. Her red hair looked stringy as it fell down a vest top. None of the pictures were tagged. Probably too challenging for him. So, Jez clicked into Colin's friends list. There were less than a hundred. He scanned down a few that looked more like dealer mugshots, before he found her. Emma Vine. A smile that looked forced. A phrase tattooed on her right hand.

"Whoop whoop!" Jez congratulated himself out loud.

He quickly clicked into another database. He was on a roll now. He inserted her name into the search field along with the town. Within seconds her address was confirmed.

The same address as Colin.

He had a couple of calls to make.

Grinning from ear to ear, Jez rang Hudson.

"Jez!" Hudson said almost instantly.

"Hudson, my man! Who is the best detective around here?"

There was a pause, and then Hudson replied, "Neither of us. I'm retired, and you're not a detective."

Jez almost stuttered. "Well, if I was, then what? And you're not retired."

"That would be you. If out of the two of us, only you are a detective, then by default, you're the best detective. It is impossible for me to be in the running."

"But you were a detective once."

"You can't say who the best detective is if we are not detectives at the same time. D'you get what I'm saying?"

A Lifetime Ago

There was silence for a beat whilst Jez let this sink in. He almost forgot the reason for his call.

"Whatever. Anyway, I've got him. Maybe."

"What?"

"Well, I mean, I think I know who took him, or who the woman is."

"Really?"

"Yep, and I've called it in."

"You know what, Jez? You are the best detective around."

"You think so?" Jez loved to be praised. He grinned even wider – if that was at all possible. *Yeah,* he thought. *I've done good.*

Chapter 32 – Robert

A few weeks back

It meant nothing to him. It really didn't.

He was part of a number of groups on Facebook, and she was just another member. Mostly, she was a lurker. Somebody who reads the posts, but never commented. Perhaps the odd 'Like', but nothing more.

Out of the blue, she'd sent him a friend request. Her name was Jade. He looked at her profile which was sparse, and generic. The picture was of a cat. He almost declined her but she'd added a few cat pictures, had some basic details about herself, and had over a hundred mutual friends, albeit ones from various other groups he frequented.

And that's when she began direct messaging him. She said *hello*, and asked how he was. He was automatically suspicious but politely replied. The usual weird tell-tale signs were absent. There was no broken English, a link to naked pictures of her, an enquiry about a financially beneficial revelation to eventually get you to click onto a link, or any intrusive questions. It was just a polite question. Innocent.

A Lifetime Ago

She instigated each time. He just responded. He was being polite. He was doing nothing wrong. It was a break from his writing; nothing more. Then she'd leave him alone. But a week later she'd message him again, slowly sharing more about herself with him. He was caught. He was intrigued, and also didn't want to not respond, but also something felt a bit wrong about it.

He thought about suddenly cutting her off. Not responding, and unfriending her, but that seemed harsh, and almost without reason. What had she done wrong? What had *he* done wrong? But it was there niggling in his mind that things weren't right.

Especially since her last post. She'd added a photo of herself. She'd coupled it with a narrative about being shy, and how she was so embarrassed about her picture. Of course, she didn't need to be. She was cute without being gorgeous. She wore glasses that made her look intelligent. They were big and suited her. It was a night out in a bar, and she was laughing, but still looking innocent.

Robert was almost disappointed. He wanted her to be grotesque and ugly. He wanted her to be from the other side of the world. It would make things all the more innocent. A random acquaintance rather than a friendship. He mulled this over in his mind unsure on whether this all just sounded shallow. The invisible angel and devil fighting it out on his shoulders, controlling his every move.

The problem was, it took him back to how his relationship with Nadia had begun. He'd been happily married then. He had a family and a wife who loved him. Then his head had been turned by the dark Eastern looks of Nadia. Whilst it was completely out of character for him, an outsider would see this as a pattern, and one that this only reinforced. He could hear people saying to him: *Why did you respond to her? Why carry the relationship on?* And he'd continue his empty defence that it was innocent. He was just being polite. But polite only got you so far.

He looked at the message she'd just sent him:
Hey, How are you?
He thought about it from her point of view. What did she want from him? He had pictures of Nadia and baby Jacob all over his profile. In fact, virtually every picture and post had them in, or referenced them. He was being completely open.

His news feed and profile said: I have a girlfriend, and I have a son.

But she never mentioned them. She'd ignored the fact. This just felt wrong too.

He sat back and looked out of the window. The sea was calm. In the distance a fishing boat was coming back to shore. He glanced at the time knowing that Nadia would be out for another hour. She was at a counsellor probably discussing him.

They'd hit a bad patch. Not really with their relationship as such, but life. Nadia was struggling to cope. He had a friend who he trusted. She was speaking to him now.

Even in this place they perceived as paradise, things can get you down. Life kept giving him beautiful things, and then the next minute snatched them away. It didn't seem fair.

He'd had enough. They both had. Somehow, and neither could explain it, they felt victimised. It was like the whole world was against them. No matter where they moved to, a darkness followed them.

Deep in thought, Robert's mobile rang. Instantly, he was worried. His heart jumping inside his ribcage. He glanced at the small screen and saw it was his agent.

"Robert!" The overly confident voice boomed out. The guy sounded like a television presenter.

"Max, how are you?" Robert was being polite again. He really couldn't care less.

The guy was all business and always straight to the point. "What's going on, huh? You looking to put me out of business? You don't want to feed your family?"

"What's up?"

"Your story is what's up. You need some variety. I can't sell this!"

Robert sighed. Part of him already knew it but deep down he was obsessed. "It's not the same as the others, Max."

"Robert… Robbie, come on now. It's a story of a child being killed in a car accident. Last month, you gave me a story of a child being injured playing too close to the road, and the time before a child accidentally poisoned…" he paused. Robert let him continue without interruption. "Look, I know what happened to you. You're a great journalist, but you need to go out and get a story, something that isn't involving kids dying."

"I know," Robert said almost in a whisper.

His agent continued, "I'm not trying to be insensitive here, right? We need more."

Taking a deep breath, Robert replied, "You know how these things work. You have to fully immerse yourself into a story to be able to write it. I… you know, it's hard. It's been hard. Only a few years since… since it happened. I have another story about a young boy…"

Max jumped in. "Unless it has a happy ending, then forget about it. Think about your son, and that beautiful woman of yours. Go get a story of something else. Maybe something heart-warming. Shit, I don't know. You might not get the big bucks for it, but I can sell it. You need to get a foothold again."

"I guess."

"Trust me, I know. Look, Robbie, I didn't want to say this but… how can I put this — people are talking, ya know?"

"What do you mean?"

"It's all about your work from years ago. It's like you're dead, mate! And you know what? To a lot of people, you are. *A lot of people!*" He emphasised.

It made Robert angry. "I don't care about them," he said instantly, and realised it did him no good.

Max paused, and huffed. "Or, you know, write about your story…" Max let the line hang. He was suddenly being unusually gentle.

"I don't know."

"Robert. Maybe it's what you're really trying to do, but don't know how to do it. I get it. It would be hard and painful, but it will get it out of your system." Robert knew what he was saying. Write about the incident. The death of his child. Get it out into the open. Name names.

"Okay," he agreed after a long time. "I'll give it a go."

"Brilliant. Brilliant. Get a draft down and send it to me as soon as possible. I'll get it circulating whilst you polish it up, okay?"

Robert nodded, even though he was on the phone, and then replied, "Okay, give me a week."

"Let it all out. Remember emotion sells."

"Okay. I'm on it."

"Bye." And he was gone. Max didn't care about the emotions involved; he just wanted to make money. Robert had made him a lot of money in the past, and now Max was losing faith in him.

He had a story all right. It was the truth and would shock a lot of people. He felt the weight pushing down on him, and deep down always knew the world had to know.

Robert reached down and pulled out the photo album again. He turned to the last picture he ever had of his son.

A lump grew in his throat. His eyes filled with tears. He would never be able to get him back, but perhaps his story could now be told.

He looked back at the message from Jade.

I'm fine, he lied. ***You?*** And pressed send. His lie was huge and tainted.

Lies were something he'd grown used to.

Chapter 33 – Robert

Nadia looked exhausted. Jacob was finally asleep having been restless all day. He'd cried so much that it had almost broken their hearts. Robert hated and loved the sound all at once. Nobody likes to hear the sound of their child crying, but he would do everything in his power to hear his first child fuss again. At least now it showed that Jacob was alive and well.

Nadia didn't get it. How could she.

She came into the room whilst he was typing. He heard her, and turned around.

"Sorry, I know you're in the zone," she said, and then after a beat added. "I miss the time we spend together."

He saved his work, and closed the laptop down. "I know," he said. He did his best to soften his words, but it was frustrating when she wouldn't leave him be. He was busy and she knew that, didn't she? How was he supposed to write a decent article if she was going to barge in every few minutes? His story was very personal, and he hated the thought of her looking over his shoulder whilst his feelings spewed out over the page.

He took a deep breath and prepared himself to put on a brave face.

She looked at him, her eyes darting back and forth to both of his eyes. "You've been crying," she said. He felt exposed. Caught in the act. A little angry, if he was honest.

He took a deep breath. "It's this story. It's about… you know… the accident." He didn't know what to say to her. He wanted to get it down.

"Oh, Robert." She flung her arms around him. She smelt of coffee, and vaguely of body odour. She'd given over to Jacob, only looking after herself when he was asleep. Today had been long and tiring. Life had worn her down. Their situation was hard and really took it out of her. They had to remain strong, each day and then week would make things easier.

"You don't look so good yourself," he commented with a gentle smile. "I'm sorry, I should've helped you out today."

She shrugged into him. Then she pulled away. "Your writing makes us money," she conceded. "I get that." It was clear she wanted to say more.

"I know but…" he started but didn't know where he was going. She looked genuinely sad, and he felt it was all his fault.

She placed a finger on his lips. "Shhh! Don't," she whispered and their lips touched together. Mouths opened slightly, and tongues caressing.

"I've missed this," she said.

"So have I."

He rubbed his hand down her back, and said, "Why don't you grab a shower, or run yourself a bath. I'll go in our room and listen out for Jacob."

"Thank you," she said kissing him again. "And maybe later…" her fingers trailed down his chest, and lower. He grinned.

"Sounds like a plan." But they both knew that later was a long way away. Many things could, and probably would, happen between now and then. That was just the way parenthood went.

He walked into their bedroom, and sat on the bed. Jacob was asleep in the small bed along the side wall. They'd talked about moving him into his own room but neither of them really wanted him out of sight. They liked to make sure he wasn't wandering off when they were not around.

The sound of the bath running was strangely comforting. Nadia walked back into the room and they both looked over at the sleeping angel.

"He's tired himself out," she said in a whisper. "Look at him."

"Our beautiful boy."

"I was talking to Ella today," Nadia said. "She's pregnant again."

"How many has she got now?"

"This will be her third." There was a pause. She looked over at him.

"Right," he said. He wasn't sure he knew what she was saying. The whole pregnancy thing was not a subject he wanted to bring up. His luck with children wasn't great. It brought nothing but heartache.

"Would you want another one," she asked trying to make it sound flippant, but the words had an edge of tentativeness. She turned her back and began to undress.

"I don't know," he said but in a neutral way. "I'd not given it much thought." Glancing at the bed with the small mound in, he wondered whether it was too soon.

"I…" she tripped over her words.

"Are you sure you'd want to go through it again?"

She shrugged. "We'd cope, wouldn't we?" She seemed to be thinking the words out loud, maybe to convince herself. "You're not against the idea?"

He surprised himself by thinking it sounded good. There was a vulnerability to having just one child and having a second now seemed almost justified. Especially considering what had happened.

"I don't mind," he replied. "I mean, sure, I think it would be a nice idea." A child that was his was all he ever wanted.

"Really?" She said sounding surprised, her face lighting up. It was a wonderful sight.

Wearing only her underwear now, she turned and kissed him. He went to grab her, but she pulled away with giggles. She unclipped her bra, and slid off her knickers and made a move towards the bathroom.

"Hey!" he called.

She stopped and turned. He said, "Let me look at you."

She smiled and looked a little embarrassed. "I'm horrible," she said blushing.

"Don't," he said. "You're beautiful." And he meant it. The lack of sleep, and stresses of a child had made her dark skin look a little paler. But her body had the wonderful natural lumps and bumps of a mother and made him only ache for her more.

"I miss seeing you fully naked," he admitted. "You hide yourself away now."

She walked up to him, now with an air of confidence. "You can see all you want after my bath." She winked and disappeared.

He was left with that snapshot in his mind. He really was a lucky man. Despite it all.

Would another child make him feel better?

He stood up and looked over at Jacob, who made some snuffling sounds in his sleep. So fragile and innocent.

Robert sat down again and thought about his story. The major problem he had was that he needed to contact the people involved again. You could do it from his point of view, but then people always questioned the facts. Assuming artistic license had been used. It was what would give the story the authenticity, the meat on the bones, and his integrity. The wounds that had managed to heal would be re-opened.

He wasn't the innocent party that people thought he was. But no one was. Everyone had a dark secret and this would open it all up.

For a second, he almost considered not doing it. But he knew he couldn't.

If he was completely honest then he'd never have another child again. But he wasn't.

And then Nadia's phone beeped. He heard her moving in the bath and looked at it.

It was a message. He thought nothing of it. Her friends were always sending them to her.

For some reason he looked at it.

His heart sank.

It was from Jade. The now familiar picture of her smiling on her night out. His Jade.

What did she want? And why was she messaging Nadia too?

This was bad. This was very bad.

Chapter 34 – Hudson

The worst thing about his job was not being in the front line. Although, that was what had started the catastrophic chain of events all those years ago. Him racing to the scene in time to catch the criminal. So now, here he was left on the side lines. He felt like the striker who had scored the goals to get his football team to the cup final, only to be left on the bench.

In front of him, the police burst into the large extended ex-council house. There was chaos as shouts burst through the neighbourhood. A pandemonium of excitement and adrenaline whipped through the air. A swarm of troops decked out in riot gear.

Gradually, from afar and in various safe places, looky-loos peaked out hoping to see something unexpected that they normally only saw on televised dramas. It wasn't unusual to see police around the area, but the raids of late had been minimal.

Hudson stood across the street watching it all unfold. Within five minutes the police came out, a couple of them escorting a cuffed woman with red hair. She looked to the ground, and her face showed shock. Behind her, and blasting out obscenities, and jumping around came her boyfriend, cuffed and not at all happy about the situation. They were put in two separate vans.

Hudson waited for the other policemen to come out. Hopefully clutching a small blond-haired child. The wait was excruciating.

Minutes passed by. That was never a good sign. It meant one of two things:

1) The child could not be located.
2) The child was dead.

Neither was a great outcome, although the former more preferable than the latter.

The vans pulled away, and disappeared down the road. Some locals shouted at the vans, and it wasn't obvious whether it was aimed at the suspects or the police. Curtains twitched. Hackneyed whispers continued behind nicotine-stained hands.

Another fifteen minutes and he sent a text to his police colleagues.

A single text came back.

He's not here.

Hudson put his hands on his head, blew out his cheeks and bent over. What had gone wrong? It was unlikely that his, and Jez's surveillance was completely incorrect, but what really did they have? Possible sightings. Confirmation of their car in the area at the time of the disappearance. A possibility of a child in the car, but there was no evidence that it was Darren.

He punched in Jez's number.

"I heard," Jez said sounding uncharacteristically sombre. "They know where he is though, I guarantee it. You know what might have happened…" he trailed off.

Hudson finished it off. "They've already disposed of the body."

"Let the experts sweat them down at the station. They'll crack. It was definitely Darren in the car. Liars tend to get found out." Jez was surprisingly thoughtful and pragmatic, his usual immaturity and general buffoonery taking a hiatus.

"Yeah, I know," Hudson agreed.

"Chin up, boss. We'll find him."

"We will. You're right." He clicked off and stared at his phone.

Hudson leant back on the lamppost. He took another deep breath and tapped Laura's number.

"Hello? Hudson?"

"Hey Laura. They've made an arrest… but Darren's not at the house. There's still no sign of him. I'm sorry."

Her voice was suddenly higher as she replied, "What? Really?"

"Yes. Two people are being questioned, but there is the possibility that they might get released."

"What? I don't understand."

Hudson sighed and continued, "We've intel that suggests they were in the area. A car was seen with a child in the back. The car was registered to the suspects, who incidentally don't have children." He realised he was saying too much.

"Okay. So they know where he is!" she demanded.

Jim Ody

"We think so, but there's no concrete evidence. It's possible they were giving a lift to another child. We need them to talk. I'm sorry I don't have better news."

"Thank you, Hudson. You've done a great job anyway. And I know you didn't have to ring me."

"It's not over." They spoke some more words that were vague and polite before finishing the call. Only then did he realise he'd not mentioned the night before, nor spoken of meeting up again. He was doing it again.

Hudson couldn't wait to move the file into the completed pile. This was the case that was becoming his life. He'd started, and he sure as hell would finish it.

Unsatisfied, he walked away from the scene, got to his car and drove home.

Back at his flat, he put on some Elton John. The crackle of static came from the speakers as the LP spun on the turntable. He made himself a pot of tea. But as it brewed, he walked into his work room and was met by all of the other hopeful faces staring back at him. He looked from one to another, hearing sad voices pleading for him to save them.

But it was the small boy with the blond hair that he went to. He felt like apologising to the picture. Telling him he'd not given up, and to hold on tight.

"We'll find you, Darren. Just hold on a little longer, buddy."

A knock on his door brought him back to reality. He opened the door, and was met by the arms of Laura as she wrapped them around him.

"I've not heard anything," he said quickly managing her expectations as best he could.

"I just wanted to thank you anyway." Her hug was tight. The smell of her perfume danced around but on a par with her hair as it all but touched his nose.

"Come in," he said stepping to the side. "D'you want a tea? I've just made a pot."

She nodded and followed him in. "It's been months of nothing. Then you take up the reins and get further than the police have."

He held his hand up. "Look, for starters we've not found him. I really hope we do, and I'm pretty sure we're close to getting something more that we can work with.

"We're surrounded by technology. It's actually pretty hard to disappear without a trace anymore. The data is being constantly collected, it's just whether or not we can access it. Jez is brilliant. He's a little weird, and needs to be micro-managed, but brilliant nevertheless." He took a breath, and laughed. "I'm babbling. I'm sorry."

She smiled. "You're fine."

A few minutes later and they were sat down at the dining table Hudson had to be creative with his meals for one. Hudson noticed that once again she wore long sleeves to hide the scars below. He'd almost forgotten about them.

"I cannot thank you and your friend enough," Laura said, her finger circling the lip of the tea cup. "I wanted you to know that I didn't just want to get to know you for the sake of Darren." She looked up and into his eyes. He knew there was more to come. There was a half-smile as she wrestled with conveying what she needed to say. "It's not always easy speaking to people. I work in a place where sadness is so overpowering, you know?" He nodded, smiling back at her with encouragement. An invisible connection fizzed between them.

"I meet a lot of people. But each one of them is caught up in incredibly traumatic experiences. Most are completely lost. I look at them, and they barely register me. Empty vessels taking each hour as it comes. Some racking their brains to find a reason to carry on. A lot believing this is their last chance before ending it all."

"It must be awful."

"I deal with a lot of PTSD victims. Did you know there is a 23% chance a victim of a single act of violence will take their own life?" He shook his head in shock.

"That seems really high."

She continued, "And if it's multiple acts of physical assault then it rockets to 73.5% But then there is the depression caused by the death of someone close. Wives, husbands, parents, children, it can have a lasting effect on people. I've seen some scary things, but one thing is certain." She paused, and said slowly, "We all handle it differently."

Hudson nodded. He knew what she meant. The reasons why he was at the session, was everything

A Lifetime Ago

he'd denied. The lies that he fed himself each time he stared at the aging man in the mirror. He could tell himself he was okay. He could bottle it up; maybe fill up another box to compartmentalise. Shove it back into the dark and dusty corners of his mind. Ignore the clutter of so many boxes.

"You come to those meetings. You know about loss." Her words were said as a soft statement. She wasn't fishing, she was stating a fact.

"I hate the meetings," he said. "No offense."

"But you keep going."

"I keep going," he agreed in a voice that had shrunk.

She smiled to herself like she was sharing a personal joke.

"And why is that?" she said, taking a sip of her tea. "Why do you keep going back?"

"You want the smooth answer? Or the honest answer?"

"I like smooth, but honesty is always king."

He couldn't argue with that. "Because, no matter how much I hate listening to the woes of others, sometimes that's what you need. What *I* need. These people have had their lives disrupted in ways I can't imagine. They're lost. They need to vent, and they need to tell their story. And sometimes, judgemental pricks like me need to sit up and listen…" he felt his eyes fill with tears. "And know that we're not alone. And whether we want to admit it or not — we're not that different."

She looked right into him. She knew this was the most he'd opened up to someone in a long time. "And that's why I do what I do, and also why I knew you weren't a lost cause."

"What?!" Hudson looked shocked, but she held up her hands quickly.

"No! What I mean is, when we first talked and you told me how much you hated it there, I knew you weren't telling the truth. You know how?"

He shrugged, still worried he was just a project rather than part of a potential relationship.

"You came back. I've seen people turn up, walk out and never return. You'd sit there and listen. You might not always agree with everyone. You might not always understand, or sympathise. You might drift off to another place that fills you with happiness. But you came back. Week after week. Always late, the rebel of the group. Still trying to be the cool kid."

Hudson took a gulp of tea. He looked at the table, and moved his fingers together.

"You know what? Sometimes it feels like a lifetime ago; and other times it feels like last week. My life was a million miles an hour. I was working long hours. But I was working on adrenaline. I felt like I was making a difference. That's huge in giving a person self-worth, and life-satisfaction… Of course, I don't need to tell you that."

She smiled knowingly.

He continued, "You must get that too… And then in one day, everything changed."

She nodded. "Yeah, I get it. I guess my line of work is slow burning. It's gently helping people, and sometimes we have to understand that some people never recover."

"I am still one of the coolest in the group though." They both grinned at that.

"Maybe," she conceded.

A silent lull fell over them, although it was now comfortable. The lack of words was filled with their own thoughts of expectation. They sipped the tea, and Hudson poured more from the teapot. Laura smiled to herself; he wondered whether she thought him a little odd.

Since when did fine crockery fit in with a cool persona?

"You don't have to answer this," she said. "Would you ever go back to the police to work?"

He was already shaking his head. "I work with the police now. I like it better this way. I guess I feel I've changed."

"How so?"

He gazed around him. "I no longer live in a beautiful detached house with a partner. Look at this place. It's small, and I'm obsessed."

"Were you not obsessed before?"

He shrugged, and exhaled. "I guess I was, but it was structured. Maybe too structured. I felt the pressure…"

"And now?"

"And now I work when I want to work. I'm giving additional help to crimes that cannot be solved, rather than the lead with everyone counting on me. I no longer deserve to be the hero in front of the cameras. This suits me. I'm behind the scenes sending other people out, solving cases but passing it on to the police to make the arrest."

"And steal the glory from you?"

"There's no glory when it comes to these kids."

"I'm sorry, that wasn't what I meant." She looked alarmed at what she'd said.

"It's okay, I know what you mean."

"I'm glad you're going to continue helping kids, in whatever capacity you decide," Laura said.

"I'm not religious, but if I was then I'd tell you it's my calling. There's something about it that draws me to it."

Just then Laura's phone buzzed. She looked at it and smiled.

"Sophie. She wants to see me. I guess she wants to talk about the arrest. You should come."

Hudson got up at the same time she did. He grabbed the cups and they both knew his answer before he said it.

"She doesn't need me there. She needs you. I'll be here waiting to hear how the interviews go."

"You'll let me know?"

"Of course."

"Thanks again, Hudson."

"You don't have to keep thanking me."

She reached over and hugged him. She went to kiss his cheek. At the last minute she pecked him on the lips. "Maybe I like it."

She walked over to the door.

"Maybe I like it too," he said as she opened it. They both tried not to grin.

"I'll call you," she said. And deep down he wondered if when Darren was found, she would still be here. Or whether the flame would disappear on their relationship forever.

Chapter 35 – Nadia

She looked at herself in the full-length mirror. She smoothed her flat stomach and wondered whether something was happening inside.

She knew it was silly. It was only last night they'd decided to have another child, and already she was expecting to have fallen pregnant. But she felt pregnant, and with her first, she'd sworn she knew the next day. Sometimes a mother just knows.

Robert was out on a walk with Jacob. It was something he'd begun doing. She thought it was sweet. A little bonding session for her men. He'd push the off-road pushchair along the track, and onto the footpath that led down to the small cove. Or sometimes, Jacob would walk, and they would go as far as his little legs could manage.

The sun was out today, and the cloudless sky inviting. It was hard to feel regrets when the sun shone so brightly.

They lived in such a beautiful area that it was a shame to not indulge in it at any opportunity they had.

She picked up her phone and smiled as she saw her online friend had messaged her. Nadia had local friends now, but sometimes it was nice to speak to someone who didn't fully know you. They seemed to like similar things, and she'd gossip away to her as a way to let off steam. An almost faceless friend who needed little back.

It looked like Jade had sent the message the night before, but she'd not had a moment to look at her phone.

She thought back to the evening. It had been nice. With Jacob, they'd not had much time together. Their life negated that; time in bed was spent either sleeping or worrying about the little lad. For the first year they'd almost slept at different times. And recently the thoughts of tragedy were never far off. It was a bit hard on mental nerves, and sometimes made you do the most inhumane things.

But last night they'd slowly turned back the years, and like hungry teenagers, had fallen quickly into their old rhythms. Nothing fancy, but it was slow and romantic. Almost discovering parts of each other's bodies again like the first time.

She pressed the message on her phone:

Hey Nadia! How r u? she'd written. It was an opening line that in the social media world wasn't so much a question designed to gain a response of well-being, as an opening line asking if she was available to talk.

No matter the hours gone by, Nadia responded with, ***Good. You?*** Again, this wasn't an honest response and further question, but another way of saying: ***I'm here now. Let's talk.***

It was complicated. A digital etiquette of a millennial age.

The dots appeared quickly suggesting that Jade was there, and writing a response.

I have the name of that architect if you still want it? I think she lives near you.

Nadia smiled to herself. They'd thought about adding a cover to the swimming pool, and re-designing the garden. With Jacob, and then Robert's work, they hadn't got around to it since they'd moved in. But now, it was another project to take their minds off the last year or so.

Jade had sent her photos of the work a friend of hers had had done. It looked amazing, and was exactly what she wanted.

Really? That would be great!

She's lovely. Her name is Linda Fletch. You'll love her!

It was great having someone who could put a smile on her face. She walked over to the window overlooking the garden, and for a second was lost imagining what it would look like. They had a limited budget, but Robert was doing well with his writing, at least that's what he'd said, so maybe he'd squeeze a little more into the budget. It would be awful to cut corners.

Thank you so much! She sent back.

You're welcome x

She sat down, rubbing her stomach once again.

Chapter 36 – May

As Luke had disappeared to swim in the pool, the two of them remained in the embrace. They were silent with neither wanting to pull away, even if both knew they should.

"There is something about you, May," Greg said. Then slowly, lips brushed cheeks as eventually they came together in a kiss.

May felt her heart flutter, but managed to breathlessly say, "I should go down with Luke." She knew it wasn't what he wanted to hear, but she was struggling with her self-respect.

"Really?" he said almost showing a flash of anger. "You're... going to walk away?"

"Maybe later," she replied, but there was something desperate that was creeping in and almost making her feel uncomfortable. She didn't want to be made to feel obligated.

"Okay..." he paused, taking it all in. Then he gave off that award-winning smile. "I understand. Look, I have to pop out but go and relax by the pool. My home is yours, okay?"

"Thank you," she replied, and both knew it was nothing to do with the hospitality.

Jim Ody

When May got down to the pool, she saw Luke happily splashing in his own world. She'd slipped back into the bikini, and soon eased herself into the water. It was cold to start with, but soon she was also enjoying the water over her body. At times she stopped and wondered what it might feel like to have Greg running his fingers down her back, and perhaps glide over the rest of her skin.

It was a beautiful sunny day again and this seemed like the perfect way to spend it. She wished she had a book. Something she could sit and get lost in.

Today would probably be their last day here. Greg had been very welcoming but he was becoming too much of a distraction. It was beginning to be a loop that they were caught up in. She didn't need the complication. That just wasn't part of the plan.

He could be part of her future.

This had been nice though. It was unplanned and gave her time to relax. She really didn't think this would happen, but sometimes you had to accept the gifts that fell into your lap.

She took a quick puff on her e-cigarette. She was slowly cutting down to a few puffs a day.

"You okay?" she called out to Luke but once again he just inanely smiled. He was happy enough despite the learning difficulties, but try as she might he was still hard to love. That sounded bad she knew that but it was also the truth. He was a boy forever in the world of a boy. He didn't talk very often choosing to regress in his communication skills. It was a coping mechanism they said, but really what did they know? They knew something about some diagnosis they were happy to chuck their hat in the ring when prescribing for, but they didn't know him. She didn't know him. Nobody knew him. She longed for him to hug her. Really hug her. To love her back the way… No, she couldn't allow herself to go there. It wasn't fair.

She was shocked out of her reverie by the voice of a middle-aged woman. It came from over the fence, and after some searching, May saw her peering over.

"Hey there?" she said again in a rural tongue. "You new?" The lady looked well-kempt. She was dressed smartly and her hair looked perfect.

"Hi," May replied not quite sure what to make of her. "We're just passing through." It felt like an excuse.

"I see. You know Greg, then?" She was late-forties, or early-fifties, and in her youth, she was probably stunning. Even now she'd hold her own.

May shrugged, not wanting to say they'd just met. That would make her seem like some cheap hussy.

"Yeah, he's a friendly chap," she said but held May's gaze a little too long. "Very popular. He has a lot of friends come around."

"Really?"

"Uh-huh. There are some wild parties here. I guess that's the life of a handsome bachelor."

"What about his wife?" May ventured.

"His wife? I don't know anything about a wife. He tell you that?" She seemed surprised, laughed it off. She was ready to start a pity-party on the poor naïve woman in the ill-fitting bikini. May was sure this woman didn't have any stretch marks.

"I've spoken to her."

She pulled a face, "His wife? She here?"

May shook her head. "No, on the phone. They've separated, she lives nearby with their kid."

"O-kay then," she looked dubious. May felt stupid. "Your child is the first one I've seen here ever. Well, unless you count a couple of girls of dubious age at one those parties I mentioned."

"Are you sure?"

"My dear I've been here for five years, you think I'd know if a wife and child lived here too?"

"Oh," was all she could manage. She tried to say something else but her mind went blank. "But?"

"But what?"

"Was there not a tragedy in this pool with his son?" As the words left her mouth, the woman was already shaking her head. She was sounding like an airhead.

"Anyway, don't pay any attention to me, I don't blame you, he's a handsome devil! I can't say as I've not thought about wandering over the fence on occasion!" And with that she turned, waved and disappeared, leaving May to feel incredibly stupid.

A Lifetime Ago

Should they get the hell out of there now? Should she confront him? She was beyond angry. No man should make her feel like this. It was just so typical!

She decided to go and put on her summer dress. That was it, she was leaving. *They* were leaving.

"I'm going inside for a bit," she called to Luke but he couldn't care less. He was splashing around, diving down to the bottom and coming back up to the surface. Each time he broke the water with a huge grin on his face.

She sloped off inside, grabbed a glass of water and went up the stairs to change into her summer dress. She was holding the glass of water when she came out, and was about to go down the stairs when she saw the room that Luke had tried to go into earlier. She stopped still.

All she had to do was take a look. When she saw the room decorated for a boy then she'd know. She had to find out what was on the other side of that door. What was it Greg didn't want them to see? Had he been lying to them? Or was the neighbour jealous of her?

She walked over and placed her hand on the door handle, and then turned it. Just as she opened it, she heard the front door downstairs swing open. She jumped, and almost spilt the water.

"Hey!" called Greg in that sing-song way again. She jumped and walked down the stairs pretending she'd come from the bedroom and not from the forbidden room.

"Oh, there you are!" he grinned and handed her a bunch of flowers. They were a wonderful spectrum of yellows and oranges with blues and greens snuck in for bonus points.

"Those for me?" she asked taken aback. The charmer.

'No, for Luke!" he grinned and winked at her. He handed them over and kissed her on the cheek.

"Thank you."

"They're an apology for making you feel uncomfortable. I'm sorry."

"No problem." But inside she was trying to work him out. What was it he wanted from her?

They stared at each other, trying to second guess each other's thoughts. May was wondering whether this was just another play to get intimate. She wondered how many other women had stood here. Gazing into those dreamy eyes the way she was. Ignoring the lies, and dismissing them as they didn't fit the fantasy.

Greg had a strange look on his face. It was hard to read when you didn't really know a person. It could be a neutral happiness, or even a slight smugness, May just couldn't tell.

"I met your neighbour today," May said, trying to sound natural. Her heart was suddenly pumping hard and fast. She knew that things could go south very quickly.

"Yes, a wonderfully handsome woman. A bit of a gossip," he said. "And slightly mad, but nice enough."

"You ever have parties over here?" May pressed, but then wondered why she was even bothering. Surely, she should get Luke out of the pool, and get the hell out of there.

"She tell you that?" He became shifty. His eyes darted all around. He looked away and chuckled to himself.

She nodded. "Said you've had a few parties here, but didn't remember ever seeing your wife or daughter."

He raised his eyebrows like she'd just insulted him. "She's a liar. She made a pass at me once and I turned her down. She's been a little vindictive ever since." He tried a smile like it was nothing.

"She made out you often had women over here?"

"Sure, my wife has a lot of friends. They come over we all swim in the pool…" he relaxed into his lies now.

"She was adamant you weren't married!"

He sighed, and said, "She's had so much surgery that she doesn't know what the fuck is going on. She's a dried-up old bag!"

"Greg, level with me. You're not married, are you?"

He nodded. "No, I'm separated. Ring my wife; she'll happily answer any questions you have." He was calm, and either telling the truth, or comfortable with the tales he was spinning.

May stood there unsure what she should do. "Look maybe we should just get going. It doesn't really matter if you're married or not. You can cheat on your wife, or march through some harem of women if you so wish… I just don't care."

Greg looked hurt. "Don't say that. This is just a big misunderstanding… Don't you like me?"

May took a breath. "It's not about whether or not I like you. I just don't need any more drama in my life. Things are not that simple."

"Stay here. Come on, stay a while, yeah?"

"I don't know. We've people to see."

"It's Luke's birthday, isn't it? Tomorrow? Let's take the little guy out, yeah?"

"Greg… I don't know. It bothers me slightly that you've lied to me."

"But…"

"No bullshit, Greg."

"As I say, I'm married, but separated. Okay, I've slept with a few other women – not many – but I have… but you're something different. You've been here longer than any other woman as it is!"

May turned away. Her stomach had sunk. She hated feeling this way. She'd only just met him and she could tell already that he used a lot of poetic license in regards to the truth.

"Okay, maybe we'll see how things go."

Suddenly Greg's mobile rang.

"Here she is!" he said pointing to the phone. "Hey babe!...Yeah great…yeah, yeah… Yes, she is… No, she felt uncomfortable… uh-huh…okay, yeah I'll put her on."

He held out the phone to May, and with a weak smile said, "Sindy wants to speak to you."

May looked at the phone like she was going to see a smiling face on the handset too. And there was a pretty blonde-haired woman saved as the photo. She held it up.

"Hello," May said tentatively. It was awkward again.

"Hi honey. You okay?"

"I'm good thank you… you?"

There was laughter. "Oh honey. Look I know all about you. I know that there is attraction between you and Greg, and honestly, I don't mind. We're separated now. If you want to kiss him… if you want to… *you know*, do other things with him then you have my blessing… I'm no longer part of his life in that way, okay?" Her voice was filled with such happiness, that it all seemed silly to think of anything else. Maybe it was just a misunderstanding.

"Uh… Okay," May replied. How do you follow that up?

"You've no need to feel uncomfortable about this, silly!"

"I don't know what to say."

"Just make him happy, okay?"

"Okay."

"Put Greg back on then. Maybe we'll meet soon? Goodbye."

"Bye." She handed it back to Greg. He smiled even without hearing what had been said.

He carried on speaking to Sindy whilst she turned, placed the flowers on the table and walked out to Luke.

He was still swimming around, periodically getting out and jumping back in.

"You okay, Luke?" she shouted. "You need anything?"

He shook his head and carried on as he was doing. She wondered whether he'd even realise if she never returned. Probably not. She walked over to her e-cigarette and took another blast for her nerves.

Life was all about choices. She smiled to herself having made up her mind. It was liberating to go and do something she normally wouldn't. She walked back in through the kitchen to where Greg was standing having finished his call.

"May…" he started but she put a finger to his lips and grabbed his hand. Without a word she took him up the stairs and into the room that she'd slept in. She was still holding the glass of water and placed it by the bed. Her bag was still open, her belongings half in and half out.

A mischievous smile played upon his lips. Slowly, and slightly awkwardly they started to kiss.

Chapter 37 – Hudson

He skulked into the building again. Another Tuesday night and what did he have to look forward to? He pictured Laura and felt a little better.

As usual he was fashionably late. Drifting in like rubbish blown from the street. Incognito like he was undercover. Wouldn't that be a hoot? What if he had never had a bereavement, or trauma? He pictured himself in a movie, the viewers unaware of this misdirection as he worked a case, getting closer to the killer.

But this wasn't the movies. He'd left a case file open whilst he'd walked away from it twice, wondering whether or not he should be here.

Deep down he knew it was a help.

Earlier that day, he'd found another witness.

He'd hit the streets around the area and was at the point of knocking on doors. People had a habit of not coming forward, assuming whatever they had to say was of no importance.

And then he found Dave. A big built guy covered in oil.

"I was workin' on me car in the garage." He said, resting his great girth against the doorframe as if standing was too much effort. I saw a red car pull up."

"Go on."

"Well this woman opened the doors and kicked the kid out. I mean it was odd."

"What do you mean kicked?"

He sniffed and wiped his bulbous nose. "She let the kid out of the car, and without a word got back in and drove off."

"And what car was it?"

His face lit up at the thought about cars. "A red VW Golf. I'd say a 2012 model, 1.9 TDi. Not bad condition."

"And the woman? Can you describe her?" This question wasn't so easy.

"Average lookin'. Black top and ginger. That's all I remember."

"And what happened to the child?"

"I dunno, I didn't look. Just walked off, I guess." It wasn't the man's fault, but it still made Hudson angry. If you saw a child as young as Darren left on the side of the road, why would you not go and see if he was okay?

It almost put them back to square one.

Hudson's mind was heavy with the outcome of the interviews after the couple had been arrested.

Colin started by denying everything until his solicitor got there, and then he clammed up and only responded with *no comment*. Emma did her very best to look down for the whole time. Despite the legal advice she received, she continued to deny everything.

And then, after another couple of hours in the cell, and another two hours of an interview, Emma, after a quick break to speak alone with her solicitor, made a surprise confession.

"I saw the boy, and tried to take him to his home," she said. "I knew his mum would, like be wonderin' where he was, but then he got confused. In the end I stopped the car and let him out."

"Why didn't you take him to a police station? Or to somewhere safe?" The detective had asked.

She looked shocked like this was a revelation. It was as if she was expecting them to just let her go after her confession.

"He was scared, and crying. I thought it best to let him go."

The two detectives looked at each other.

Colin McGill still denied being involved, or even knowing anything about it. He was happy to advise the police that his girlfriend was a liar, and a junkie.

Hudson shared his findings from the witness which corroborated Emma's story, and both suspects were released pending further investigation. Their car had still been seized for testing.

Hudson was brought back to reality as he looked at the poor woman currently speaking at the meeting.

She was a short, but robust woman gesticulating with her hands as she talked. Sometimes they moved so frantically it appeared she had something sticky on them that she was hoping to remove with the vigorous action. It was just so sad and depressing. She had gone there and opened up her heart to them. Her feelings exploded from every pore, as they sat either nodding in sympathy, joined in her wallowing and self-pity, or simply judged her.

At times, he had to wonder how many people slouched in the same chairs, and instead of listening to the details of the story being told, just sat and questioned religion. Asked the questions about God, and why he thought it such a good idea to make these people feel the way they did.

He'd held off beforehand, but now looked over and saw Laura. She turned, smiled and wiggled her fingers in a small wave gesture. He smiled back. She was also another very good reason why he was there.

He also found it useful, whilst the meeting was on, to sit back and think over cases. On one level it seemed a little disrespectful to those sharing their stories, but it was a time he could sit and indulge in contemplation. He'd heard this from a number of people who frequented church. Some of them weren't deeply religious, but found it to be a good time for reflection. To relax, and mull over a few things without the common distractions of life.

A new guy was the next to speak. He was painfully thin, and had chosen to stand up, and almost address everyone like it was some proclamation.

"I've learnt some things from this already," he started, and whilst there was the slight quiver in his voice, he made an effort to speak to each and every person.

"Time is so dear to us all. We don't know how long we've got. We need to make that time to spend with each other, 'cause one day…" he paused and looked at every single person. "We'll be gone." He raised a finger to hit home his statement. Hudson saw the backs of nodding heads, and one woman began to sob.

His shirt was hanging off him, and Hudson had to wonder whether at some point he'd actually filled it out. Tragedy had a tendency to either drive you towards, or keep you away from food.

There was a sadness in the way you could see a patch of stubble missed from that day's shave. Even from where Hudson sat it was noticeable. The normal functions of daily routine were being neglected. Trauma's dark cloud dulling the brain's abilities to perform simple tasks.

As usual, at the break Hudson was the first to the coffee. He poured two, and turned around to see the smiling face of Laura. He handed one to her.

"A gentleman," she said accepting it.

"You're welcome." They stepped aside so the others could grab a cup too.

Laura looked like she was about to ask a question even before she spoke. "Something I've been meaning to ask you," she started. "You drink tea from a teapot, but here drink coffee! What's that all about?"

"D'you see a teapot anywhere?"

She grinned, but looking around quickly hid it. "You're making me break the rules again!" She hissed. "Laughing is prohibited!"

He shrugged as they walked further away from the sadsacks around them.

"Let's not be strangers," she said suddenly. "Honestly, I like you."

Hudson was taken aback a little. He wasn't used to a woman being so forward with him. "Good to know," he said. "You're not bad yourself."

"You do good work too, remember that. Kids are lucky to have someone like you fighting for them."

"But unlucky to need me."

"You have a habit of that, you know?"

Hudson looked at her with a frown. "What'd'ya mean?"

"I compliment you, and you turn it into criticism."

He nodded. "I know," he paused. "I've a few trust issues. I'm working on them."

"Work harder." She winked, and let another smile escape, before adding. "Well let's get back to it then."

He liked that. They separated back to their chairs, and he threw her a last glance that he hoped spoke out to her. He wasn't sure what they had, but it helped him get through the next half an hour.

Laura had been upset when Colin and Emma had been released. He'd explained that even suspicion wasn't enough to hold them. But suddenly the trail turned to ice again.

Outside, they stumbled over words, not knowing which move to make, until Laura made an excuse to leave, and Hudson was left kicking himself for not asking her to stay. She was meeting Sophie. The case dominating both of them, and driving a wedge between any chance they had of anything more than whatever they currently had.

He was too emotionally involved in the case that he struggled to be able to sort out how he felt about Laura. He had a good idea, but she deserved his undivided attention.

The problem was, when he thought about it, he came up with the same conclusion: would she ever get it?

Chapter 38 – May

Hands quickly roamed over and under clothing. There was a sexual electricity in the air as they both let themselves go.

"You have coffee breath," May said which stopped the moment.

Greg stopped, "Really?" He looked shellshocked.

May grinned, and pointed to the glass. "Have a drink of that," she said.

"You want me to stop kissing you to drink water?"

"If you want more kisses, then kill the stale breath!"

He shook his head and grabbed the glass. He took a swig, then lowered it.

"Ah-ha," she said waggling her finger. "All of it, mister!"

He let his frustration be known by huffing, but still did as he was told. When he put the glass back down on the side, it hit with a heavy sound.

It wasn't long before May was laid back on the bed. She was still wearing her dress, but it was now hiked up and showing a lot more of her thighs than normal. Her underwear, now removed, was crumpled and forgotten on the floor. Greg leered over her with a deviant and predatory look in his eyes. His arms held him up in a press-up pose. His breath tickled her neck.

His kisses brushed her skin, as his hand worked its way along her thigh. Heartbeats quickened and expectation grew.

May wriggled and twisted, flipping Greg over so that he was then on his back. He grinned, enjoying the sudden dominance by her. She covered his mouth with hers. Lips parted and tongues touched.

She moved her hips gently over him. Still wearing his underwear, she felt the hardness of him underneath. With one hand, she teased his underwear down slightly. His breathing quickened, as his head tilted.

And then his eyes rolled back into his head. He became still.

She looked at the empty glass. The one she'd dissolved the tablets in earlier.

He was out cold. He'd be like that for a while.

Men lie. They do whatever they can to sneak into a woman's pants, she thought.

She no longer saw Greg. She saw the face of her ex-husband instead.

She moved to squeeze his windpipe with all of her might. But stopped, and instead reached in the drawer and removed the cuffs. She snapped them first onto his wrist, and then to the headboard.

She looked at him as she got her clothes on. She couldn't help it, she slapped him.

"You fucking cheating bastard!" she spat the words out. His face slowly morphing back into

Greg's. It made no difference — he was just as bad.

She walked out of the door and along to one of the other rooms. She glanced out of the window at the pool below.

Luke was still lost in his own world. She knew she had to leave and disappear.

May packed her bag. She grabbed the glass and wiped her prints off it. She knew she wasn't doing a great job, but she placed the glass in the cupboard of another room. She'd added a huge dosage of tranquilizer and in all honesty wasn't sure whether it had been too much. She hadn't meant to kill him, but just in case things went south she wanted to stay out of it, and figured it would be less likely to be checked for DNA if it didn't look part of the crime scene.

It was his fault. She couldn't believe what he'd made her do. She did her very best not to get involved but he insisted on pushing her further and further until she couldn't stop anymore. She hated men and their needs. She thought he was her knight in shining armour, helping her, but all the time all he really wanted to do was sleep with her. Use her like some naïve teen.

Whilst her son was outside too!

She'd had years of marriage to a man who seemed a slightly fun side of boring. The bastard then found refuge in the panties of her neighbour. Her friend! She'd been clueless to the fact. Of course she had. His sneaky little sexpeditions next-door fucking that conniving slut, with her stupid grinning face, big boobs and exotic look.

A Lifetime Ago

And she was left looking after the house and making sure Luke had everything.

She thought they were in love but it turned out it was only her that was. He couldn't give a shit. She was just the fool who kept the house in order whilst he went off to have his kicks!

She threw him out and moved away.

It should've just been her and Luke living together until the end of time, but even that little dream turned to shit.

May shook off the bad memories and explored the house. She had time on her hands now.

She felt in a daze. She suddenly couldn't believe what she'd done. But then she saw the room.

The forbidden room.

Slowly, she opened the door. *Just what's in here, Greg? What did you not want us to see?*

The room looked normal albeit for an unused room it looked lived in.

But there was nothing to suggest it was the room of a little boy.

And then she heard the phone ring. Greg's mobile.

She ran to the spare room, smiling at the almost naked body on the bed exactly how she'd left it. She bent down, and took out the phone from the pocket of Greg's trousers.

"Hello?" she said but the face had already told her who it was.

"May? Hi. Where's Greg?"

"Hi Sindy… he's just popped out."

Her happy-smiley tone dropped slightly. "Without his phone?"

"Uh, yeah… he must've forgotten it."

She laughed but it sounded a little off. "Silly man," she said. May wasn't sure how she felt. Guilty? Sad? Sorry?

May walked back to the forbidden room again feeling awkward.

"You did it, didn't you?" Sindy suddenly said her voice sounding slightly different. May stopped in her tracks. But before she could reply there was something happening at the other end of the phone, and then there was the small voice of Bee.

"Hello? May? It's Bee. Where's Dad-dy? Is he o-kay?"

"Hi Bee. Um, your daddy's just gone to the shop."

"Are you lying to us, May?" the little voice asked. "Are you telling lies? Mummy doesn't like lies!"

"No, of course not. He left his phone. Why would I lie?"

There were no toys, or children's books. Nothing. It just looked like a regular spare room. She looked at the clothes on the bed and then she saw the photo-frame…

"You had sex with my daddy, didn't you?"

The photograph showed Greg but his arm was around the shoulders of the man who had attacked her. They were smiling together. Like best-buddies. Or brothers.

"I'm sorry?" she said not believing what she was seeing nor what the child was saying. It looked like Greg and the man knew each other more than Greg had admitted. He'd said he was just a work colleague of Sindy's. This suggested otherwise. They knew each other very well. Why would there be a picture up of a man who had attacked his wife here, proud in this room?

Unless it was all a lie. Another fucking lie.

"*Are you sorry?* You fucked him hard!" The child was angry. May's heart was pounding, and she could feel sweat beading on her forehead, and down her back.

May walked up to the picture, and then she saw the ID card. The man's name was Martin. She looked around the room again.

This was Martin's room!

"I, er, I…" The air in the room got thick. She stepped back but then the sound on the phone got funny.

"May?" The voice said quietly. It seemed to have calmed.

"Yes?"

"Turn around," the small voice said.

May whipped around to find Martin stood there talking into a voice-box. In his other hand was a large hunting knife.

"Surprise!" he said in the same little girl voice. He then clicked a button and spoke in the voice that sounded like Sindy.

"You had sex with my husband, May! Naughty slut!"

"What is going on here?" May said, stepping back further into the room, and knocking something off the side.

Jim Ody

"You think this was all Greg? The big handsome guy? It was me," he chucked the box down so only his true voice could be heard. "You've been speaking to us both online." He grinned. "I liked the picture you sent." He winked. "I looked at that a lot! Greg knew you were coming here. You told him as much."

"What? No, I didn't."

"You said you were taking a trip down here. Greg told you about the café, didn't he?"

Then she remembered. She'd been thinking about Robert and her mind was foggy. She had said she was driving through the county, and Greg had been talking up the town.

"He's been working on you for weeks! We knew the best way to get a girl was to play out the hero routine, but then you decided to get all worried about cheating, for fucksake! Who gives a shit! I guess we got no disruptions now, huh?"

"No," she mumbled, her hands held up in defence.

He had those big crazy eyes again.

She suddenly glanced behind him and shouted, "Greg! No!" and in the split second that Martin turned around she charged at him knocking him off his feet. His head cracked the corner of the wall, as he crumpled to the floor. She grabbed the knife and looked at him. She wanted to plunge it deep into him. Instead she kicked him in the face as hard as she could.

She hated men! All of them nothing but bloody liars.

She almost ran down the stairs. She knew she had to leave. Martin could come around at any moment.

She ran outside quickly, to where Luke was stood out on the side, the towel around him and looking worried.

He'd heard the shouting.

"Time to go, buddy. Okay?" He nodded.

Her eyes looked all around, hoping the nosey neighbour wasn't peeking over the fence.

She held his hand, and they went out the gate and straight to the car.

She put him into his seat, noting again hat dark roots were beginning to show in his hair. She needed to get more peroxide again. Luke hated it. But it had to be done.

Luke didn't have brown hair, only Sonny.

She got into the driver's seat, started up the car, and without looking back drove away.

She didn't even notice the man hobbling out behind them, one hand rubbing his dazed head.

"Well that was some excitement, wasn't it, Luke?" she said hoping he couldn't detect the fear in her voice. That had been close.

That was what happened when you were foolish enough to trust a man.

This changed nothing. In fact, it only reinforced what she had to do. Her plan was still on. Men couldn't be allowed to run around about their business trying to manipulate women for their own sexual gratification. They had to be stopped.

He had to be stopped.

Things had to be put right.
"You okay, Luke?" she asked him.
He nodded. Even if that wasn't really his name.

Chapter 39 – Hudson

The next day Hudson was hard on the case. He'd read the background again, and he'd stared at the face of the boy. The pictures on the wall spoke to him in a way that made him feel guilty to sleep at night.

He'd made a fresh pot of tea and sat having a break whilst watching the local news. He did this periodically hoping to see one of his cases solved before his eyes. It had happened once. He lived in hope that it would happen again.

His mobile went and he smiled when he saw it was Jez.

"Jez, are we not friends?" He started, messing with him. It was the only humour he had nowadays.

"Eh? What d'ya mean?" Jez was confused. He was a genius when it came to computers, but like a child to speak to.

"It's been days since you sent me a video of your wife in a compromising position. And now? Nothing. Not even a nipple-slip. I assumed I'd done something wrong?"

There was silence. Jez was digesting this. "Ah, I see. A joke."

"Yes, I apologise for the act of humour."

Then in an excited voice, Jez added, "'Cause I have videos. She dressed up as Britney Spears once. And the photos…"

"No, it's okay, Jez. Really, it was a joke. Not that your wife is not great to look at, of course."

"Of course," he agreed. "Anyway, the reason I called was I've come across something a bit weird."

Jez was the epitome of weird. In fact, he could also be described as strange, bizarre, odd, goofy, kooky, and even at times a little hinky, so when he stumbled across something he thought was unusual, Hudson knew it was going to be bad.

"Go on."

"I'm running more cyber checks on the Darren Hughes case—*like you asked me to do*. And there are a few people I'm checking backgrounds for, and one of them is someone interesting. Someone you know."

"It's not you, is it?" Hudson was messing again.

There was another beat of silence. "It's not me."

"I know a lot of people, Jez. Should you be telling me this?"

"It's about an ongoing case which involves you so I reckon that's fine."

"Okay."

"This person used to live next door to you. Her husband was over your place a lot."

Hudson felt his stomach drop and his heart rate increase. That was one way of putting it. Apparently, he came over a number of times.

A Lifetime Ago

Mostly when Hudson was out. He had a habit of removing his clothes each time too.

It was too much to take in.

He knew who he meant. But he couldn't imagine she'd have anything to do with a missing child. She baked cakes for the cubs, for Christsake!

"I know who you mean. How many people are on the list?"

"Four."

"Shit. Is she linked to any of the others?"

There was the sound of keys being tapped in the background. "Not really."

Hudson was suddenly frustrated. He got like this when he wanted information and wasn't in control. "What does that mean?"

"Just that," Jez said. "There's no indication that she knew the others. They were not friends on social media apps, or part of the same groups. There's no email or phone correspondence. Nothing."

"Mutual friends?" He pressed.

"Sure. A handful, but so what? We're probably all connected some way or another." Of course, he was right. Mutual friends, whether on social media, or even in person was hardly the same as 'known associates'.

"And the husband?" He didn't want to say his name.

"They're no longer together." He knew that already. He'd moved away and had done all he could to forget about them.

It was impossible, but he'd tried nevertheless.

"So how is she connected to this then? What have you got?"

"Not much. A vague sighting, and a missed phone call."

"Not exactly watertight then. And the others, anything stronger?"

Jez was puffing out his cheeks. "It's all pretty clean. But they all look similar. Apart from Emma Vine."

"Who claims she let Darren go when he was crying in her car, and who we have a witness who agrees with that."

"Yes."

"Any of them make phone calls?"

"No. Allegedly, one of them knocked on Sophie's front door a few days before, but again they didn't know who she was so it was down to description. This woman was known to have been in the area about that time."

"Jesus. I don't know," Hudson said. "I just don't see it."

"And that's the problem, boss. We never do."

"I'm not your boss, Jez." Jez just laughed. Loudly. Jez assumed everyone to be his boss.

"Keep me posted," Hudson said and was left looking at his phone.

Again, he just couldn't see it. She was a lot of things but she wasn't evil.

She just couldn't keep hold of her man.

And who was he to be so critical. He couldn't keep hold of his woman either.

He got up and walked into the room. Third from the left was a boy with brown hair and blue eyes. He had a huge grin on his face, and seemingly not a care in the world. If only he knew, he thought. If only he knew.

He'd been missing now for months. As hard as they tried, they couldn't pin it on Emma and Colin, and whilst it seemed likely Emma knew a lot more than she was letting on, it also became more apparent that Colin knew absolutely nothing. The pair didn't seem clever enough to be able to carry out an abduction, and then murder and dispose of a body. Her car had been searched, and later cleared. Cadaver dogs had also been through it without luck.

This was how it went sometimes. Maybe one day he'd have a whole team working around the clock to find these children, but until that time, he'd do the best he could.

And live with the consequences later.

Jim Ody

A Lifetime Ago

Chapter 40 – The abduction

Four years ago

Darren was going up and down the slide and giggling loudly. Then he ran in the waddling way small children did, to go underneath the climbing frame to the car, when his uncle's phone rang. Simon glanced over and, satisfied Darren was fine, answered it.

It was his sister. She'd been in a state that morning when she'd been called in for an interview. It was in the town centre of Swindon, and was a great opportunity for her. She couldn't pass it up and had got Simon out of bed when she'd called him. As usual his schedule was pretty slim. He'd already decided to blow out college for a few hours of *Call Of Duty* instead, so he was happy to step in and look after Darren.

"Oh my god!" she had been saying to him. "They want me!" she went on to tell him at great length all about the interview. Proudly, he stood listening, and looking over at the attractive mothers fussing over their little darlings.

Darren looked up at a woman waving to him. She was smiling and looked like she had something. Darren looked over at his uncle, but he

A Lifetime Ago

was on his phone. He thought he could run over to the lady, and be back before he was missed. She looked friendly.

He giggled to himself, thinking this would be a fun trick.

He'd already slipped his coat off. His uncle made him wear it but now after running around the park he was hot.

The woman got closer, and waved him over to her. She looked really happy to see him.

Darren passed other children, weaving in and out. It was busy now. He walked to the gate, and with all his strength managed to open it. He turned and closed it gently so as not to make a sound.

His uncle was moving his arms around, and still looking in the other direction.

Darren giggled and ran as fast as he could towards the woman.

"Hello!" she grinned. "Have you seen my dog?"

Darren shook his head and saw her pushchair. It was big.

"No?" Darren shook his head again.

She looked down at him, and glanced once at his uncle. "Could you run to those bushes and see if he's in there? I'm too big!"

Darren nodded and smiled. He then took off the few metres into the undergrowth.

The woman suddenly jogged after him pushing the pushchair in front, and went around the other side. They were now hidden from the playpark.

"Is he there?" she called.

Darren came out and shook his head. She looked sad, and even pretended to cry. "Come and help me, please?" she held out her hand.

Darren glanced through the bushes at his uncle.

"It's okay, I've just texted him. He knows you're with me, okay?"

Darren looked a little scared, but nodded.

"Hey, get in the pushchair, and I'll wheel you to the end of the path, and then I'll take you back to your dad, okay?"

Darren looked up at her with trusting eyes. "Uncle Simon," he corrected her.

"Yes, Uncle Simon. Come on, I'll show you how fast this thing can go!"

Darren slowly got in.

She pushed him off. A normal pace at first, then she quickened it.

They left the park and continued down the road. The street was long, but the area was nice. The woman wished she lived nearer.

Darren began to grizzle as they continued to go further from the park. Eventually, they came to her car.

"Come on, jump in. We'll have one more look and then I'll take you home."

Darren stood still.

"Don't worry. I'll get you an ice-cream. You like ice-cream?"

He nodded and reluctantly got in.

She started the car and pulled away. She felt the relief. But then the boy started to cry. Not just sobs, but huge wails. She panicked. It was too much. She hadn't actually thought it would work. And now she had no idea what to do.

She pulled the car over in an area that seemed deserted. She opened the car door.

"Go on," she said. "Off you go."

He stopped not sure what to do, and not understanding about making a break for freedom.

"Get out!" she shouted, suddenly wanting no further part of it.

He got out. But instead of running away, just stood there snivelling. She looked at the pitiful sight, and got back in the VW Golf and left him.

Darren looked all around him. He was alone, lost and petrified.

So later, a little way down the road, when the stranger came up to him and took his hand with a promise to take him home Darren accepted it. He just wanted to see his mum.

He was too trusting, and the stranger took full advantage of that.

Chapter 41 – Hudson

Some days you were staring at a monitor, looking at data or trawling through security cameras, and other times, with one phone call the world hit a supersonic pace.

Hudson had been sat for a couple of hours following up leads, and trying to piece things together. He'd just stopped and was looking at his phone, and thinking about sending a text message to Laura. Nothing much, but enough to let her know he cared. He hated to think their relationship could end before it had even started.

And that was when everything kicked into action, and his good intentions got lost in the whirlwind.

It started with another call, and from there the ball kept rolling and building up speed.

"Hudson, it's Pete." Why Pete needed to introduce himself each time, god only knew.

"Hi Pete."

"Look, we've had a sighting on the Darren Hughes case."

Hudson sat up straight ready for action. It seemed things were suddenly moving on the case. "Yes?" he said.

"Thing is, the sighting is vague and has come from Devon & Cornwall police. They've spoken to the witness, but don't have much…" He trailed off.

"You want me to dig deeper?"

"Yeah. It's a big case but we're on a skeleton crew as it is, and the serg is not going to authorise us driving across the country on a vague sighting. I know how much you want these cases solved. I was thinking if you could take a trip down there, maybe check them out yourself?" he was babbling, and Hudson was slightly amused that driving a couple of hours south was considered across the country. He was probably paraphrasing.

Despite being on the phone, Hudson was nodding, and ready to wrap up the call to leave and jump into action.

"Sure. When was the sighting?"

"Yesterday," Pete replied. That was good. They were only 24hrs behind.

"Email me the details. I'll get straight onto it."

Could this be it? The break they were looking for? A sighting away from Thornhill and Swindon made sense, and a sighting of Darren meant he was still alive.

Hudson rang Jez to let him know.

"Sure," Jez said with real excitement. "I'll just clear it with her indoors and we'll be on our way!"

"Whoa, there! You don't need to be with me. You can stay here. I'll ring through any information I need and you can find it."

There was a silence before Jez laughed. "Haha! Good one. You almost had me!"

Hudson rolled his eyes. A thing he did at least once in every single conversation he had with Jez.

"You're not coming."

"Sure," Jez replied.

*

Hudson started the engine ready for the drive.

The passenger door opened and Jez folded himself into the passenger seat. He wore an open shirt with a white vest on underneath. Perhaps he thought he'd fallen into an episode of *Hawaii Five-0*. "Jesus, who've you had in here, mate?" He complained.

Hudson took a deep breath. This was going to be a long journey.

"Jez, you're like seven-foot-tall, everyone seems short to you. Get in, and belt up, so we can get going."

"Yes, boss!"

They pulled away from Jez's house, his wife was stood blowing kisses from the doorway. Jez was pretending to catch them and then blow them back. Hudson really didn't know what to make of it. He was slightly embarrassed for them.

"Shall I put my mix tape on?" Jez said the minute they pulled out onto the main road that would eventually take them to the M4 junction.

"I'd rather you didn't," Hudson replied. He meant it too. Jez had an interesting taste in music. One minute you might get classic rock, and the next you'd be hit with either Gangsta rap, or Europop. As a mix tape it was definitely a mix.

Hudson gave in somewhere around the Bath junction. Jez acted like a school girl as he squealed and plugged his phone into the dashboard.

Suddenly Steps blasted out their sugary-pop, to which Hudson commented, "For fucksake!"

"You don't have to dance too," Jez said as if that was the source of his frustration.

"I wasn't planning on doing so," he said and hoped the world would allow the next two hours to pass quickly.

When the music wasn't blasting, Jez was talking. He was a big talker. Just like a small child who hasn't seen a parent for a week, he continuously reeled off story after story hardly taking a break. He didn't require any acknowledgement, or confirmation that Hudson was listening, or gave two shits about the story content. He just kept on. Mile after mile. Past Bristol, and onto the M5. The odometer continued to clock up the miles, and the towns passed them by: Bridgewater, Taunton and Exeter, and Jez went with his stories, observations and sometimes even his fantasies. He took a deep breath as they got onto the A30, and momentarily went quiet, but by Oakhampton he was verbally going at it like an assault rifle. Bang, bang bang!

"I'm hungry," Jez said as they had left the main road and were headed down into the seaside town.

"Well, we're going to a café, so you're in luck. They appreciate silence though, so why don't we pretend you're mute?"

"Really?" Jez said, tapping his fingers.

Jim Ody

"Or you could stay in the car and I could bring you a doggy bag."

"Haha! You're joking again, Huds!"

The town was pleasant enough. None of the large chain stores had bullied their way in there yet, and there was a general hustle and bustle of locals and holiday makers. Small shops had an assortment of colourful inflatables, and racks of T-shirts outside.

"Here we are," Hudson said as they pulled into the busy carpark.

Jez was already out. "Come on, slow-coach!"

Hudson thought this must be what it's like to take your twelve-year-old son on a trip.

"Hang on," he said, but Jez was already inside.

When Hudson caught up, Jez was sat in a booth by the window and looking so intently at the menu that his tongue was hanging out. He was like a mash up between Scooby-Doo, Shaggy and Marilyn Manson. He was a living caricature of a human, possibly more cartoon than human.

"Stay here," Hudson said feeling the need to tell him that. Jez held up a hand by way of a response not taking his eyes away from the edible delights on offer.

Hudson managed another eyeroll, then turned and walked over to the counter. A young girl behind it did her best to smile at him. Her hair was pulled back painfully into a ponytail, and she had huge hooped earrings that budgies could most likely swing on.

"Take a seat, sum'un'll be wiv ya in a minute." It was said without feeling. A stud in her tongue bobbed with each word.

"Yeah, my friend has a table," he replied. "I'm actually looking for Beth. She here?"

The girl huffed like this might be above her minimum pay grade. She turned her head quickly which whipped her ponytail around in a slightly dangerous fashion. Hudson almost had to duck.

"Havin' a fag, I fink."

"She's here though?"

The girl nodded.

"Can you send her over when she's back? It's about something she told the police."

"Right," she replied bored. "You orderin'?"

"We will after we've spoken to Beth."

"She's 'avin' a fag."

Hudson turned away and muttered, "I think we've already established that."

"Jeez!" Jez said. "You should see all the great stuff they have here!"

"You do remember why we're here?" Sometimes Hudson admired the way Jez could switch on and switch off. It certainly brought him less stress.

Jez nodded, but he wouldn't have even heard the words. Food had a habit of doing that with him.

Defeated, Hudson grabbed another menu and had a look at it himself. When in Rome and all that.

The menu was loaded with stuff to block your arteries and increase your chances of a heart attack. He'd considered going vegan of late. Not because of the animals, but because of the benefits of the diet. Every once in a while, when a bandwagon drove by he'd hitchhike on it for a while. He soon got off.

But the burgers did look good. Really good.

"Hello there!" a voice said full of cheer. Hudson looked up at a huge pair of breasts, and the chubby middle-aged owner of them. "You wanted to speak to me?"

Jez looked scared. Strong women had that effect on him. It was strange that he'd chosen to married one.

"Beth?" she nodded at the mention of her name. "Yes, please take a seat we have a couple of questions."

"O-kay." She looked worried. "Are you the police?"

"Sort of. More like associate detectives."

She looked confused but bought it.

"I'm interested in what you told our colleagues about the woman and child. They were here yesterday and had a meal, yes?"

She smiled like it was such a happy memory. "Yes, they did. The little boy was such a sweet little thing. Mind you, he didn't speak at al…"

"What, at all?"

"Nope. Not a dicky-bird. I looked up a few times and he just looked scared. It's why I remembered them so well."

"And the woman?" Hudson didn't want to say mother, the waitress was already seeing them as a sweet couple, and not as a potential victim and abductor.

Beth pulled a face, which was a slight gurn. A strange movement in her mouth showed that not all of her teeth were real. "She was good for her age. Looked like one of those sporty-mums. You know, does yoga, and goes to the gym. That sort." She chuckled. "Puts the likes of me to shame!"

Hudson nodded and offered a smile, and Jez kept glancing at his menu, desperate to place an order.

"Anything else about her?" Hudson pressed. He hoped there was more. They'd driven a long way to hear she was good for her age and they were a sweet couple.

She thought hard. "I dunno, medium height, with beautiful red hair. Like I say she was skinny."

"How old would you put her?"

"Forties? Late, I guess. I'm forty-one, and she was stunning."

"But you could tell she was older than you?"

"Leading the witness!" Jez jumped in with a grin. Beth looked at him and grinned.

"Ignore him," Hudson said. "He's read too many Grisham novels, and he's been eating sweets on the journey."

"He's alright," she said with a wink. "I love your shirt!" Hudson couldn't believe it. She probably felt sorry for him. "Maybe it was just the way she carried herself. She seemed so in control."

"Any idea which way they went? Or which car was hers?"

Beth puffed out her cheeks. "It was a silver car. One of them German things. I was out the back havin' a fag when they pulled in." Then suddenly she clicked her fingers. "Martin was talking to her. He left not long after, and I'm sure I saw them talking by her car."

"Whereabouts was the car parked?"

She raised a freckled hand, and pointed one of her only fingers that didn't house a ring towards the back. "Out the back."

"You were having another cigarette?" She nodded, and Hudson wondered what the smoking to working ratio was per hour, and whether her pay was a reflection of that.

"And who is Martin?"

"Oh, Martin is a local. He's a funny guy. Likes the ladies if you know what I mean."

Hudson took notice. "He ever cause any trouble?" It was a leap, but you had to look at every angle.

She shrugged. "Not really. I mean sometimes I'd have to tell him to stop – like I did that day. He was trying to sit in with the lady and kid. They didn't seem interested. The kid looked petrified, in fact. I told him to leave them be, and he did."

"He come in often?"

"Yeah, he's a regular. He flirts with the staff. I've caught him on many an occasion looking at my boobs!" she giggled, and then glanced to Jez. He suddenly looked up at her face. "I wasn't looking at… I…"

"You look all you want, Sweetheart!" she winked again.

Hudson cleared his throat. "Anything else?" He asked. This was often the time that people would either open up with something completely out of left field, or else they'd shut down and end things.

She shrugged, which only caused her boobs to bob up and down more. "I have Martin's address if you're interested? You know, to follow up and stuff."

Hudson threw Jez a glance, and then replied, "Most definitely."

"One minute," she said and rushed back towards the kitchen.

"Get your laptop," Hudson said to Jez.

Jez looked at the menu, and then said, "But I haven't eaten yet."

"We'll eat, but you can do research at the same time. That is why you came, right?"

Jez unfolded his large skinny frame from the vinyl booth, and wandered out in a disappointed stride. He was like a spoilt teenager that wasn't getting his own way. He loped out unenthusiastically to the car.

Chapter 42 – Hudson

Half an hour later, and they were sat back against the vinyl chairs munching burgers and fries. Jez had his laptop open and was frantically tapping the keys between huge mouthfuls. He was like some wild animal ripping off large amounts and then slowly chewing it down.

"Okay," Hudson said whilst sipping on a Diet 7Up, "What've we got?"

Jez chewed a couple more times, held up a finger to bide some more time and then spoke, "I've checked the CCTV, but there's nothing. I mean, as the police report stated the system went down a week before and it looks like it's still not back up."

"Any others?"

"There's one down the road that way," he swivelled around and pointed to the way they had come in. "It shows a couple of cars that might've been theirs, but the registration numbers can't be seen." He then turned to the opposite direction. "There's another down there. Well two in fact. One on a corner shop, which has nothing, and another on an eye-in-the-sky. The last might have more of an idea on which way they were heading but it's too far out to recognise much detail. Especially if we don't know what car to look for."

"A German one apparently." Jez almost spat his burger out at that.

Hudson thought about the suspect. The person he'd known. Could it be her?

"And this Martin guy. What do we know about him?"

Jez clicked and tapped a little more, then pulled a face which meant either that he was reading, or that he had wind. Either was possible.

"Ex-squaddie. Looks like some sort of altercation had him leave the army early. It's not exactly Dishonourable Discharge, but a softer, and more subtle version to get him out quickly. He has a police record, mostly violent threats and aggravated assault. A few drunk and disorderlies, a criminal damage charge, and one act of disturbing the peace. There are also allegations of sexual assault, inappropriate behaviour, and stalking but none of those have ever stuck."

"Jesus. A nice guy then. Beth didn't mention any of that."

"Maybe she doesn't know."

Hudson shrugged. "Look around, Jez. He's a local, everyone knows, it's just sometimes they choose not to know."

"There are a few addresses for him, but the most recent suggests he lives with his brother, Greg."

"Anything on his brother?"

Jez took another big bite, then as his jaws worked, his fingers tapped away on the keyboard, leaving greasy marks. Hudson was itching to clean them off.

"Nope, nothing."

Hudson sat back in his seat and glanced around. He wasn't so much as taking in his surroundings as letting the details drop into place. The mind is a powerful thing, and sometimes you had to just relax and let it do its own thing.

With his 7Up drunk, he turned to the tea he'd also been brought. Jez was amazed they'd found a tea pot, but there it was, sat there, looking completely out of place. Beth had been only too pleased to dig it out for him.

"You got any pictures of the suspects there, Jez?"

Jez looked up like he'd just been asked something really simple. "Of course I have."

"Brilliant. Get them together, let's get Beth to take a look and see whether she recognises anyone. If she's not out the back smoking again."

It wasn't long before Beth was back over to check on them. A fresh waft of stale cigarettes on her breath as she spoke. "You boys okay? Everything alright with your meal?"

Jez grinned and nodded, before stuffing the last of the chips in his mouth.

"Perfect," Hudson said. She was about to turn around when Hudson spoke up, "Actually, would you mind having a look at a couple of photos for me?"

"Photos?" She repeated.

"Yes. Just in case you recognise anyone."

"Okay."

Jez turned around his laptop and showed the montage of half a dozen women. All different. Four of them suspects, and two were random people added to make up the numbers.

Beth was quiet as she stared intently. Hudson could see she was giving each photo a good few seconds to look closely at. He was always glad when a witness took their time.

"It's fine if you don't. Please don't think you have to choose one. There is nothing…"

"Her!" Beth said suddenly, her voice rising an octave. "She looks exactly as I remember her!"

"Really?" Hudson said, glancing up at Jez.

"Yes, definitely. I mean she looks better here. Less tired."

Hudson's heart beat fast. He looked at Jez. "Can you get a few kids' pictures up too, mate? Just the same."

Jez understood what he was saying. Hudson was asking him to get together a group of missing kids including Darren. If she picked him out too, then that was the breakthrough they were hoping for.

Hudson tried a bit of small talk with Beth whilst Jez got it together. He wasn't great at it. He asked her how long she'd worked there, and it came out like a cheap chat up line. She'd blushed when answering simply, "Too long." Luckily, before Hudson could embarrass himself further, Jez was done.

He turned the laptop around again.

"See if you recognise any of these children, Beth. Again, no pressure."

Beth once again took her time with each. She shook her head slowly as she got to the end. Then she stopped and with her finger drew a line back. She stopped at one of them, biting the inside of her mouth through concentration, and tapping the screen.

"What is it?" Hudson asked. He sensed that she'd found something. She was squinting at it, then covering something with her finger.

"That's him, I think?" she said quietly.

"You think?" Hudson challenged.

Beth turned to him looking concerned. "The face looks a little familiar, but the hair…"

"What about it?"

"Here it's brown. The little boy that was here was blond."

"Are you sure?"

"Yes, it's the eyes. Those beautiful eyes…" She then clicked her fingers. "Luke! That was what she called him. I remember now. I couldn't remember before when the police asked."

"L-Luke?" Hudson struggled with the name. For all of his silliness, Jez understood and took over the questioning.

"You're quite sure it's the boy?" Jez reaffirmed. "And she called him Luke?"

Beth nodded, "I'm pretty sure. I mean he looked sadder. Not once did he smile like this but I'm sure that's him." And then glanced over at the kitchen. "If there's nothing else, I need to get back."

Hudson had sunk down into the chair. Jez nodded to her. "Yes. Yes, of course. Thank you. You've been a great help!"

Hudson looked up and managed a smile as she departed.

"Jesus fuckin' Christ," he said pushing the rest of his tea cup away, wishing to God he had something a little stronger to hand.

Jez struggled to know what to say. He was apt at putting his foot in it at times like this. He looked at his phone, and satisfied there was nothing new, turned back to his laptop.

Hudson felt like he'd been punched in the stomach and kicked in the nuts. There were only so many times he could tell himself how unbelievable this was.

Jez looked up. "What shall we do now?"

Hudson shrugged. "Find them, I guess."

"What? His brother Greg's place?"

"May as well." But Hudson was starting to look a bit more into it. The whole motivation of why she'd be here so far away from Swindon.

"I need to loo," Jez announced loud enough for the whole place to hear.

Hudson looked at his phone, and when directly to social media. He pulled up the person he'd tried to forget, and began to scroll through his pictures.

He looked happy. But most people even lied with pictures on social media. Fool the world into believing your life was perfect. But his looked pretty much just that.

Jim Ody

The house was as huge as the smiles on their faces. But sometimes it's not about what you are being shown. It's about what's not being shown.

He clicked into a couple of his friends, and looked at their pictures. So often it was so telling. Pictures that people were caught in.

Suddenly, Hudson had a theory. Just a hunch. He swiped into his email and tapped out a quick request to a friend of his.

He sent it just as Jez was clicking his finger-pistol at someone and saying, "Hello." Then he was tugging his shirt as if they'd be impressed with his tropical fashion. It was a couple of women sat catching up on gossip. They grinned back at the fool as he joined Hudson.

"What was that?" Hudson asked.

He glanced back, just in case his mind had forgotten them already. "Just being polite."

"O-kay," was all Hudson could think of to say. And with that they got up and began to move.

"Hey?" Hudson said to Jez.

"What?" Hudson glanced at the table and made a motion with his thumb and forefinger as a sign for money.

"We paid," he said.

"Tip?"

"Why do I have to leave the tip?"

Hudson pointed to Jez's laptop. "You used their Wi-Fi," and then using his fingers as speech marks, added, "it's a *thing* down here."

Jez sighed as if this made perfect sense to him, fumbled in his wallet, and floated a fiver down.

"Good man."

A Lifetime Ago

They said their goodbyes and headed out to the car.

Chapter 43 – Hudson

Jez directed the way out of the town, and on to the main road that climbed up out and along the cliffs above. The roads in true Cornish fashion were winding and would often go narrow, whilst a covering of trees above gave the impression that they were driving through a tunnel.

"Take the next right," Jez said, Hudson slowed down and waited for a break in the oncoming traffic before turning into a road that seemed to be no wider than a single lane.

In front of them they could see the sea, but soon they were heading down a steep gradient and the trees covered their view.

"This must be awful in the winter," Hudson remarked.

The car bounced, and every few seconds lurched to the side. Hudson eased up on the accelerator.

"Just off here," Jez said as things levelled out.

In front of them were a couple of large white houses. Hudson could only imagine their cost.

"This one here," Jez said pointing towards a hedge, with a driveway poking out.

A Lifetime Ago

When they crept into the driveway, the house stood proudly in front of them. It looked minimalist from where they were. Large clean lines, and a huge bank of glass. There were no other cars anywhere to be seen.

"Stay here," Hudson said as he turned off the engine.

"Why d'you always say that?" Jez whined.

"Because if I didn't, you'd follow."

Jez nodded, then thought about it. "Why's that so bad?"

"Because," Hudson responded, leaning back in. "Then I have to look out for you as well as persons unknown. Understand?"

"Okay." Jez didn't, and Hudson knew that, but like a kid it would give him something to mull over until either they were back in the car, or he was calling for his help.

Hudson walked to the large front door. He rang the bell, but also pounded a couple of times with his fist too.

He stood back and waited.

He glanced at Jez, who put two thumbs up at him and grinned the way a child with ADHD might. Ignoring him, Hudson turned back and tried the bell again.

Then a voice called out from behind them. "Hello?"

Hudson turned and saw a well-dressed older woman. She looked like a former film star.

"Hi," Hudson said. "D'you know if the owner's home?"

"Well, you never can tell with that one! He was in earlier… oh," she suddenly said. "Are you the husband?"

"I'm sorry?" It was a strange thing for someone to say.

"It's just… well, there was a lady-guest there lounging out by the pool. I assumed she was another woman tempted by Greg."

"Not Martin?"

"Oh, no. Have you not seen him? Oh, my, he went to seed a long time ago! No, it's the handsome Greg, who attracts the ladies."

Hudson walked over to her so as he wasn't shouting. "Did she have a child with her?"

This time the woman grinned, and looked at him knowingly. "So you do know her then?"

"Yes, I do," he said. "Okay, you got me. I'm her husband."

She laughed. "Oh dear," she said in mock sadness. "You're not the first, you know!"

Hudson shrugged, and hoped that Jez didn't decide to join in. His cover would certainly be blown then.

"Well, I saw her and the child disappear off in their car a little earlier. They seemed in an awful hurry."

"Today? Or yesterday"

"Less than an hour ago. And before you ask, no, I have no idea where she was going. I'm assuming by your sorry state, that it was home to you."

"Was she on her own?"

She nodded. "With the child."

"I see," Hudson said. "Thank you."

She nibbled her lip and looked him up and down. "No problem. If you're ever at a loose end... well, I'll be happy to answer any further questions you might have... I live next door. Alone."

"Okay," Hudson said inching away. "I'll bear that in mind."

He got back in the car and started the engine.

"Who was that?" Jez asked.

"Neighbour."

"She looked like she wanted to do bad things to you, mate. And from what I could hear, it sounded like she was offering it to you too."

Hudson checked his phone. He saw the small envelope in the top right hand corner, and opened the email.

He sat back, and went onto the page he was on at the café. He looked at the pictures again, but this time he looked closely in the background.

"Uh-ha," he said.

"What? You trying to find her on Facebook?"

"Not quite, my strange buddy. But I think I might just have found the motivation for the crime!"

"You gonna tell me, or are you going to do your usual Velma thing, and reveal it later?"

"Jinkies!" Hudson said in a poor Velma impression.

Jez blew out his cheeks and shook his head slowly. "Thought so."

"Let's just get out of here." Hudson said, turning the car around. They pulled out onto the road and headed back up the steep hill again.

"You know May's ex-husband Robert bought a house down here a few years back. It's the other side of Woolacombe."

"So?" Jez replied. Sometimes, if it wasn't on a computer screen, you had to join the dots for him.

"So, it's all a little coincidental. Don't you think?"

"You think she's headed to her ex-husband?"

"The man who cheated on her," Hudson shook his head. It was like one of the magic eye pictures. At first it was just a jumble of details – people, places, names and dates, but then when you looked more closely, everything came together. This had been where she'd been heading all along.

"It's all because of that day. And I was part of it. Get the postcode in the Sat Nav, I think I know where to find her."

"I would if I knew it."

Hudson rolled his eyes. "Hold your horses, I'm just about to give it to you!" He pulled over, grabbed his phone and scrolled.

"You have the new address of your ex-girlfriend in your phone?" Jez said in a sly way.

"What's wrong with that?"

Jez chuckled. "What's *right* with that!"

"It's for the case."

"Ah-ha." Then under his breath he added. "You keep telling yourself that, buddy."

Hudson looked up at him and narrowed his eyes. "I heard that."

A Lifetime Ago

Jez looked out the window with a huge smirk on his face.

"Here you go," Hudson said handing over his phone.

Jez popped it in, and off they went. Was this really how this case was going to be?

Jim Ody

A Lifetime Ago

Chapter 44 – Nadia

Nadia had made a batch of chocolate chip cookies. Since having a child she'd suddenly found her love of baking. It was almost unexpected, seeing as before she would snack rather than spend time preparing a meal.

Robert had a few more culinary skills, although by all accounts his ex-wife May was the main chef. Maybe that was what had put her off. Not wanting to compete. But then she'd made some cakes which had turned out surprisingly well. The cookies were just the next step. Not only did they taste good, but there was something about the smell of them that was inviting. Not to mention it made her feel like a mother catering for her family.

The designer Linda Fletch was booked in to see them today. Nadia knew it was silly, but she wanted to make a good impression. It was important that Linda liked her. Liked *them*.

That she thought nothing was strange.

It had been a peculiar year. No wait, a peculiar few years to be exact. An emotional see-saw. Up and down. But surely now they were over the worst part.

Nadia grabbed a couple of the cookies, still warm from the oven, and took them on a plate with a mug of coffee to Robert.

He was up in the study, hunched over the laptop the way he did when he was deep into a new story. He was slipping back into an old obsession again and that was never a good thing. It dredged up the past, which was the exact thing she was trying her best to forget.

"I brought you a snack," she said walking up behind him. He stopped, turned around and removed the glasses he'd recently started wearing. She happened to think it made him look the part, whereas he saw it as nothing more than a validation of getting old.

"Freshly baked?" he grinned grabbing it off the plate before she could place it down.

"Hey!" she laughed playfully slapping his hand, and then placing the empty plate down anyway on top of the old photo album.

She pretended it wasn't there. It was a reminder of what he was missing out on, and of course what she was not. All those pictures of *that woman* looking perfect. Milky white skin and strawberry blonde hair. She looked like she'd slip nicely into one of the Bronte sisters' novels. An English rose.

"Hmmm," he said, his mouth full and spraying crumbs out as he spoke.

"Pig!"

"I know!"

She glanced over his shoulder. "What're you working on? Or is it a big secret?"

He went serious. This was often the way. His work meant the world to him.

"It's about the… er… accident. I thought it was time I got it down. My agent thinks it would make a good story."

"Oh, Robert," she said, not so much out of pity, but out of surprise. He didn't like to talk about it. Maybe this was exactly what he needed. Maybe it was the best type of therapy for him. God knows she'd exhausted trying to get him professional help. He'd lost his voice with excuses, and it wasn't something he'd budge on.

He shrugged. A gesture that should've been followed by a reason for it, but he was lost for words.

"I think it's great you're doing it. Even if you don't sell it, it's time. It's not always about money."

He nodded. "I know. I'll read you it when I'm done."

"It's just about the accident, yeah?"

"Of course," he lied for the very first time to her.

Just then the doorbell went. Nadia's face lit up.

"It's Linda! The designer!" And off she went, quickly but still aware that there was a child slowly growing inside her. She didn't see many people anymore. She'd kept herself hidden away so any opportunity to speak to someone new was something she relished. She saw this as an opportunity to make a new friend.

She glided down the huge staircase that turned on itself, and saw the outline of the woman through the frosted glass of the door. She couldn't believe how excited she was. There was something about redesigning, even to a house that was virtually perfect, that made you feel great.

She swung open the door. "Linda…!?"

She took a step back. Her mouth hung open.

She knew this woman and her name wasn't Linda. It was May.

It was Robert's ex-wife.

"Na-dia," she said, stringing her name out and grinning. "Haven't you done well for yourself?"

Many responses ran through Nadia's head. So many things she wanted to say. Instead, all that escaped was the obvious. "May? What're you doing here?"

"Charming," she said. "You going to invite me in? Or am I going to stand out here all day?"

Nadia's heart pounded inside her chest. She hated this woman. She never wanted to see her again let alone invite her in. She was pretty sure this woman hated her too, so what could this be all about?

"I really don't think that's a good idea, do you?" Nadia said.

"Maybe I want to see my husband."

"Your *ex*-husband! And he won't want to see you, I can assure you of that!" Nadia was struggling to hold down her temper.

"Really? You speak for him now, do you?" May pulled her arm up quickly showing Nadia what she'd been holding behind her back. A large kitchen knife.

Instantly, Nadia held up her hands in defence.

"May, no. I've done nothing wrong. It was a long, long time ago!"

"Really?" she said taking a step forward. One foot inside the front door. "You fucked my husband when we were still married."

"No. It wasn't like…"

"That? How was it then?" And then May's face screwed up. Her eyes like black pearls. "You screwed my husband and you stole my son!"

"No! That's not true!" Nadia didn't like this. May looked crazy.

"Luckily for you, I remember! I know how it went!"

Nadia continued to walk backwards deeper into her house as May pushed forward. All the while, the knife was held out threateningly in front of her. She looked coiled and ready to spring at any moment.

"Easy for you to forget when you're regularly having sex with my husband. I've come for him. And I've come for your son too!"

Nadia screamed as May thrust forward. *This can't be happening!* She screamed inside.

A few years ago

Chapter 45 – May & Robert

2017

May pulled her long red hair back into a ponytail. She was dressed for a meeting today. A power suit that was both tight-fitting and smart. Authoritarian but sexy. She had been to the gym, and when she got back had made breakfast for herself, Robert and little Luke. Her bowl held less food than theirs as she was watching her weight.

"Wish me luck," she said bending down and kissing her husband.

"You don't need luck, you'll be fine!" Robert said distracted. He shovelled in a heaped spoonful of porridge.

They'd been married for eight years, having met at university many years before. They'd had their ups and downs, mostly surrounding May being extremely focused on what she liked and what she didn't like, and Robert being too laid back. Most people saw them as the perfect couple, but every relationship had its cracks. You could mend the chips, and small nicks but ultimately everything could become brittle if you didn't look to repair whatever was wrong.

"What are you working on?" she asked as an afterthought. What she was actually asking was when he was going to get paid. She supported him in his investigative journalism to a point, but she didn't like the fact that he was freelance, so his wages were never guaranteed. A big pay out was often followed by months of nothing.

"It's an exposé on a prominent banker skimming cash to pay for call-girls." He had a glint in his eye.

She screwed up her nose and said, "Sounds like sleezy-trash."

"Sleezy-trash sells."

"Not enough," she replied, blowing him a kiss and with a wave left for work.

Robert was left feeling a little deflated. It was hard. He had such a passion for what he did, but without his wife's full support, he never felt he could go for the big one. The story that would make him the big money. Maybe even win him an award. But money and financial stability was the thing that drove a wedge between them. They lived well. In fact, very well by most people's standards, but May wanted to holiday in the Caribbean every year. She wanted city breaks away, extensions to the house, a string of new cars and shoes that cost more than he'd paid for this first vehicle. He wanted it too, but he also wanted to write stories that mattered, not do regular small gossip columns like he'd been offered. Now he was stuck with the fun stories. The sleaze stories as she saw them, but they were easy. Little research, and easy to bang out, if you pardoned the pun.

"C'mon, buddy," he said to Luke. "Time for school."

Luke smiled. He loved school. His thirst for knowledge was insatiable and he looked like he could really do something with his life — even if he was only four! Robert and May couldn't be prouder.

"Okay, Da," he said in his little voice.

Ten minutes later and they left the house to walk towards the school. Luke's little hand almost lost in Robert's as they went.

Robert spoke briefly to other parents, and smiled at the teachers as he dropped his son off, kissing his forehead before turning back.

He walked back thinking about his story. He knew he needed to get out there and find that big one. In some respect May was right; there was something sleazy, and snitchy about the whole thing. Bankers weren't the most loved of people as it was, so did people really care about another one skimming cash? Most people thought they earnt too much as it was. Even the call-girl aspect no longer seemed to have the shock value or titilation of the past. He now worried he wouldn't be able to sell the story. May had made it obvious that he needed to start contributing more. She had a great job, with a big wage, and she was only too pleased to point this out at each and every opportunity.

He loved his house, and he smiled as he turned into the drive.

A Lifetime Ago

Just then a voice called out to him. "Rob?" He turned and saw his smiling neighbour Nadia.

"Hi," he replied. He was genuinely pleased to see her. He'd had bad neighbours in the past so it was a blessing that she was anything but. She had an exotic look, all black hair and dark skin. It sounded bad, but there was an element of mystery to her. Maybe he'd watched too many old films.

"This is a bit embarrassing, but the electricity has just gone off…"

He held up his hand. "No problem. You want me to take a look?"

"Would you mind?"

"Of course not."

He followed her into the house.

"Where's your fuse box? Is it in your downstairs toilet like ours?"

She shrugged, which only made him grin. She was a few years younger than him and always seemed to be smiling. He knew her family originally came from India, although she had very little connection with her roots anymore. She lived with her boyfriend. He was a rugged-looking policeman. Annoyingly nice enough too. They'd been over each other's houses a couple of times, but they all seemed to have busy schedules. On a number of occasions plans had been cancelled or changed.

She led the way to the toilet. And there it was up high on the wall.

"Is that it?" she said.

He nodded, and then carefully reached up to look at all of the switches. Sure enough, one was down, and this had tripped them all, also turning the main one off too.

He clicked one, and stretched for the other. He clicked it on but lost his balance and fell backwards. Nadia caught him, which gave them both an awkward moment where they were holding on to each other.

"Thank you," Robert said, and he felt something deep down. He did his best to supress it. It wasn't right.

Their eyes locked, as her voice in almost a whisper replied, "You're welcome."

They pulled away, and both guiltily rubbed hands on their own trousers as if to wipe the memory of intentions away.

"Check your electricity now," Robert said trying to get things back on track.

She nodded, and went first to the light switch. Light appeared at the same time as the sound of the click. She then popped her head into the kitchen and saw that the clock on the cooker was now flashing.

"All good!" she called.

He walked out to the front door with her following.

"Thanks Rob. I really appreciate that."

"You're more than welcome. Anytime, just give me a shout, okay?"

Nadia hugged him. She'd always been the touchy-feely type. But this time, she pulled away looking a little embarrassed.

"Sorry, was that too much. I'm a hugger, that's all."

"That's fine," he said. "I didn't mind."

And he didn't. Not at all. In fact, for the rest of the day it was all he could do not to think about it. He felt so strange. The more he thought about how good his feelings towards her were, the worse the feelings of guilt were towards May.

Chapter 46 – Nadia & Hudson

2015

The case had been a bad one. The child had been missing for well over a month. Then, out of the blue, there had been a ransom note to the family and it gave a 48hour deadline. The media were all over it.

Ransom notes were never a good sign. Often, they reeked of desperation, and that only increased the likelihood of the child not being found alive. In the case of children being taken and a ransom note not being sent for a few weeks it meant that money was not the motivation of taking the child. It was either a family member due to some custody battle — and that was the good one — or it was a sexual or a control thing, and these were more likely to end in death. Disposing of a body to keep hidden the guilt, or urges.

Hudson had been leading the investigation. He was completely immersed and obsessed with the case. He was the one that the family was looking to in order to bring their little angel back. He was at the office until 9pm, sometimes later. When he got back, he was like a zombie, the pressure building up inside of him but he was unable to let it out.

Nadia was proud of him. He was an unsung hero. She couldn't believe how much of his energy he put into the investigations. Even smaller cases, he had to oversee. But when something huge happened, she was invisible to him. She got it. She was here at home safe and sound. She was a children's author, which meant working from home, or having lunch with her agent. It just didn't seem important. She waited like some family pet for Hudson to come home to her, and then when he did, he was a guy who constantly acted like he was going through a bereavement.

He'd kiss her cheek, sometimes if she was lucky their lips would touch. He'd ask her how her day was, but no sooner had the words left his mouth than he'd switched off, his mind deep into the recesses of his brain on the current case.

She hated how she felt about it. She was jealous of the grieving parents, or those who he was fighting for. All she wanted was the dark and handsome man to notice her again. To grab her hand and lead her up to the bedroom. She wanted to be kissed like she was a teenager, and have those rough hands tug her underwear free. Even rip them like he'd done before.

Hudson was at the office when the call came in.

"We've got an address!" the caller said.

"Really?" Hudson said. "Can we get a warrant?"

"No, not enough to go on. It's all rumours and hearsay. There's a guy called Jack though that we're interested in, and we're told he's staying at the residence."

"Okay, and who is this Jack guy?"

"He's something to do with the family. Intelligence have something on him but I'm waiting for the details to be sent. We're going to stake the place out tonight. See if he turns up."

"I'd like to join you."

"The more the merrier, Huds!"

Hudson smiled. He was sure this was going to be the break in the case.

He called home and told Nadia that he was going to be out all night. She wouldn't mind, it was getting late now anyway. He'd be back by morning.

Nadia put her mobile down and cried.

Again, she was just a ghost in this relationship. Watching the world go by, listening to friends go on about the romantic holidays they were going on, the nights out with their other halves, shit, even the sex they were having. She topped up her glass of wine and sat down on the sofa and cried again. Big wet tears. The more she thought about it, the more it made her sob.

And then, completely out of character she did something silly. She walked to the downstairs toilet and flicked off the switches in the fuse box again, immediately plunging her into darkness.

She grabbed her phone and sent a text to Robert.

Sorry to bother you, but it's happened again! Can you pop around and get the power back on? X

She'd sent it before she realised she'd added the kiss.

And that he'd know she'd seen him flick the switch.

She took a deep breath, felt stupid and was about to turn it back on when he responded.

Of course. On my way x

He put a kiss too.

She opened the door for him when she saw him coming up the driveway.

"Sorry!" she said as he walked in.

"Really, it's no problem." He could smell the alcohol on her breath.

She grabbed his hand. "So you don't get lost," she giggled.

"I'm sure I'll find the way."

They got to the toilet.

"Rob, thanks for coming so quickly. I really appreciate it."

And then in the dark, her hands were on him and he wasn't pulling away. He felt her body against his. Her breath. Her lips. Her breasts pressed against his chest. Without moving away, or even speaking a word, their tongues were together.

When her hand reached for his belt, he pulled away. "I shouldn't do this," he said trying to catch his breath.

"I know," she replied.

Jim Ody

He turned and in the dark fumbled to find the switches. It took a while to realise that only the main switch was off. He knew then that she'd orchestrated it. He smiled to himself, his hand hovering over the switch. He flicked it and the light flooded in.

He opened his eyes and she stood there, topless and slightly embarrassed.

"Surprise."

He drank it all in. He was taken aback with how even more beautiful she looked. Something inside stirred. Her very dark nipples on large brown breasts.

And then he was touching them. And they were kissing again.

But before more clothing could be removed, he conceded that he had to go home. His wife and child were next door, albeit both in bed.

"Are we going to do this again?" she asked as he left.

He turned and simply replied, "I hope so."

As he walked out of the driveway, he saw Sven, a guy he knew from football. He stood there smoking a cigarette and looking amused.

"Evening Robert," he said with a knowing look in his eye. "Everything alright?"

"Hi," Robert said back but scurried off, only showing more guilt.

He went upstairs to see if May was awake. He stopped and looked at her, listening for her breathing.

And then a sleepy voice asked, "Did you sort her out?"

And with a huge dollop of guilt he replied, "I think so."

And from there things were never quite the same again.

The next day when Luke was at school, and May and Hudson were at their respective works, Robert slipped around to his neighbour.

The door was on the latch. He walked in and up the stairs. From there he had the best sex of his life, and never looked back.

Chapter 47 – That Day

2017

Life was a whirlwind. There was electricity in the air. The whole world was in a hurry. It had to be something to do with the moon, or some such.

May had overslept, which caused her much panic. She liked to be in control and playing catch up with the time meant anything but. Luke was also playing up, acknowledging the lack of attention he was getting due to the tension in the air.

"I don't feel well!" he cried, but May insisted he still get ready for school.

"Let him stay home, love," Robert said looking up from his laptop. "He looks pale."

Her face was evil. Medusa without the snakes. "That would really mess your plans up wouldn't it!" she spat, and it was then that he realised that she knew.

He went to respond, but was lost for words. How could he respond to it? Deny it? Confirm it?

"See! You think I don't know what's going on around here? Why your writing never seems to go anywhere anymore!"

A Lifetime Ago

"May, just calm down, yeah?" he tried, but it only seemed to make matters worse.

"Calm down! Why should I be the one to calm down? My husband is out fucking the neighbour, and he wants *me* to calm down!"

Robert sat there. Rooted to the spot like he was weighted down. It was the beginning of the end. The problem was, he had no idea how it would play out. He wasn't thinking long-term. He was riding the wave and enjoying the ride, but refusing to think about what would happen when the wave was nothing more than wetness in the sand. And he was left stranded on the beach.

It was a Mexican stand-off. Both stared at each other. One with a rage that looked ready to burst, and the other resigned to feel the full force of it. A condemned sinner.

Their love was flatlining, and neither of them was reaching for the paddles to shock it back to life again.

*

She had lain awake all night. Nadia looked over at her boyfriend sleeping, and wondered where they could go from here. Of course, by sleeping she meant watching him wriggle, turn and moan out in his sleep. The names of victims all too familiar as being the soundtrack of the bedroom deep into the night. At one stage he'd called out her name between the sheets. Well, he did it once, but at least it was her name. Those days of pillow confessions, and naked truths seemed a lifetime ago. Here was a handsome man aging with rapid speed each day. Stressed out by his job at playing an undercover Superman.

She got up and looked at herself in the full-length mirror. Her body was aging, but still looked good. She thought about hands roaming over her body, but they no longer belonged to Hudson. It was the journalist from next door who had made her feel like a woman again. She couldn't say whether it was so much better than her boyfriend, or just the excitement of it being different.

She wanted to tell him. If for no other reason them to see some sort of emotion aimed at her.

And then his mobile rang. Its loud ringtone making her jump at the same time that he shot awake.

He grabbed it, hardly even noticing her at the foot of the bed holding herself in front of the mirror. She was virtually naked and he wasn't paying her any attention.

"Hello? When? Okay, give me fifteen minutes and I'll be there!"

He jumped out of bed, and almost took her out.

"Sorry, I didn't see you there. I have to go into work."

She nodded, and her mouth hung open. She wanted to ask more, but knew he couldn't, and wouldn't say. He wrestled with his trousers and ran down stairs without further word.

Hudson felt the adrenaline pumping through his veins. It had all come down to this. They had the warrant, and intel of where the guy was. This was it. Now or never. He wanted to be part of it. He needed to be part of it. He wanted to look into the monster's eyes, knowing that he would never have freedom again.

Forgetting to even say good bye to Nadia, he was out the door in a flash. It banged behind him, as he beeped open his car.

*

"Sit down!" May shouted to Robert. "You think about what you're going to do and I'll take him! I'm late already, so who cares! Luke! Get your coat on now!"

"But, Mum!"

"Shut it! I don't want to hear your whining!"

Luke grabbed his coat, and struggled to get it on. He picked up his bag and walked out of the door.

"See ya, buddy!" Robert shouted, but Luke was already out of earshot.

May slammed the door behind her, and stormed purposefully down the drive. She could hear her neighbour getting in his car, and wondered whether she should tell him what his slut-girlfriend had been up to with her husband.

"John!" Luke shouted and suddenly took off.

It happened fast and hard.

Hudson's mind was on getting to the scene as he reversed his car. He wasn't going fast, but focused on his friend, Luke didn't see him until it was too late.

The boot hit the boy in the side, and with him running, sent him crashing to the ground. Unfortunately, his head cracked the side of the curb with a sickening thud. A woman screamed, and then May hearing the sound before turning out of her drive, screeched in a way only a devastated mother could.

"Jesus!" Hudson said, flinging his door open.

"There's blood!" May screamed.

With blood draining from his own face, Hudson made a call that later he wouldn't even remember doing. People gathered around the broken body.

Robert appeared and tried to get to Luke, but May slapped him hard. "Stay away from my son!" she shouted loudly. Shocked looks were shared with the passers-by. Nobody knew what was going on. The horror of it all unfolded in front of them.

Then Nadia appeared. "Oh my god!" she said her hand covering her mouth. "Is he okay?"

May stood up. "Does he look okay?"

"I…I," she stammered, tears suddenly streaming down her face.

"You what?" May screamed and went for her. Hudson jumped up quickly and got between them.

"May…" he started, but couldn't follow it up. He'd just knocked down her son. What could he possibly say that could help her?

"I have nothing to say to you," she said to him, and then looked over his shoulder to Nadia. "But you! First you fuck my husband, and then your boyfriend runs down my son! What sort of an evil bitch, are you?"

If those around thought that Hudson already looked bad, then they were wrong. Before their eyes he aged rapidly. He looked up at Robert looking as guilty as a cheating man could.

"Really? Rob?"

Robert looked directly at him, and then his gaze dropped to the floor, as he shook his head. It wasn't in denial though, just at the total shock of the situation.

Hudson slipped down to the floor, his back against the back nearside tyre.

Panning away from the scene as the ambulance arrived, those around were left with many questions, and very few answers. A hundred what ifs, and a thousand separate scenarios of how that day could've played out.

A miasma of sorrow engulfed the scene. One that would never be the same again. The five lives that day would be blown apart like a shotgun blast, sending them all off into separate directions.

Luke fell into a coma. The heavy trauma to his head started internal bleeding. He was operated on, and then wired up to machines that only made functional robotic noises. All they wanted was for little Luke to breathe for himself without the noisy ventilator doing it for him. The constant sound of his life support machine.

Often Robert sat as an empty shell of a man, whilst either his wife sat scowling and blaming him for hours at a time, or else he sat praying to someone he didn't believe in, in the hope that a miracle would happen, and his little boy would walk and talk again.

He was a month into living in a rented flat when he received the call.

Luke had woken up, and no sooner had they tried to take away the breathing apparatus, he fitted, and flatlined. The doctors did all they could, but eventually they had to stop.

Luke was dead.

Hudson was initially investigated. But witness accounts said that he didn't reverse any quicker than was legally plausible. Luke suddenly running past the driveway was more to blame. May had initially rebutted the decision, but eventually conceded the point having not been able to see over the wall that split the two properties.

At first, Hudson did desk duties, away from the outside world, but his nights became longer as he could only sleep with a bottle of booze. The walls of the flat came in on him claustrophobically. He hated not living in the large house anymore, but how could he live next door to a woman whose son he killed?

Nadia moved back home to start with, but eventually she met back up with Robert, and their relationship grew. The tragedy ruined many relationships that day, but somehow, through it all Robert and Nadia felt stronger than ever before.

But even they could no longer live in Thornhill anymore. They had to move away. And Robert fell into a deep depression having lost his son.

Chapter 48 – Present Day

Robert was on a roll with his writing. He got like that sometimes. In his mind he was thinking he'd just write one more paragraph, but then the clock would fast forward another hour.

He was so caught up in what had happened years ago, that he'd forgotten about the arrival of the designer. It would be nice to get the pool area completed, but for him, it was far from his top priority. He knew he should go downstairs and make an appearance. The design of the garden was important to Nadia, and he wanted to support her.

The truth was he felt himself spiraling. He felt dark. They'd moved here and had a child, but that wasn't the end of it. He rested his hands on the desk, and glanced out of the window and over the sea. Why couldn't that have been it? His happy-ever-after?

He clenched his jaw tightly with anger, but the worst thing of all was he had nowhere to channel it. Maybe that was why he ended up doing what he did. Caught up in a rash decision he'd now have to live by.

He glanced for the last time at the confessions sat on the innocent white background of his Word file, and knew what it meant. A flashing cursor promising more but perhaps no words would ever follow.

Resigned, he left the study, walked down the hall, and had just turned to go down the staircase when he saw his girlfriend laid on the floor and another woman on top of her.

"Hey!" he shouted for want of something better to say. So many things were rushing through his mind. The horror of it all, not to mention the fact that Nadia was pregnant.

"Get off her!" He shouted again. She looked up, and as she did, Nadia bucked her off.

But now he recognised her. How could he not. His ex-wife looked at him with the same anger as she had that very day of the accident all those years ago. It felt like some PTSD flash back. This couldn't be happening. Was it his mind? Had he finally lost it?

He froze in an action pose that promised so much but currently delivered nothing.

She stood up and showed him the knife. "Here he is. The knight coming to save the damsel in distress! The hero, and the slut! What a fuckin' fairytale!"

"May, come on. Leave her! It's me you want to hurt not her. It was my fault you slept in that day. Not hers! All of it was my fault."

"She was the one you ran to! Her foreign looks, teasing you in her skimpy clothes!"

Slowly, he began to walk. A careful look each step forward on the stairs. "No, I chased her. It wasn't her fault."

"Why, Robert? Why?" A soft whine crept it, but he wasn't fooled. She could do this. Lead him into thinking her rational side was taking control before she exploded again.

"May? Please put the knife down. It doesn't have to be like this. We can't bring him back, can we?"

She stood there rigid. She looked confused, not sure how she wanted it to play out. She'd been obsessed for so long about hunting them down. Making them pay. But now stood in front of them she was torn.

"We had it all," she said, her voice almost normal. "We had such great times together. I just don't understand why you both had to ruin it."

Robert nodded. He was too scared to disagree. "We did," he conceded. "I sometimes think back to those times too… Our marriage? Remember?" She did. He could tell she did. The corners of her mouth twitched. Another time it would've been the beginning of a smile.

"And our honeymoon? How great was that?"

She nodded slowly. Tears streamed down May's face. "So why did you ruin it, Robbie?"

"I… I don't know," he said. He wanted to just launch at her, and protect Nadia from the knife.

And then suddenly Jacob began to cry from above. He'd been in his room taking a nap. All eyes shot to the sound.

Nadia turned to run up the stairs, but May arched an arm and swung. The knife slashed Nadia's leg, not deep, but enough to stop her in her tracks.

"It's okay!" May shouted. "I'm coming!" Robert made a grab for her and they both fell backwards down the few steps.

Nadia screamed but gritted her teeth, and hobbled up the rest of the stairs. Her child was now her only concern.

May fell on top of Robert which knocked the wind out of him. The knife fell out of her hand and skidded across the slate floor. They both made a scramble for it, but still winded, May easily kneed him between the legs. She grabbed the knife and hit him with the handle. The force snapped his head back, hitting the hard floor below.

"I'm sorry it came to this," she said getting up. "We could've been so happy but you ruined it!"

She placed a foot on the stairs and shouted up, "Luke? I'm coming for you, honey!"

She kicked Robert again, and slowly made her way up the stairs to look for them. Above her, the sound of scrambling feet could be heard.

Chapter 49 – Hudson

Hudson went over the full incident again with Jez. As usual, Jez was focusing on all of the wrong things.

"I still can't believe your girlfriend was cheating on you with your neighbour? Wow!"

"Seriously, Jez. Out of all that you want to home in on my girlfriend's infidelity?"

"You didn't suspect a thing?" He almost looked concerned. Whilst Jez knew about that day, Hudson had never gone in to the specific details. He'd been a completely closed book towards it.

"No, I was heavily involved in a case. Did you not hear what I said? I killed a child!"

"Nah," Jez replied looking out of the window as he said it, like he was disagreeing with Hudson's choice in socks. "The kid ran out in front of you, or rather behind you. He was distracted, and fell awkwardly. It's unlucky, but not your fault. Look, mate, I've heard the story, I've read the files, you were no more to blame than the parents, or even the kid himself."

"You have a strange way about you."

"So I've been told. Anyway, you were cleared, weren't you?"

"Yes. Standard procedure that I'm cleared of any wrong doing, but it still doesn't stop the fact that if I hadn't jumped in my car that day, then Luke would still be alive today."

Jez was shaking his head again. "Not convinced mate. Also, you were off to arrest the leader of a paedophile ring, not to mention finding a missing child! You were hardly a drunk, or a boy-racer showing off."

"I didn't have to be there though. I was being egotistical, wanting to take him down myself. I was so obsessed with the case; I just wanted to see him and the others behind bars."

"I still think you're being too hard on yourself." Hudson appreciated the words, even if he didn't believe them.

"But you should learn from it."

Hudson wasn't sure what Jez was getting at. "What d'you mean?"

"Laura. When's your next date?"

"We don't have one."

"That's my point, mate. This is an important case, of course it is, but you're going to lose her if you're not careful."

Hudson went to say something. He knew it was a weak defense, but Jez was already waving him down. "No, I don't want to hear it. It's just excuses. You have to make time for her, or else one day you're going to be too old to race around the country being a hero, and then what will you have?"

"You still bothering me," Hudson half-heartedly joked.

"True, but I won't be in your bed. You'll be alone mate."

Hudson knew he was right. He was doing exactly the same with Laura as he had with Nadia. He'd loved Nadia but she'd grown bored and frustrated.

Hudson pulled over the car into a layby. Without a word to Jez, he grabbed his phone and fired off a text.

I want to see you. When I get back let's have a date. A proper date. x

He sent it, and pulled away, trying not to engage with the grinning buffoon next to him. The case was clearly getting to him — that was the second time he'd taken Jez's advice when it had come to women.

"You're not going to ask what I sent?" Hudson said as they continued.

Jez was still grinning and looking out of the passenger window when he replied, "I'll look when I get home."

"I thought the app only worked when the phone was nearby?"

This time Jez looked over at him. "Not my new version!" He winked.

They turned into another lane, which climbed up a hill. The sea was in front of them albeit out of sight for the moment.

At the top of the hill, they saw a large house sat on its own. It was a magnificent sight.

"Nice place," Jez said. "I'd love to buy a place like this."

"You'd be bored."

"Probably."

They pulled into the driveway, and saw a large Mercedes, a Jaguar and a small Range Rover.

"Nice cars."

Jez looked at the registration numbers. "That's May's," he said pointing to the Mercedes. "You probably already knew that."

And then they saw the front door was left open.

"Shit," Hudson said. "Call it in, I'm going to check it out."

Jez grabbed his phone. "Yeah, best I stay here with the car, right?"

But Hudson was already jogging in.

As he pushed through the door, he saw Robert lying on the floor. He was starting to move, but looked out of it.

"Rob?" Hudson said. It didn't even register that he was talking to the father of the child he'd killed. "What's going on?"

Robert moaned, some nonsensical words trying, but unable to form.

And then he heard a crash from upstairs.

*

Outside, Jez was looking out of his window when he saw something move in the Mercedes.

Someone was in there!

He got out and jogged over. At first, he squished his face up against the window, and then seeing it was a child, he jogged around the side and opened up the door.

A Lifetime Ago

"Hey, there!" he said, trying to act like a presenter on CBeebies. "What's your name, Pal?"

The child just looked down and refused to speak.

"Okay. My name is Jez. Is your name Darren? It's okay, you're safe now."

The child slowly shook his head.

"It's not? What is it then?"

The child suddenly looked up with his big blue eyes, at the same time that Jez noticed the dark roots.

"You not speaking?"

The boy just shook his head.

Chapter 50 – Nadia

It seemed so clichéd. She sat in the large wardrobe amongst the clothes, and hugging her son for dear life. She'd never felt so scared. This was it, the climax. The final scene.

She heard May patrolling around the rooms. She wondered whether or not she could make a run for it, but with Jacob it was highly unlikely.

May stopped outside, the bedroom and listened.

"*Luke?* Mummy's here?" she called out in a sing-song voice. "It's time to come home and be a family again!"

Jacob sobbed, and Nadia hugged him tightly doing all she could to muffle the sound. The boy was scared. So much had already happened in his little life. She pulled him close feeling his pale skin and brown hair against her.

"She's not your mummy, Luke? She's lying to you." The voice now closer.

"Shhh," Nadia hushed into his ear and held her finger to her lips.

"You can't escape me!" There was a defiance in her voice now as it grew closer. May was now in the bedroom. Each of her movements could be heard.

Suddenly there was the sound of the knife dragging along the slats of the wardrobe door.

"Knoc- knock!" May shouted and whipped open the door. "Boo!"

Nadia and Jacob both screamed, as May stood there with the knife that now looked huge.

"Let him go!" she screamed about to lunge, but suddenly a man was on her. Huge arms around her body, with one grabbing the knife.

Behind her stood the man she'd first fallen in love with many years ago. Hudson Bell.

"Hudson!" Nadia cried out. "She was going to kill me!"

"I don't think so," he bent down, picked the knife up, and said, "D'you wanna let me have Darren now?"

Even with her dark skin he could see her pale.

"What? I don't know what you're talking about. This is my son Jacob. Our son. Robert and I." The babbling words of lies. People often talked too much when they weren't telling the truth. Skirting around in circles and tripping over their own tongues.

"Cut the crap, Nadia. Your son Jacob died a few months back."

"No. It's not true!" she looked angry, before suddenly she began to cry in floods of tears. His eyes looking past him hoping for Robert to save her.

"Nadia. You can't lie to me. You never could. A friend told me. Even though you did your very best to keep it to yourselves.

"I did a check on you. It's also funny what you find on the internet. I found a recent picture of you with a child that didn't look like Jacob. You did a good job of keeping him off social media. But you were in the background of someone else's photo. It troubled me. The boy was so different from your son."

May was still shrugging Hudson off. "I'm okay." She said and slumped to the floor in tears. "I suspected it," she began. "I know Robert was devastated with Luke's death – but not as much as me! There is no bond like a mother and their son!"

Nadia went to say something, but Hudson held up a hand to stop her. He could see May had more to say. She buried her head into her hands. Then continued. "I was Facebook-stalking him for years – I couldn't help it. Part of me was pleased for him when he had another boy. I'd check out the pictures and watch the child grow, and then suddenly everything stopped. No more pictures. Nothing. That was so unlike Robert, and you."

"You suspected from that?" Nadia spat.

"No, I knew they were back in Thornhill when the child was taken. I was out looking to run into them. I was near the park that day, in fact. But I just missed them."

"We had you as a suspect," Hudson admitted.

Nadia grabbed the boy suddenly, but Hudson was already there, knowing her every move. He prized the child away. "Leave him!"

Suddenly there was noise and then movement outside of the door. Everyone turned.

"Ha!" The figure of Jez appeared doing some sort of kung-fu move he'd seen in some 80s movie.

"Jez! What the fuck!" Hudson said, then quickly looked at Darren. "Sorry 'bout the language."

"Oh, looks like you got her then," Jez said. "We should like tie her up, or something."

But then they heard the sirens.

And behind Jez was a small boy.

"And who is this?" Hudson said in a calming voice.

May looked embarrassed when she admitted, "I call him Luke. It's not his birth name, but it's what I call him."

"What's his birth name?"

"Honey?" she said to her son. "What's your real name?"

He surveyed the situation. His bright blue eyes looking at them all. He looked down at small hands that fidgeted, and just when they thought he was refusing to speak, he looked up and with the biggest grin you'd ever see on a child confidently said, "Sonny! My name is Sonny!"

It melted May's heart.

"Who cares!" Nadia shouted.

And then, ever the one to cut the tension, Jez stood and pointed at both Nadia and Hudson, the penny dropped and increased the smile on his face. "Ah, yes. You two, er…" He winked and made some strange juvenile noises.

"Not the time, mate," Hudson hissed.

Then just as unexpectedly, Jez pulled out something. It was a pair of fluffy-pink handcuffs.

Hudson rolled his eyes for the hundredth time to him. "Why does this not surprise me?"

"They're mostly clean."

"Stop talking."

Hudson pulled Nadia's arms behind her back and clicked on the cuffs. It was the strangest move of his life. The last time he'd cuffed her had been in a hotel room in Paris under completely different circumstances. And now it was making a citizen's arrest. Life had really changed quite dramatically for them both.

Then Robert appeared at the door, one hand nursing a large lump on his head, and a rumbling of footsteps behind saw a group of confused policemen.

"Ah-ha," Jez grinned. "This is a bit awkward!"

A few minutes later and the place was filled with policemen. Darren was quickly taken away.

Hudson grabbed his phone and was about to call Laura. He saw her reply.

That would be great. I'm really looking forward to it. xx

He smiled as he rang her.

"Hudson?" she said as if not expecting him to ring her again.

"We've got him. Darren is safe and sound."

There was a pause, and then a huge squeal, before she replied, "Oh my god! How can I ever repay you?"

Hudson chuckled. "I could think of a few ways." They laughed, and spoke some more

A Lifetime Ago

before agreeing to meet up when he was back in Thornhill.

What a huge tangle of lies it was. One of the policemen took Hudson up to the study and showed him Robert's computer. There in black and white were the details of the whole abduction. A confession from a guilty mind. Robert had told his story right from the beginning but unable to stop, he'd continued on from moving to the coast. The tender description of having another son, and then the anguish and despair of losing him too. Some medical issue never picked up until it was too late. He'd almost lost it. Really lost it.

One night he'd walked out into the sea ready to end it all. He'd shouted at the top of his lungs to be taken. He didn't want to live anymore. But the desperate hands of Nadia grabbed him and they wrestled in the freezing cold water until she was able to get him at least back onto the sand.

They'd collapsed into each other's arms. The frigid cold night air attacking them until, under the light of the moon, the made a huge decision.

They would replace Jacob.

*

Hudson joined Jez, May and her son Sonny. They had a lot to catch up on.

"May, you need to get help," Hudson said, matter-of-factly and then looking towards her son and added, "Look at your beautiful boy, here? You cannot bring him up in Luke's shadow any longer."

May looked defeated. She had a lot of questions to answer. She did her best to argue that she was in complete control of herself but Hudson wasn't buying it. He couldn't. For his own piece of mind he wanted her checked out by professionals.

"I wanted the truth to be known," she said, but with her head bowed down, Hudson wasn't sure which truth it was she meant.

"I know I'm the last person on earth you want to listen to. I cannot tell you how much the death of your son has affected me. I'm still in counselling now. And that's exactly what you need to do."

May looked up at him, and acknowledged what he was saying.

"I don't blame you, Hudson. You're a good person. I just found it hard to speak to you over the years…" She swallowed hard, and quickly rubbed away the tears. "Not anymore. I… I don't know what I was going to do. That's the honest truth." She looked at her son and then pulled him in. The little boy hugged her tightly.

She turned to him. "I'm sorry, Sonny," she admitted. "I'm the worst mother. I promise I'll see you as you. I love you."

He pulled away just enough to look up to her. His big blue eyes filled with love. Children were so forgiving.

"I love you too," he said in small voice.

And then a car pulled up.

A lady got out with a huge smile on her face, seemingly oblivious to the circus that was going on. She was well-dressed in an array of bright colours, and dangly-bangly jewelry. Her blonde hair was whipped up, mostly long, but shaved one side. She walked purposefully up towards where May stood, a cross between an art student and a professional, but oozing confidence. She was creativity on legs.

"Hello everyone! I'm looking for Nadia? I'm Linda Fletch! I believe you have something you want me to make beautiful for you!" She was infectious with her positive attitude, and for some reason this just made everyone laugh.

"You've just missed her," Jez said. "She's been arrested."

"Oh my," she replied. "That will never do." And without another word she turned, power walked back to her car, and drove away.

Hudson's mobile rang. He looked at the screen and saw it was Pete.

"Well done, Huds! Great work. The sergeant is over the moon with you. He's singing your praises! He wanted me to pass on his thanks."

Hudson chuckled at that. "But not enough to do it himself?"

"Don't be like that, Huds. You and Jez are a real asset to the team."

"Thanks Pete. It's another one down, but I have an ever-growing pile left to plough into."

"The sarg did say you should take a few days off."

"I will," Hudson said. "Just as soon as my in-tray is empty." He finished the call before Pete could respond. Hudson would apologise to him later, it wasn't his fault. He was just the monkey. It was the organ grinder who annoyed him.

"Everything alright?" Jez asked.

"That was Tom Selleck on the phone," Hudson said looking Jez up and down. "He wants his shirt back."

This time it was Jez who rolled his eyes, and muttered under his breath. "Funny."

The End.

A Lifetime Ago

Acknowledgements

A big thank you to my family and friends. Your support it massive.

A huge thanks to the members of *Jim Ody's Spooky Circus* - my street team, and specifically my group of advisors Simon, Angela, AJ, Cheryl, Dee, Terry and Ellie who listen to all my crazy ideas and advise me whether or not they are worth pursuing!

I had some wonderful BETA readers for this, so thank you to, Lisa Howarth, Eileen Parascandola, Simon Leonard and Caitlin Brosseau.

Thank you to Caroline, David and Jason for your continued support. Also, to Andy Barrett, Maggie James, Sarah Hardy, Valerie Dickenson, Bella James, and Kerry Watts who also try to steer me in the right direction. Or try.

A special mention to Emmy Ellis @ studioenp for her wonderful design direction. You truly bring my book covers to life!

Thank you to Alan Moss for his knowledge on policing. You really took time out to answer all of my questions!

As ever a huge thank you to my editor Shelagh Corker who tireless corrects everything, keeps me in check. I don't always listen, but she is still there shaking her head at me, ready for my next maverick idea.

And finally thank you to you, the readers. For reading, for enjoying, and for getting behind me. Without you there would really be no point!

ABOUT THE AUTHOR

Jim writes dark psychological/thrillers that have endings you won't see coming, and favours stories packed with wit. He has written ten novels and well over a dozen short-stories spanning many genres.

Jim has a very strange sense of humour and is often considered a little odd. When not writing he will be found playing the drums, watching football and eating chocolate. He lives with his long-suffering wife, three beautiful children and two indignant cats in Swindon, Wiltshire UK.

Connect with Jim Ody here:

Facebook: www.facebook.com/JimOdyAuthor
Jim Ody's Spooky Circus Street Team: https://www.facebook.com/groups/1372500609494122/
Amazon Author Link: https://www.amazon.co.uk/Jim-Ody/e/B019A6AMSY/
Email: jim.ody@hotmail.co.uk
Twitter: @Jim_Ody_Author
Instagram: @jimodyauthor
Pintrest: https://www.pinterest.co.uk/jimodyauthor/
Bookbub: https://www.bookbub.com/profile/jim-ody

Want to read more books by this author?

Here are details of three more books for you to get your hands on!

The Place That Never Existed

For Paul and Debbie it was meant to be the happiest time of their lives.

A small village wedding in front of their family and friends, followed by a quiet honeymoon in Devon. Not everyone had been happy to see them together. A woman from their past refused to accept it. Her actions over the previous year had ended in tragedy, and had almost broken the happy couple apart.

Now, away from it all in a picturesque log cabin, Paul and Debbie look forward to time spent alone together... But she has found out where they are, and she will stop at nothing to make sure that the marriage is over... forever.

But Huntswood Cove isn't just a beautiful Devonshire fishing town, it has its own secret. Recently, people have begun to disappear, only to turn up dead in suspicious circumstances. The locals begin to question what is going on. Soon everything strange points to the abandoned house in the woods.

The house that nobody wants to talk about. To them, it is the place that never existed.

?

Question Mark Press

Beneath The Whispers

Scotty Dean didn't expect to run into his childhood sweetheart deep in the woods. Especially having just been dumped by a woman well out of his league.

But Mary-Ann needs him to get back a USB stick that has fallen into the wrong hands. He knows he shouldn't get involved, but as old feelings resurface, so do the hidden secrets.

His past collides with the present and Scotty is surrounded by whispering voices – but what is it they're trying to say?

?

Question Mark Press

A Cold Retreat

Penny was a naïve child, only ever wanting to please. And men can be evil, and quick to take advantage of her. Forcing her deeper into a dark world.

Only when Penny hits rock bottom, does she finally wake up with a new sense of worth, and an appetite for retribution. The men had known what they were doing was wrong, and now it's her turn to make them wish they'd never messed with her.

Love can be a real killer.

?

Question Mark Press

How many have you read?

Coming soon:

Question Mark Horror

A new series of YA Horror books. One series by a handful of authors.

Are you ready?

1 – Camp Death
2 – Ouija
3 – House of Horrors

Printed in Great Britain
by Amazon